"What ha... ...an cannot aid a p... ...n pins came loose, and her locks cascaded, satiny curls that brushed his knuckles.

Desire pulsed thick and urgent in his veins. He fought the urge to wind his fingers through her hair, tip her face to his, and ravish her full, lush mouth.

"Fetched a saddle, did you?" Maeve asked, all innocence.

"I wanted to ride with you."

His words took on a meaning that made him growl with frustration. Had he no decency? She trusted him like family, looked to him as an older brother.

"You wish to take me riding? Me, a kitchen maid?" She ran her fingers smartly across his chest. Playful, hot little taps that made him ache for her.

"Since you are off duty, you are not a maid until tomorrow morning arrives."

"Flawed reasoning, but you are a nobleman and it's to be expected. Have you become such a dandy that you need a saddle?" She stole the bridle from him and swished into the shadows, leaving him alone in the aisle.

Alone and desiring . . .

From "The Keepsake" by Jill Henry

BOOK YOUR PLACE ON OUR WEBSITE AND MAKE THE READING CONNECTION!

We've created a customized website just for our very special readers, where you can get the inside scoop on everything that's going on with Zebra, Pinnacle and Kensington books.

When you come online, you'll have the exciting opportunity to:

- View covers of upcoming books
- Read sample chapters
- Learn about our future publishing schedule (listed by publication month *and author*)
- Find out when your favorite authors will be visiting a city near you
- Search for and order backlist books from our online catalog
- Check out author bios and background information
- Send e-mail to your favorite authors
- Meet the Kensington staff online
- Join us in weekly chats with authors, readers and other guests
- Get writing guidelines
- AND MUCH MORE!

Visit our website at
http://www.kensingtonbooks.com

IRISH EYES

Tina Donahue

Jill Henry

Elizabeth Keys

ZEBRA BOOKS
Kensington Publishing Corp.
http://www.kensingtonbooks.com

CONTENTS

FINALLY AND FOREVER

Tina Donahue

One

Captain Aidan O'Rourke was in the Swan Inn quietly enjoying his ale when the door behind him was pushed open with such force it crashed into the wall.

Before that sound had an opportunity to fade, a female voice rose above it. "Seamus Fahey," said she, "I want what's mine!"

Well, now. Aidan had no idea what might be hers, but sensed it could very well include Seamus Fahey's life. The man was seated at a table to Aidan's left and had already gone quite pale.

"I don't know what you'd be talking about," Seamus said, even as he scrambled backwards over the plank seat.

The men about him also scattered fast as the woman approached.

Aidan caught only a glimpse of her before she passed. He could see she was young—no more than eighteen—and was quite serious about this matter for she had come armed with a cudgel.

Aidan took another sip of his ale, while Seamus's watery blue eyes remained on the girl's club.

"You'd best put that down," he warned.

"In the middle of your head," she promised.

Seamus scrambled backwards over another table as she continued to approach.

Aidan turned to a fellow on his right. "What would this be about?"

The man fled without answering as the girl's cudgel slammed into the table Seamus was now scrambling over.

"Thief!" she accused.

"I took nothing!"

"Liar!" she hissed.

Just in time, Aidan leaned back as Seamus clambered across his table with the girl in murderous pursuit.

"I want me Claddagh ring," she said, slamming her cudgel onto Aidan's table.

Seamus jumped off and continued to back away. "Are you daft? What do you mean *your* Claddagh—"

"Aye, *mine*," said she. "An heirloom from me dearly departed mother."

Seamus laughed, until her cudgel hit the wall to the right of his head.

"Will no one stop this woman?" he cried.

The rest of the men fled the inn, leaving only Seamus, Aidan, and the girl.

"You took me ring, admit it!" she cried with unexpected sorrow in her voice. She spun around as Seamus ran to the right. "I hid it from the likes of you, but you found it, you did, in me sack of flour!"

Aidan quickly swallowed the last of his ale and turned to look at the girl. Now, as before, he noticed that she was the only one with flour on her person.

There were streaks of it everywhere—on her worn brown dress, on her hands, face, and even in her dark hair.

It was lovely hair, thought Aidan, the same as her large green eyes. Sadly, though, the rest of her features were decidedly plain. She was rather on the skinny side, too, except for her breasts, which were quite ample and fetching.

Not that Seamus Fahey noticed this, or that he was far taller than she and presumably stronger. His gaze remained fixed on her cudgel. As he ran outside, he kept looking over his shoulder for she was right behind him and still swinging that club.

Aidan pulled some coins from his pocket, tossed them onto the table, then followed these two.

By now, the girl had backed Seamus against a wall as she continued to call him a thief and a liar.

Despite those accusations, the man continued to shake his head and deny everything, including the fact that he was the Seamus Fahey she sought. "You have the wrong man!" he shouted.

"You believe there would be another like you in this town?"

He frowned. "There would be two with me name."

"Aye," said she. "One in his eightieth year, and the other not yet old enough to walk!"

Seamus mumbled, "The older of the two must have taken your—"

"You think I'm daft?" she interrupted, then continued before he could answer. "Very well, Mr. Fahey. Say your prayers." She lifted the cudgel.

Before it could come crashing down on the wall

next to Seamus—or worse, in the middle of the man's head—Aidan grabbed it.

Briana MacCullen paused at this, then looked over her shoulder to a very tall, red-headed man dressed in a captain's uniform, a look of authority in his brown eyes.

Her gaze lowered to his broad shoulders and chest, then returned to his thickly lashed eyes. ". . . And what would you be doing?" she asked.

There was a hint of a smile on his full lips. "Saving you from the gaol."

Her gaze again dropped to his broad chest. It was as powerful as his voice though he was still a fairly young man, surely no more than five and twenty. ". . . And how would you be doing that?"

"By not allowing you to murder this fellow."

All at once, Briana remembered Seamus. Not that she was about to look at him, for she far preferred this captain. "Though I would love to see Mr. Fahey in the ground," she said, "he *should,* at the very least, be in the gaol."

"Perhaps. But you must allow the authorities to handle—"

"No, no," she quickly interrupted. "Seamus Fahey's the goal's warder paid to watch the prisoners. He *belongs* there."

"And should be returning there about now," Seamus said.

"Stay where you are," Aidan warned.

The man gave Aidan the same sour look he had been giving the girl.

Aidan turned to her and was again taken with her

eyes. Not only were they lovely, but beneath her fury, he saw intelligence and true sorrow.

All too quickly, he wondered if Seamus were or had been one of her lovers, and wondered why that disturbed him.

Aidan gestured to Seamus. "How did you come to know this lad?"

"He stole me ring." Her frown deepened. "Have you not been listening?"

"Only a deaf man could be blessed with the power to do that," Seamus said.

"Quiet," Aidan warned him, then said to her, "That's not what I meant. How would he have known where to look for your ring?"

"How else?" she asked. "Me no-good brother, Conor, told him about it."

"And where is this Conor?"

"Where he *always* is," Seamus said, as if Aidan were daft. "In the gaol."

"That would be where they met," the girl quickly said. "Together they conspired to steal me Claddagh ring." She briefly paused, then glanced over both shoulders before leaning forward and continuing in a soft voice, "It would be an heirloom from me dearly departed—" Her words paused at Seamus's laughter. She glared at him. "It *is* from me mother! And me brother—"

"Who is also a warder in the town gaol?" Aidan asked.

Briana laughed, then quickly sobered. "Conor would be a debtor, Captain, which is why he wants to sell me ring, and now has it with this one's help." She briefly glared at Seamus before yanking her cudgel from the captain's grip.

Before she could use it on Seamus, the captain again wrapped his large hand about it.

"I shall handle this," he said.

Will you now? thought Briana. To her way of thinking, men of his rank never bothered with those of her station, unless it was to cause more trouble. Because of this, her tone was quickly skeptical. "And why would you be doing that?"

The captain not only seemed surprised by the question, but quite unsure of his answer. Even so, he narrowed his gaze at Seamus and spoke in a voice even deeper than before. "I believe I can avoid bloodshed." Taking the cudgel from Briana, he tapped the top of it against his opened palm. "Can I not, Mr. Fahey?"

Seamus's spindly arms were shaking as badly as his spindly legs. "Now look here, Your Honor, I—"

"Fool," Briana said, "you must use the man's rank when addressing him." She turned to the captain and smiled. "Is that not right?"

The captain didn't rightly say. His gaze drifted to her mouth and remained there.

Briana wondered why. Her smile finally faded, which oddly enough brought the captain's gaze back to hers.

In that moment, the desire in his eyes was so naked and unashamed, Briana's heart paused, then fluttered. She might even have stepped a bit closer if not for Seamus loudly clearing his throat.

Both she and the captain looked at the man.

"*Quiet*," the captain ordered.

Seamus frowned. "I only cleared me throat, Your Hon—"

"Did you not hear the young woman? You will address me in the proper manner, *and*," he said, speaking above the man, "you will return her Claddagh ring."

"It's hardly hers!" Seamus said.

"It *is!*" Briana cried.

"Quiet!" the captain ordered them both, but added to her, "If you please."

Briana couldn't recall another time she had been as pleased, and that caused her to blush crimson.

The captain gave her a fast smile before turning back to Seamus. "You obviously know about the ring, so give me the truth, or you shall soon regret not only the crime, but your lies."

"Will I now?" Seamus said, then growled, "And what would a ring from the likes of us matter to someone like you?"

The captain stepped closer. His proximity and superior height now fully blocked the man. "I have just come from battle that was long and hard, and am now looking to amuse myself before returning to my estate." He swung the cudgel to the right and left of Seamus's head, then swung it to the side of Seamus's legs and between them, too, until the fool was nearly dancing.

During this, the captain said, "I believe knocking the truth from you with this weapon should amuse me quite nice—"

No confession was given faster than Seamus Fahey's, though it did little to please Briana.

Her heart fell as she cried, "What do you mean you

sold me ring and spent the money? How could you *do* such a thing? How could he *do* such a thing?" she asked the captain.

"Quiet now," he said in his gentlest tone that turned quickly hard as he spoke to Seamus. "Who purchased her ring?"

". . . Dermot Fitzgerald, a servant in Mrs. Walsh's employ on Stephen's Green. But no matter," Seamus said, then pointed to Briana. "The ring was never hers to claim."

"It *was,*" Briana cried. More than that, it was her one hope of being wed; it was a powerful omen that a man would someday want her, that he would cherish her forever. Only now, that hope was gone.

Holding back tears, Briana lowered her head.

"Take heart," the captain quickly said to her, then spoke to Seamus. "You will leave this town at once and never return."

"Leave?" he said. "Never return? But I am the town's warder!"

"No more. You will leave now while you still have full use of your arms and legs." To hurry Seamus along, he swung the cudgel.

"Will no one stop this man?" Seamus cried as he sidestepped those swings.

"Have a care," the captain warned, "or the good people in this town may very well assist me." He swung again, barely missing Seamus's knee.

The man yelped as if he had been struck. The captain frowned. "Come now, quit dancing so. Since you've decided to stay, I must show you the full extent of my wrath and put this cudgel to good use."

No man had ever run as fast as Seamus Fahey did now, his haste finally making him trip and fall. He remained sprawled in the dirt for only a moment before he was crawling on his hands and knees, then running as fast as he could from the captain's wrath—and this town.

It was a pleasing sight that would have once made Briana laugh, but that was before she lost her ring and the hope of ever being wed.

The captain seemed to realize this, for he shifted from one foot to the other, then at last said, ". . . I am quite sorry about your ring."

No more than she, but his kind words so touched her that Briana gently nodded.

"Rest assured that Mr. Fahey will not trouble you again," he said.

"I wish he would," Briana muttered, "for I would surely love to put him in the ground."

The captain was briefly silent to that threat, then asked, "Might another ring restore your good spirits, sweet disposition, and lovely smile?"

If it were to come from him, it would. Briana met his gaze with such delight and naked hope, the captain's face blushed to the roots of his red hair. He even took a step back.

"I would be pleased to purchase one for you," he quickly said, then immediately added, "as a replacement for the other."

As high as Briana's heart had just soared, it now sank to a place far lower, though she kept that disappointment from her voice. "A Claddagh ring cannot be purchased," she explained, though she sensed a man his age should surely know that fundamental rule. "It must be gotten in a special way."

". . . As an heirloom from one's mother?" he asked.

Well, yes, though there were surely other ways to come into possession of it, one of which Briana was more than familiar with. Not that she was about to tell the captain that, of course.

At last, she sighed. "Me ring was all that I had. It was me only future, Captain."

He was momentarily silent, then said in a soft voice, "Come now, your entire future is not in peril because of this one ring. How could it be when the item is surely lost?"

Briana surely did not like that talk. "It is not lost, Captain. You heard Seamus. Me ring would be at Mrs. Walsh's on Stephen's Green."

"You intend to claim it?"

Of course. Why had she not thought of that before? "I do," she said, taking her cudgel from him.

His gaze went to it, then returned to her eyes. "You would be foolish to use that club to threaten a woman of position."

"I would be foolish not to, as the ring belongs to me. And I mean Mrs. Walsh no harm . . . I intend to use me cudgel on her servant."

The captain rubbed his hand over his mouth, though that hardly hid his smile. "What if you never see the ring again?"

"I will," Briana said, then quickly interrupted his words of doubt. " 'Tis plain that you don't know how determined I can be. But how could you? You hardly know me any more than I know you, save for the fact that you are quite a brute that scares the truth from poor souls like Seamus Fahey."

The captain's hand dropped from his face; he arched one brow. "Poor soul, you say? You do not know me, you say? Very well." He made an elaborate bow from the waist. "I would be Aidan O'Rourke, a captain in the Irish Army and a landowner in Galway County."

With that, he straightened and so quickly approached, Briana was obliged to keep dancing back or be run over by the man.

"I would also be the brute that scares the truth from poor souls like Seamus Fahey," he said.

Briana wasn't about to counter that as he had just backed her into a wall. She glanced over her right shoulder, then her left.

"And who might you be?" Aidan asked, placing his right hand on the wall next to her head.

Briana's gaze slid sideways. She studied his long, strong fingers, deciding she liked them. She looked at his broad shoulders, deciding she liked them, too. She noticed that his coming beard would be darker than his red hair, perhaps even the same shade as his lovely brown eyes, which she liked best of all.

". . . Come now," he said, his voice coaxing, "what's your name?"

If Briana could have recalled it, she might have given it to him. As it was, her mind was blank and her heart was beating far too fast as she met his gaze and smiled.

For Aidan, it was the second time he was held by her smile—no, he was surely lost in it. Never in his life had he seen such a smile. It was a fey smile, straight from the fairies. An enchanting smile, surrounded by dimples.

To Aidan's way of thinking, this girl had far more dimples than any mortal should be allowed and her skin was fair beyond belief. He saw not one mole or freckle on her throat, and certainly none on the swell of her fetching breasts that were barely contained by her brown dress. The garment seemed to be a relic from her girlhood days, though Aidan was hardly complaining.

Each time she breathed, her breasts pressed against the fabric. And they fairly trembled as she murmured, "Take care, Captain."

His gaze slowly lifted to hers, then returned to her fetching breasts. ". . . Take care?"

"Aye," she murmured, "for a fortune-teller once told me that the first man to ask me name would also be the one who would wed me."

Aidan did not counter that. His heart was beating far too fast for him to find additional words, much less adequate breath. He continued to stare at her breasts, completely bewitched by them . . . at least, until his mind heard what she had said about a fortune-teller and being wed.

With great care Aidan lifted his gaze and was again lost in hers. How long he remained that way, he could not be certain, but at last the noise of the town caused him to regain part of his good sense.

Arching one brow, he said, "Did she now?"

The girl's smile became even more enchanting . . . and all too assured. "Aye, she did."

Aidan briefly glanced to the side for protection

against this girl's charms, though he doubted he would be safe for long. Even so, fey smile or not, fortune-teller or not, he had no plans for the altar with any woman, in particular one he'd just met. However, a bit of fun might be in order.

"Well now," he said, as he lifted one of her flour-streaked tresses, then risked meeting her gaze. "I would surely not be the first man to have asked your name, dear girl."

Her smile instantly paused, even as her eyes narrowed.

Aidan wondered why. He had no idea how his words had offended her, but offended she was, so he spoke quickly. "Come now. There's no reason to be—"

"Oh, but there is," she said, "as I am hardly your *dear girl*, Captain."

Planting both hands on his chest, she gave him a quick shove.

As Aidan stumbled backwards, she turned on her heel, but paused after only a few steps.

Looking over her shoulder to him, she spoke in a proud voice that also held great sorrow. "Nor am I a fancy woman that gives men what they want so long as they meet the price."

Aidan stopped rubbing those areas she had bruised on his chest. His cheeks burned with shame. "You must forgive me," he said.

"For thinking so poorly of me?"

"For causing you such distress. My intent was not to wound you."

Her frown briefly paused as she considered whether

he was telling the truth or not. At last, she faced him, but kept her proud tone.

"Be certain you don't. Though you are a gentleman and used to the very best, I'll have you know me mother was no fool—she was a skilled bonesetter. When me no-good brother Conor broke his arm, she fixed it quite well, she did. And from the time I was born, it was her greatest wish to teach me the trade, but she was forced to give up on the notion for if I had Conor between me hands, I would have broke his other arm and both of his legs after that."

Aidan laughed.

Her face flooded with color. "Why do you laugh so, and at a true story? Do you not believe me mother was a bonesetter?" Her frown returned. "Or is it you think I am no more than a simpleton?"

Aidan quickly sobered. "No."

Her frown deepened. "You doubt me mother set—"

"No!" he fairly shouted, then spoke quick as could be for he could not bear her being angry with him. He needed to see her smile. "I believe your mother set bones. And I have never claimed that you are a sim—"

"I can read," she interrupted. "You may be a gentleman and far better schooled than me, but I can read." Turning on her heel, she quickly walked away.

Aidan was so dumbfounded, he could do little but watch. Never had he met such a spirited girl, one who possessed such sweet, fierce pride—and one that he had twice wounded.

Fool, he chided himself, then ran to catch up with her.

When at last he was by her side, he said, "My dear—that is, lass—that is—"

"Me name is Briana MacCullen." She abruptly stopped, then looked sideways at him. "But that would be *Miss* MacCullen to you."

Aidan nodded, fearful of further offending her. "Miss MacCullen," said he, "though I must say Briana is a lovely name."

Her gaze drifted away, but she did smile, then quickly pointed to the right. "Look there."

Aidan did, though all he saw were the town's shops. Had she changed her mind about having him purchase a new ring to replace the last?

He was looking for the town goldsmith when Briana said, "I can read that sign."

Aidan looked at her, then back to the shops. "Which sign?" After all, there were several.

"The very first on the left. Cob-be-ler," she said, slowly enunciating the word.

Aidan suppressed a smile as he looked at her, and all too quickly became lost in her gaze.

She fared no better, for only the sound of a slamming door caused *Miss* MacCullen to come to her senses. Blushing scarlet, she looked past Aidan and pointed to another sign. ". . . see that one to the right?"

He did and nodded.

"Mill-en-er," she said, again enunciating each part of the word.

"Well done," Aidan said.

"I know more," she said, though his compliment brought a brief smile.

As Aidan listened to her sweet voice, Briana read sign after sign until she came to one that at last puzzled her. "An-ee," she said, then paused and breathed as hard as she appeared to be thinking. "An-ee—"

As she continued to struggle with the word, Aidan finally glanced over his shoulder. Without thinking, he said, "Animal and Bird Preserver."

Briana looked at him, then averted her gaze, though not quickly enough to hide the shame in her eyes. She had tried to impress him with her reading when it was a skill she hardly owned.

Once more, he had wounded her pride and so very easily, too. Would he never treat her with the respect she craved and surely deserved?

It appeared not as she continued to back away from him.

Aidan had no choice but to follow. "Does it not?" he asked.

Briana stopped, but it was a long moment before she finally lifted her gaze to his. Her cheeks were still reddened, her voice quite hesitant. "I don't rightly know what you would be asking."

"Of course you don't, as I'm hardly making myself clear. What I want to know is—does that sign say 'Animal and Bird Preserver'? You must tell me, Miss Mac-Cullen, as I fear reading is not one of my best skills." Nor could it be in this town as many of the signs were so misspelled, Aidan could barely make them out.

Briana hardly knew this, of course, for she continued to search his face as if to uncover a lie, or to see if he were making light of her.

Before doing that, Aidan would have forfeited his

life. He wanted only to please this woman, though he hardly understood why.

At last, Briana seemed convinced of his sincerity for her enchanting smile had returned.

"You are quite right, Captain, that is the correct reading of the sign. And should you have further trouble reading the others, I shall be glad to assist you."

Now, Aidan smiled. "I am most grateful, Miss Mac-Cullen. And to return your kindness, I intend to help you in retrieving your ring."

Before she could say no to that plan, Aidan offered his hand.

"Come," he said, though his voice was exceedingly soft, "we must go to the Walsh residence."

Briana's gaze lowered to his hand. Her cheeks reddened still more, she lingered for a very long time, but at last she placed her hand inside his.

Two

The captain's touch was strong yet gentle as he held Briana's hand with great care.

Minutes passed as they walked in silence with him stealing glances at her and her stealing glances right back. When their gazes finally met, he struggled to suppress a smile.

"Would my pace be too fast for you?" he asked.

He could have broken into a run and Briana would have kept up. "Your pace would be lovely."

At last he smiled as if that were the end of it.

Briana knew better; it was only the beginning. Her gaze lowered to their fingers so completely entwined. Her heart beat quickly as she murmured, "Take care, Captain . . . the first man to hold me hand with both strength and gentleness will also be the one who will wed me."

His step briefly paused, while his gaze seemed reluctant to meet hers. "What did you say?"

No more than his future and hers. Not that Briana was about to tell him that, for now was not the time. She looked from their joined hands to the cudgel she still held.

The captain's step completely stopped. "You are still in possession of that?"

She was, but hardly meant to use it on him. When he wed her, it would be of his own free will; Briana would have it no other way.

". . . Do you believe we will need this weapon at Mrs. Walsh's house?" she asked.

He gently squeezed her hand, then gave her another smile as she looked at him. "I think not."

"Very well." She tossed it to the side, then glanced over her shoulder to a man's startled cry.

The shopkeeper, who was moaning, was also hopping about on one leg while rubbing his other shin. This, while her cudgel lay nearby.

"Fool girl!" the man shouted at Briana the moment she saw what her carelessness had done. "Simpleton! Cursed wen—"

"Enough!" Aidan bellowed loud enough to wake the dead. He pulled Briana behind himself as he faced the man. "You will show this young woman no disrespect!"

Briana looked up at Aidan, then around his arm as the shopkeeper suddenly noticed her protector's superior height, youth, and rank.

"Forgive me, Captain," the man said. "I did not see you."

"You saw Miss MacCullen," Aidan said with fire in his voice. "And you will now offer her your sincerest apology."

Briana's eyes widened as the shopkeeper did just that. Then the man was on his way, muttering curses beneath his breath as he hopped on his good leg and limped on the other.

Turning to Briana, Aidan again took her hand. "Would you be all right?" he asked.

She glanced at the shopkeeper. "Me leg's in a better state than his, of that you can be sure."

He laughed.

So did Briana until they were required to move out of the way of an approaching carriage.

"Best we go," the captain said, then commenced walking at the same easy pace so that she might keep up.

Briana did, and through it all she kept her gaze on him. Never before had a man so quickly defended her, especially one who was also above her station. Never before had a man treated her as if she were equal to him.

And that set Briana to wondering—was it because she was somehow special or did the captain treat all women in the same manner?

She looked even harder at the man. At last, he met her gaze.

". . . Why do you stare so?" he asked.

Why else? If ever there were a man to be stared at by a woman, he was the one. Not only was he just and kind, but not at all hard on the eye. His nose was quite manly, which went well with his firm jaw and chin. He wasn't what others would call a handsome man, but Briana thought his features were lovely all the same. Not that she was about to tell him that or how he had already captured her heart.

"No one never gives you trouble, do they?" she asked, wondering what it must be like to be so tall and strong and powerful.

He unexpectedly smiled. "Those in battle give me plenty of trouble."

Briana's gaze lowered to his uniform, then returned to his lovely brown eyes. "Have you been injured?"

"At times—though I was never in need of a surgeon or bonesetter."

For that she was grateful . . . but would he ever be in need of a bonesetter's daughter? ". . . Do you battle a great deal, Captain?"

His gaze briefly turned inward. "In truth?" he asked. "What else?"

"Then yes," he said, looking at her. "But only now."

"Now?"

"Aye, with you. You have given me more resistance than any enemy I can recall . . ." He paused briefly, then added in a wistful tone, ". . . And have allowed me to win far less often."

Briana arched one brow, though her voice teased. "Am I so difficult, Captain?"

"That you are." He gently squeezed her hand so she could not pull it from his. "You fight me even now. You continue to address me as Captain rather than Aidan, and you refuse to allow me to address you as Briana . . . a lovely name if ever there was one."

The warmth in his gaze touched Briana more than his words, and all too quickly had her blushing. "You are far too kind, Aidan."

"I am hardly too—" He paused abruptly, then asked, "Aidan?"

"Well, that would be your name, would it not?"

"It would, Briana."

She lowered her face to hide her smile.

They walked in contented silence after that. Aidan and Briana, thought she. Briana and Aidan. The names fit quite nicely, though the man and woman who belonged to them did not.

As they continued down the long, narrow streets of town, Briana saw how the others paused to stare at her and Aidan walking easy as can be and holding hands.

What an odd couple they must have presented, thought she. Him with his superior height and fine graces; her with nothing to be proud of save for the ring they were now seeking and the respect he continued to show her.

Thankfully, that was enough for Briana to finally meet those disapproving stares and do some hard staring of her own. All of the women quickly glanced away, with the men doing the very same.

Except for one—a goodman who was just below Aidan's rank. The man's clothes were of a fine quality, his wig powdered white, his reputation untarnished, and his pipe dangling from the corner of his mouth as he gaped openly.

Briana knew why. Just last week, she had to apologize to the man when the edge of her skirt had brushed against his boots, dirtying them, he claimed.

Now, she held her head high, straightened her back, then asked in her haughtiest tone, "And what would you be staring at, Mr. Rooney?"

Aidan glanced at the man, then leaned down to her. "Why you, of course."

Briana's gaze lifted from his mouth to his eyes.

"Well, he surely can't be staring at me," Aidan said, "as I'm hardly a comely lass."

Briana laughed, then paused. "You believe me to be comely, Aidan?"

Did he believe her comely? He instantly stopped and cupped her face in his hands, knowing he had never felt skin softer than hers. It grew quite rosy beneath his touch, while there was innocence and wonder in her beautiful eyes and the promise of passion in her lush mouth.

How could he have ever thought her plain? Why, the girl was a beauty, pure and simple. "You are more than comely," he murmured. "You are lovely beyond compare."

At last she smiled, and his enchantment only grew.

"I take after me mother," she said.

"The bonesetter."

She slowly nodded, then looked to the side as a group of children giggled.

Aidan gave those brats a hard stare which set them to running.

"Best we go," Briana said.

He released her face, but recaptured her hand and resumed walking. "You must tell me about your mother, Briana."

Her step paused, then stopped. Her gaze and voice grew cautious. ". . . And why must I?"

Why else? Aidan was hungry for this dear girl's history, a matter he had never considered with any other woman and wondered if he should pursue now. Briana's caution puzzled him, until he remembered that he was still no more than a stranger to her. "So that I might tell you of my own."

"Tell me now," she demanded. "Tell me first."

"She passed when I was but twelve years old."

"Oh, Aidan, how sad I am for you."

"Then you don't think me foolish for still missing her?"

"Foolish?" Briana frowned. "How could I? Me own mother passed but a year ago, but I shall miss her as much ten years from this day as I do now."

"Then it's well a part of her still remains."

"That would be two parts," she muttered. "Me being one and me no-good brother, Conor, being the other."

Aidan smiled. "I was speaking of the Claddagh ring she gave to you."

". . . Aye, the ring," Briana said, averting her gaze. "Me mother wanted nothing more than for her daughter to be wed—it was truly her dying wish." She resumed walking, but Aidan did not.

Looking over her shoulder to him, she asked, "You all right?"

He was not. He was aroused to his very core by this young woman and frightened by the power she seemed to have over him. So where had she learned to be so enchanting and determined, in particular when it came to being wed?

". . . About your mother," he said.

"She was a wonderful woman," Briana offered, then pulled him along as she resumed walking. "And a great comfort to all, in particular her sisters."

Aidan wondered if the dear lady had wanted them wed, too, and for good reason. ". . . She supported them?" he asked.

Briana unexpectedly laughed, then abruptly paused. ". . . She set their bones."

Did she now? "All of them?" he asked.

"Surely not. Only an arm on one, and a leg on another, and yet another's thumb, and—"

He interrupted before she went through her entire family. "I hardly meant every bone in each of them."

"Well, I would hope not, Aidan. So many injuries to one person would have surely done them in."

He suppressed a smile. "How is it that so many in your family have met with so many accidents?"

Briana lifted her shoulders in a careless shrug, but there was a moment of shame in her eyes. "Living's hard, but you do what you must to put food in your belly."

Indeed. Trouble was, Aidan had never been forced to worry about that, nor had he considered the plight of others until now.

"Did your mother set any of your bones, Briana?"

The girl quickly straightened her shoulders and held her head high. "She did not. I gave her no cause then, nor would I now."

Aidan had no idea what she was talking about, nor did Briana give him an opportunity to ask. She directed him to the right.

"This street would be a quicker way to Mrs. Walsh's."

"You've been there before?" he asked.

"Aye, many times."

He didn't understand. "Why?"

Briana arched a brow as if he were daft. "Why, to see the lovely houses and ladies in their fine dresses." She smiled. "I always wait until dark so that no one troubles me with questions or chases me away. I always hide behind one of the trees, afore I peer into the windows. How lovely everything is. So clean and bright."

And so very different from what she had always known, Aidan thought.

Not that Briana seemed to mind. There was no envy in her gaze as she glanced at the fine buildings they approached. Instead, her expression was filled with wonder, in particular as several ladies passed.

The women in question turned completely around to stare at Briana's flour-streaked dress, face, and hair, while she did the very same to better see their fine taffetas and silk.

"Oh, Aidan, look at that one," she cooed.

He caught only a glimpse of the blue embroidered gown before that woman turned and hurried away.

Briana sighed. ". . . 'Twould be a shame if she tripped and fell in her haste to flee the likes of me. Why, she would surely soil that precious gown."

'Twould be what the arrogant woman deserved, thought Aidan. "How do you know she wasn't fleeing the likes of me?"

"The woman's surely not daft."

Aidan arched a brow, then held onto Briana's hand even though she was trying mightily to take it back. "What would you be doing, Briana?"

"I wouldn't want to be shaming you in such a fine part of town. If you walk on that side of the street and I walk on this, no one need know we have come together."

"No one need know?" Aidan frowned. "Come now, girl, where's your pride?"

"Why, in me heart, Aidan, safe from the likes of them."

His frown quickly faded and was replaced with a tenderness he never knew he possessed. "You are a wonder, Briana MacCullen."

Her smile grew even more enchanting, but hardly changed her determination. "I would be a wonder who remains poorly clothed." She pulled her hand from his. "Go on, Captain—get yourself to the other side."

"I will not. I have a better plan." Taking her hand, Aidan not only went in the wrong direction, but walked so quickly, Briana was soon running to keep up.

Breathing hard, she asked, "Would your plan be to run me about the vicinity in hopes of shaking the flour from me dress?"

He slowed his pace, then stopped. "There would also be flour on your face and in your hair."

Briana's eyes widened in surprise. She quickly pulled a tress to her eyes, then looked down at her nose.

Even crossed, her eyes were beyond compare. How easily she continued to bewitch him, thought Aidan, but knew of no way to protect himself, except to leave.

Sighing deeply, he moved still closer. "You have heard of Mrs. O'Donnell, have you not?"

Briana rubbed her eyes before lifting her gaze to his. "Would she be one of Mrs. Walsh's servants?" She frowned. "Would she be the one who has me ring?"

"No. Come." Aidan led Briana down this newest street, but was mindful to keep his pace on the slow side so that she might keep up.

As she did, Briana glanced at the couples who passed. They gaped at her, raised their brows at Aidan, whispered to each other, then shook their heads or quietly laughed.

Briana sighed. "Aidan, what has this Mrs. O'Donnell to do with me ring?"

"Nothing. She would be a seamstress." He glanced over both shoulders. "To my recollection, her shop is somewhere near here."

Briana glanced past him to the only shop in the area and surely the one that belonged to the seamstress. She stopped and pointed. "Would that be her establishment, Aidan?"

He looked. "If the sign reads 'Seamstress' it would."

Briana had no idea what those letters read, but the needle and thread carved into the wood surely told her this was the correct location. Only why? "And what would you be needing with her services, Aidan?"

"They would be for you. She can mend and clean your dress."

"No." Briana pulled her hand from his and so quickly moved back, she stepped on another gentleman's toes.

Both of them gasped, with Briana's being the loudest. First she had injured the shopkeeper with her cudgel, and now this fellow with her feet. Was there no end to her troubles?

Aidan apparently thought not. Before this man could call her a simpleton or throttle her with his cane, Aidan stepped forward.

"You must take care and watch where you're going," he said in a tone that was civil but brooked no argument.

The fellow's gaze darted from Briana to Aidan. All at once, he gave the captain a sly smile.

One that Aidan did not return.

The man now seemed confused. "She would be with you, would she not?" he asked.

"I would be with her," Aidan corrected, "in the role of protector."

The fellow's gaze flew to Aidan's broad shoulders and superior height. "You must have a good day," he muttered, then hurried away.

"Now, Briana," the captain said as if the last few moments had not occurred. "The seamstress can—"

"What she can do is one thing, what I can do is surely another," Briana said, wondering how a man who was so kind to defend her could be so daft about the obvious. "I cannot pay to have me dress cleaned or mended."

"Then I shall pay for the service."

"No. I cannot accept such a gift."

"You mean your pride cannot."

Briana planted her hands on her hips and gave him a frown. "When I showed me pride to Mr. Rooney because of the way he stared, it pleased you—do not lie, I saw that on your face."

He arched one brow. "That was before, this is now. And I was hardly offering you a gift for you shall surely pay me back."

Oh, she would, would she? Glancing over her shoulder, Briana saw that no one stood behind her, so she took another step back.

The captain not only followed, but boldly took her hand. "Before you bolt from me or injure another gentleman, allow me to explain. You shall return my kindness by telling me if I am correct or not when I read the coming signs."

Briana held back a sigh. Of all the things he might have asked for, she most dreaded that and now knew she should never have offered to assist him in that task. It was clearly plain the man could not only read signs, but surely books, and was only pretending she owned the same skill so as not to shame her. At last, she mumbled, ". . . I will do me very best."

"I have never doubted that."

She glanced down to his hand gently caressing hers. "Would you be doing this in hopes of getting a kiss?"

"Would you be offering one?"

Briana craved that more than she craved a filled belly, but was not about to succumb to the pleasure. Her need of Aidan's respect was as great as her passion for him, and so she pulled her hand from his. "I would not."

His smile paused.

With that, Briana's heart sank. She worried that a kiss might be all he wanted and would soon expect. She feared that if she again refused him, he might then take the kiss by force, or turn and bolt, leaving her here alone and unwanted.

He did neither. Glancing to the side, he breathed hard, then returned his gaze to her. "Did your mother, the bonesetter, raise her daughter to be an anchoress?"

Not likely, thought Briana, even as she fell more in love with this man. Not only had he not stolen a kiss, but he remained staunchly by her side.

". . . I am no religious recluse, Captain. Nor," she quickly added, her voice soft, "am I a fancy woman as that other gentleman surely thought. I am simply on a quest to retrieve me ring."

"Then you must act the part," he advised. "To that end you must say *my* ring."

Briana didn't immediately comment. She paused to consider the wisdom of telling Mrs. Walsh that the ring now belonged to him. ". . . Would that be because of your position being so far above mine, with you not only being a Captain, but a gentleman?" And a person Mrs. Walsh would surely respect?

Aidan gave her a queer look. "What?"

Briana was now as confused as he appeared to be. Did he want her to say that the ring was his because he truly wanted it? "Did you want it, too?" she asked.

His gaze dropped to her lips. ". . . What?"

Why, the ring, of course. What else could there be that he wanted? Unless he was also speaking of her. After all, the ring was only to be got in a special way— it was to be a gift from the heart.

Briana knew she would gladly give it to him if he were to offer his love in return.

"If you want me Claddagh ring," she said, "with that being a mark of true love and everlasting wedded bliss, then—"

"No—NO," he said, quicker than required, while also dropping her hand so that he might take a step back. "The ring shall always be yours, dear girl, *if* you heed my advice. When you speak of it to Mrs. Walsh, you will say 'I demand *my* ring,' not *me* ring."

Briana's face reddened as she finally realized this was not about love, but position. ". . . the manner in which I speak offends you, Aidan?"

"No, not at all," he said, even quicker than before, then paused before he stepped closer. "I simply don't want Mrs. Walsh treating you with any unkindness. As a gentleman, I would deplore upbraiding her."

Briana tried to picture that scene. She sensed it might be as satisfying as when he had run Seamus Fahey from town, and all that he was willing to give at the moment. As he had clearly said, he was now her protector. ". . . But if you are somehow forced to take that woman to task, might you have also made use of me—my cudgel? Should we go back to fetch it?"

He smiled. "No need, dear girl, as words have far more power."

Briana was not about to counter that. She recalled the words people in this town had used when speaking of her and her family. She recalled, too, those bumps and bruises she had known over the years. How easily her flesh had healed, while her pride and heart had yet to mend, or to be fully wanted by this man.

". . . I will speak as well as I am able," she promised, "but you must make certain to correct me as often as you think necessary."

"I will do my very best." He took her hand. "Now quit your dawdling—we must go to the seamstress."

Briana still held back. "Can you not find a needle and thread for me to use?"

"You are a seamstress by trade?"

No more than he. "I can make do with the proper tools."

"Why should you wish to when there is a seamstress near at—"

"Oh, Aidan," she sighed, "can you not see I have never been inside such a fine establishment as that?"

He laced his fingers through hers and gave her hand a gentle squeeze. "That I know. But take heart, Briana. You will come to no harm, of that I can assure you."

"I am hardly worried about coming to harm. I simply don't want to make a fool of me—my—" She sighed deeply, not knowing what word to use. "I don't want to be thought a fool."

"Threaten the woman with no weapon and all will go well."

She laughed, then wanted to cry.

"Briana," Aidan said, "you have visited Mrs. Walsh's home, but only in the dark. You have peered through her windows, but only when you were hidden behind a tree. You have feared that someone might see you, then chase you away. But today, you will do none of that. You will walk up the street with the sun to your back and your head held high. You will knock on her door and you will demand to be admitted. Once inside, you will state your business. And you will do all of that in a dress that has been cleaned and fully mended."

"Sad thing, too, for the lady will most likely tear the clean and mended dress from me—my back."

Aidan laughed, then narrowed his gaze at her. "To the shop on your own feet or in my arms, Briana Mac-Cullen, the choice is yours."

Though Briana would have preferred his arms, she finally walked to the shop on her own two feet.

Three

A short time later, Briana was wrapped in a sheet with naught but her undergarments beneath. Although they also needed to be mended, she was not about to give them to Mrs. O'Donnell, the seamstress.

"It is hardly the tragedy you are making it," Aidan said.

Briana's gaze slid sideways to him, then back to what remained of her dress since Mrs. O'Donnell had cleaned it. The right sleeve was now gone—*It surely turned to dust when I simply brushed it!* the seamstress had cried—while the patches on the skirt had been brushed so well, they now had holes in them just like the ones they were intended to hide.

Briana covered her eyes with her hand. "That would be me—my only dress."

"Then we shall have to get you another," Aidan said.

Briana dropped her hand and looked at him, then the seamstress, who seemed delighted at the prospect. She took what remained of Briana's dress and tossed it outside for the dogs to play with.

Briana cried, "I liked that dress, I did!"

" 'Twas surely made when you were no more than a girl," the seamstress countered, "as it hardly fit."

Briana regarded the woman's stout frame stuffed into her well-made dress. "It surely fit better than this sheet I now wear."

Aidan glanced over his shoulder to her, then continued moving about the shop, touching one fine gown after the other, in colors as lovely as any rainbow. "Perhaps one of these will fit," he said.

The seamstress was quickly at his side. "Oh no, Captain, those would be for Mrs. Sweeney."

Briana's hand again covered her eyes, for she knew Mrs. Sweeney quite well. The woman had often come to town to give Briana's mother and aunts trouble when Briana had been small. At the time, Briana had been prone to kicking Mrs. Sweeney in the shins in the hopes of getting rid of her.

To this day, Mrs. Sweeney had not forgotten those kicks.

Aidan, of course, knew none of this for he easily dismissed Mrs. O'Donnell's concerns. "Mrs. Sweeney will simply have to make do with one less gown, will she not, Briana?"

She moaned behind her hand.

"I could make the girl a dress of her very own," Mrs. O'Donnell said. "It would surely take me no more than four full days."

Briana whimpered.

"One of these will have to do," the captain said, then offered a sum that had Briana gasping and Mrs. O'Donnell squealing in delight.

"Very well, Captain, which dress do you want?"

Briana hoped against hope that he might pick the one the dogs were currently playing with, only he did not.

"The one that matches the color of her eyes," he said.

Briana lowered her hand and saw the gown in question. It was constructed of a pale green taffeta with a quilted petticoat that had delicate flowers embroidered into it.

"Do you like it?" he asked.

Briana liked it so well, her eyes filled with tears.

"Perhaps the rose one would be more to her liking," the seamstress said.

"No," Aidan said, his gaze still on Briana. "This is the one she wants and it shall be the one she has."

She looked at him, then back to the dress as tears rolled down her face and over the flour on her cheeks.

Aidan took in the scene and felt such a wave of tenderness, he feared he might weep. What power this wee bit of a girl had over him! Clearing his throat, he turned to the seamstress. "You will help the young woman get dressed." He leaned close and whispered, "Would you also have a basin of water so that she might wash her face and hands, and then give her a brush to be used on her hair?"

The woman quickly nodded, then went to Briana. "Come, dear girl, we have much to do."

Mrs. O'Donnell did not own a light touch. She scrubbed Briana's hands and face, then brushed her hair with such fervor, the girl was surprised she had any hair or flesh left.

At last, though, she was clean and in the gown with a lace-edged linen cap upon her head.

". . . Oh my," Mrs. O'Donnell said, as Briana commenced weeping. "There, there," she cautiously added, "dry your tears and take off the gown and—"

"Take it off?" Briana cried. "Not on me life!"

"What goes on here?" Aidan asked, stepping into the room.

"Not on *my* life," Briana quickly corrected herself, though Aidan hardly seemed to notice.

His gaze went from her hair to her face to the gown, then returned so that he might take that same journey again.

"My apologies, Captain," the seamstress said, "the gown does not fit, so I shall—"

"Not fit?" Briana protested. "It fits me as well as the other I come in."

"Came in," Aidan absently corrected even as his gaze remained on her breasts.

"The gown would be far too snug at the top and too loose at the waist," Mrs. O'Donnell said.

"Aye," Briana said, "the same as the dress I *came* in."

Aidan briefly smiled, then lifted his gaze to hers. "Do you like it as it is?"

"I do!"

The seamstress frowned. "Then why are you weeping so?"

Why else? This was the most beautiful thing Briana had ever seen . . . save for her Claddagh ring, of course.

"Her tears are ones of happiness, are they not?" the captain asked.

Briana nodded shyly.

"Then the gown is yours," he said.

". . . Oh my," Mrs. O'Donnell said as Briana buried her face in her hands and truly wept.

Aidan turned to the seamstress. "Would you be kind enough to leave us for a moment?"

The woman hurried from the room, making certain to close the door.

At that moment, Briana ran to Aidan, throwing herself into his arms.

As he staggered back, she cried, "I cannot thank you enough for this!"

Having her pressed against him was surely thanks enough, though Aidan was not about to voice those thoughts. "It's only a gown, Briana."

"But surely the loveliest one in this world!" she said, then pulled her arms from him and stepped back. "We must go outside and get my other dress from the dogs."

It was a moment before he understood what she had said for he was still feeling the loss of her sweet body against his. "And why would we want to do that?"

She used the back of her hand to wipe the tears from her cheeks. "Why else? So I can mend it and wear it once more." She looked down at her new gown. "This is far too lovely for me to be wearing every single day—I shall have to save it for something special . . . perhaps the day I am wed."

Aidan's heart started beating fast. He pulled at the neckcloth about his throat, but it did not ease his breathing. Deep inside, he told himself he should run from this room and never look back. Still deeper inside, he told himself he was not yet capable of leaving and that made his heart beat even faster until he feared he might swoon.

At that moment Briana finished blowing her nose on a piece of cloth. "You all right?" she asked.

He never was when she was about . . . or so close, for she had unexpectedly moved toward him and was gazing into his eyes.

He whispered, ". . . Why do you stare so, Briana?"

"You are not at all hard on the eye," she said in reply.

"And you are beauty beyond compare."

Her cheeks pinked up quite nicely. "I believe I will give you a kiss for making me so."

Aidan was completely stunned, then quickly eager—at least, until she cupped his face in her hands, turned it to the side, then pressed her soft lips to his cheek, kissing him as if he were her brother—one whose bones she did not wish to break.

Aidan frowned, in particular when she began to pull away, a matter he was not about to abide. Keeping her to him, he was of a mind to take her right here and now, and would have if she had been any other girl. But she was Briana MacCullen, the bonesetter's daughter and a young woman who demanded respect.

To that end, Aidan simply pressed his cheek to hers, but also gave her a warning. "Briana, you must not tempt me so."

Her body trembled against his, but her voice was strong. "Then I shall not."

"Just a moment," he warned, keeping her to him. "I am not yet finished with you."

He held her close, enjoying how she finally softened in his arms. She would make a worthy bedmate, thought he, for she would be both strong and yielding, and that set his heart to beating even faster until his passion was nearly out of control.

So, too, was Briana's, for her arms were now about him.

As luck would have it, the seamstress took that moment to pace in front of the door, most likely wishing to come back in.

"We must leave," Briana said, her cheek against his chest. "We must get *my* ring."

Aidan smiled at her proper speech and breathed hard in response to every other part of her. Lowering his mouth to her ear, he whispered, "Take care, girl, for I *shall* know the sweetness of your lips."

Briana withdrew her arms, but she did not push away. Instead, she pressed her hands against his chest and lifted her face to his.

He saw beauty and innocence, softness and strength. He saw what he wanted.

Trouble was, the seamstress wanted entrance and was now shouting loud enough to wake the dead. "Might I come back in, Captain? Has the girl stopped weeping?"

Not only had she stopped weeping, she had taken to blushing and was quickly moving away from him.

"I warn you," he said, "I shall not be put off forever."

Her blush deepened, even as she arched one brow. "And I warn you, Captain, the first man to kiss me shall also be the man who will wed me."

Aidan's heart was again beating fast.

"You may come in," Briana finally called to the seamstress.

"Would all be . . . well?" the woman asked as she looked at Aidan, then over her shoulder as Briana fled the room.

"Where would you be going?" Mrs. O'Donnell called out.

"To get *my* dress from the dogs!" Briana shouted back.

She was able to save nothing but the remaining sleeve and that was only because the dog coveting it was but a pup.

Sighing deeply, Briana glanced at Aidan's hand that was extended to her, palm up. She placed the damp sleeve on it.

Aidan arched one brow, threw that sleeve to the side, then took her hand in his. "To Mrs. Walsh's," he said, and commenced walking.

Those who passed them this time were far different from the last. The men all tipped their hats to Briana and offered their greetings to the captain, with the women being even friendlier.

"My, what a lovely gown," one of them said, giving Briana a dear smile before turning to her companion. "I believe Mrs. Sweeney told me she was having one made in the very same fabric."

"Careful," Aidan murmured, holding tight to Briana's hand. "If you run now, they will know the truth of the matter."

Indeed. She lowered her voice to a whisper. "Might we, at least, walk fast?"

Aidan nodded, wished the women a good-day, and hurried along with Briana to Mrs. Walsh's house.

It was only when the dwelling was in sight that Briana's step slowed.

Aidan saw the wonder in her eyes and the doubt in her heart. He also saw the tree she was wont to hide behind, and led her past it.

"Go on," he said, when they reached the door, "use the knocker as if you belong here."

"As I do not, I see why they have placed it so far above my reach." That said, she lifted her skirt and thrice kicked the door with her foot.

Aidan resisted scolding the girl *and* laughing at her antics, for her unorthodox manner of knocking surely brought a servant running.

"Yes, Captain," the elderly man said, then turned to Briana. "Good afternoon, Miss—do come in."

Briana's breath caught as she stepped onto a rug that was softer than new grass. She gaped at the circular staircase, nearly high enough to reach the clouds, and the walls covered with the loveliest paintings she had ever seen.

"What might I do for you, Captain?" the servant asked.

"You will address the young woman," Aidan said, "as she is the cause of this visit."

The man turned to her. "Yes, Miss, what may I do for you?"

Holding back a sigh, she squared her shoulders, lifted her chin and said, "I have come for *my* Claddagh ring."

The elderly man briefly arched his white brows. "And would you have lost it here during one of Mrs. Walsh's gatherings?"

Briana started to laugh, until Aidan squeezed her

hand. Quickly sobering, she said, "Ah, no, Your Honor—ah, that is," she amended when Aidan again squeezed her hand, "no, I did not."

"I believe the young woman needs to speak to the lady of the house," Aidan said. "Would you be so kind as to tell Mrs. Walsh that Miss Briana MacCullen and Captain O'Rourke await her?"

Minutes later, the lady in question was fairly beaming as she hurried into the gold-and-ivory drawing room where Aidan and Briana had been asked to wait.

Seeing Aidan first, Mrs. Walsh retained her smile. Seeing Briana next, that smile surely paused, then turned to an outrageous frown.

"You!" the woman said, then quickly turned to Aidan. "Good work, Captain. Did you catch this one peering into my windows? She does that, you know." She turned on Briana. "Whose gown is that you wear?" She looked back to Aidan. "Did she steal it from someone you know, Captain? Did she tell you she stole something of mine? Did she—"

"Something of *hers* has been taken," Aidan said, his voice icy and low.

Mrs. Walsh's mouth moved for a moment more, but produced no words.

Aidan spoke to Briana. "Go on," he said, in a voice that was now quite soft, "tell this woman what you've come for."

Briana looked at Mrs. Walsh's stunned expression and could not help but smile. Oh, how she loved this moment and this man. How ably he protected her! Though now, Briana knew it was her turn to shine.

Making certain to keep her voice subdued and ladylike, she announced, "I am here to claim *my* ring." That said, Briana looked at Aidan to see how she had done.

His broad smile said she had done quite well.

Mrs. Walsh, however, seemed quite confused and on the verge of a very bad headache.

"*Your* ring?" the lady asked. "And what ring would that be?"

"Her Claddagh ring," Aidan quickly answered before Briana could. Then he added, "It would be an heirloom from her dearly departed mother."

Briana's grin promptly faded. She looked at Mrs. Walsh, who was laughing.

"Why, St. Patrick himself could not have made me believe *that* lie," the lady said.

Briana had already lowered her face. At this moment, she would have given anything to leave . . . perhaps even to die.

Aidan, on the other hand, was quite ready to fight and made his voice harder than he ever had with one of the gentler sex. "It would be no lie, *madam*. Your servant, Dermot Fitzgerald, has Miss MacCullen's ring—*an heirloom from her dearly departed mother*—an heirloom he purchased under false pretenses. Now, you will order the man to this room and have him produce Miss MacCullen's property, or I shall call the sheriff to do so, and then you and your servant will have to answer to him. Is that understood?"

Mrs. Walsh's sudden pallor said that it was more than understood.

"Do forgive me, Captain," she said, her voice trembling. "I knew not the importance of your request."

"You do now, so bring the man forward at once."

As she fairly flew from the room, Aidan gently squeezed Briana's hand and whispered, "You shall have your ring in a moment."

Her eyes filled with quick tears.

"What is it?" Aidan asked.

What else? "You believed me over her. If you had had my cudgel, I believe you might have saw fit to use it on her and all in my behalf."

He regarded her for a moment, then leaned close so that he might lower his voice even more. "I would do it again and again, I can tell you that."

"Oh my," she said, her voice thick with tears.

"Come now, Briana," Aidan said quickly, "you mustn't cry. Show them what you're made of. After all, you're the daughter of a boneset—Briana?"

She had already taken her hand from his and turned away, for if she met his gaze a moment more, she would weep for days on end and tell him everything, including how much she loved him.

"Briana," he said, his voice truly concerned, "do tell me what is troubling you."

What wasn't? thought she, but could not discuss that now. At last, she said, "I need a moment to me—myself."

"Of course," Aidan said, then moved to another part of this room.

Briana held back all the tears she could, but some still escaped. She was using one of the couch's silk pillows to dry them, when she heard someone approach. Throwing the pillow down, she turned and saw Mrs. Walsh glaring at her—at least until Aidan returned to her side.

Quick as could be, Mrs. Walsh gave Briana a dear smile. "Would you require a handkerchief, Miss Mac-Cullen?"

"No. Just my ring." She glanced at the young man behind Mrs. Walsh.

The lady turned to her servant. "Go on," she ordered the lad, "tell her."

"Tell me what?" Briana asked, not liking the sound of that, or anything else that followed.

Her shoulders sagged as the servant told her that he had purchased the Claddagh ring not for his own use, but for another servant in a neighboring town, and had since sold it to that friend.

"My apologies, Miss—Captain," the boy said, "but me friend wanted the ring to give to this girl he means to wed." He looked at Briana. "Knowing the girl, I am quite certain she will not be giving it back."

Briana's heart fell even further.

"Very good," Mrs. Walsh said to the lad, then ordered him back to his tasks. "I am quite sorry about your loss," she said to Briana in a tone that said she was not sorry at all. "Will you now be on your way?"

"We will," Aidan said, his voice quite cool as he took Briana's hand and led her from this cursed place.

Once outside, he headed to the right, but Briana sorely tried to go to the left.

"What would you be doing?" Aidan asked. "If we are to go to the neighboring town, we must—"

"You heard the man as I did!" she cried, pulling her hand from his. "The ring is lost!" As was her hope of ever being wed.

Turning on her heel, Briana ran to the same group

of trees she had so often hidden behind when she had peered into Mrs. Walsh's house. Slumping against the first, she finally wept.

Aidan felt completely helpless as he watched Briana's narrow shoulders trembling with those wrenching sobs. Swearing beneath his breath, he turned and thrice kicked Mrs. Walsh's door, then went to Briana's side.

"The ring is not lost," he said, his voice gentle as could be to her, then raised to a shout as Mrs. Walsh's elderly servant called from the kicked door.

"No!" Aidan told the man. "We did not knock again!" Turning to Briana, he said, "The ring has simply traveled to another town. One we must now go to in order to reclaim it for you."

She shook her head, then moved to another tree that hid her from the passersby.

After a moment, Aidan joined her. "You no longer wish to claim your—"

"The town is too far!" she cried. "It might as well be on the other side of the moon!"

"The town is hardly that far, in particular when one is on horseback."

"Oh, well then," she said, looking at him, "that would be far different, *if* I had a horse."

He smiled. "I do, and will allow you to ride it so that we might continue this quest for your ring . . . a matter I will not deem settled until the blasted thing is yours again." Cupping her chin in his hand, he said, "Come now, give me a smile."

It took her a moment, but she complied. Aidan's tenderness so quickly flared into passion he could barely catch his breath, and was surely unable to stop his words. "How you tempt me, Briana . . . I am mad to kiss you."

Unlike times past, she offered no retort. Instead, her gaze lowered to his mouth, even as her own lips parted. And when Aidan gathered her into his arms, she did not resist.

How small she was, thought he, but with an inner strength that humbled him, making him want her all the more. At last, he closed his eyes and gently touched her lips with his own.

Her breath was hot and sweet, her words whispered as she said, "I am mad to kiss you, too, Aidan."

His heart soared.

"But you must also take care," she said, "for the first man to kiss me shall also be the man who will wed me."

He heard the warning, of course, but could not stop. He covered her mouth with his own, then quickly deepened the kiss as he slipped his tongue inside.

There was no hesitation in Briana's response. She suckled his tongue, drawing it still deeper into her mouth. She wove her arms about his neck, pulling him closer still.

She had no guile, and for that Aidan craved her even more. He had kissed many others—some of them considered beauties and quite a catch—but they had always shown a lingering reluctance as if good manners did not allow full passion. Not so Briana. With this young woman, Aidan felt truly wanted for the first time in his life, and so he held nothing back. He gave her his all.

She wanted only his heart and respect; she needed his love. Her flesh tingled as he kissed her with a need that said she was special—*that she was his*. Her heart beat out of control as he pressed her still closer until she could feel the strength in his body and the promise of his passion.

They kissed for a very long time, and might have spent the rest of the day in each other's arms if not for the sudden sound of children nearby.

As Aidan's mouth finally broke free of hers, Briana slumped into him, for her legs felt far too weak for support. Resting her head against his broad chest, she heard his heart beating as fast as hers, while his breathing remained as strained.

At last, he lifted one of her tresses, then wound it around his palm. "We must do this again," he said.

For the rest of our days, she thought, but knew this was not the moment to bring up the future, so she teased, "You mean me leaning against you so that you might play with me—my hair?"

"You know very well what I mean," he said, his voice husky and low. "Were it not for those brats nearby, I would kiss you again and yet again."

"Were it not for my ring, I would let you."

Laughing, he eased back, then took her hand. "Come," he said, "we shall get my horse and ride to the next town for your ring."

Four

Although the neighboring town was not on the other side of the moon as Briana had once claimed, to Aidan's way of thinking, it was still not far enough away.

With his arm about her waist, and her head resting against his shoulder, he was hard pressed to want this journey ever to end. Given that, he kept his horse at a very slow pace—and at times completely stopped—so that he could turn Briana's face to his and taste the sweetness of her lips.

It was after the seventh or eighth pause in their journey that Briana finally said, "At this pace, Aidan, we might never arrive."

She was on to him, of course, but also smiling and that made him want her all the more.

Holding her even tighter, he kissed her with a passion that would have frightened even the most experienced of women. Not so Briana. She was with him every step of the way and, at times, even surpassing him.

Never had Aidan been so besotted by a woman. Trouble was, he also feared he was losing his heart.

With that, the blasted thing started beating hard

enough to bruise his chest. Oh, this had gone too far. Pulling his mouth from hers, Aidan mumbled, "To the town." It was either that or go back to the first, wed the girl, and be done with it.

Aidan was not ready for that now, or as far as he could see, anytime in the future. So, he kept his gaze straight ahead as he prodded his horse to a canter. During this, Briana continued to stare at him.

"You all right?" she finally asked.

Of course he was not. The girl's body was pressed to his as a wife's would be to a husband's, and her lips were all too close.

"Turn around," he said. "Not to face me," he quickly added, when he saw she was prepared to do just that.

She lowered her leg and seemed quite confused. "If I'm not to face you, then which way should I turn?"

"To face the road," he said.

"Why?"

He risked looking at her, and wanted her all the more. ". . . It will serve to keep you on this horse."

"Your arm would be doing that." She eased it still closer, then folded her own arms over it, so it could not be withdrawn.

Aidan swallowed, but that hardly calmed his galloping heart. He lifted his gaze to the passing countryside and noticed that although the hills were of a velvety green hue, their color was not nearly as lovely as Briana's eyes.

"Would you care to kiss me again?" she asked.

His gaze shot to her even as he recalled her words.

. . . you must also take care . . . the first man to kiss me shall be the one who will wed me.

Aidan so quickly reined in his horse, they both nearly fell from the saddle. Before Briana could recover or he could regain his good sense, Aidan was kissing her even more fiercely than before.

It was near dusk before they finally reached the town, with Briana's belly growling louder with each passing moment.

Aidan pressed his lips to her ear and murmured, "You must eat."

"I want nothing at all," she said, despite her stomach's newest growl.

"Perhaps you don't, but your belly surely does."

"Then it must find the funds to pay for the meal as I am sorely lacking."

"As you well know, I shall pay."

"If I allowed that, you would surely want another kiss."

He smiled. "I shall get that in any case. No more arguments," he warned as she started to protest. "We are pausing to eat." Not only did Aidan wish to fill her poor belly, but he wanted this part of the journey to last. He feared the moment they reached their destination, Briana's ring might truly be gone, and he was loath to see her in tears.

Thinking of that, he directed his horse to the town's sole inn. It bore a curious name.

Briana glanced at the sign and asked without thinking, "What does it say?"

Aidan swallowed, then was forced to clear his throat before he was able to speak. ". . . The Good Wife Inn."

"Oh my."

Oh my, indeed. Was there nowhere on this earth that he might go to flee the two words he dreaded most— *wife* and *wedding*?

"You all right?" Briana suddenly asked.

Of course he was not. He was fully prepared to ride to the next town or even the one after that for a suitable place to eat—a *safe* place to eat—when Briana's rumbling belly reminded him of her discomfort.

". . . I would be fine," he said at last. "Is this inn to your liking?"

She gave him a dimpled smile. "I think it's quite lovely, I do."

Indeed. Suppressing a sigh, Aidan helped Briana to dismount, then led her inside.

The dining hall was hardly one Mrs. Walsh might have enjoyed, but given the way Briana continued to smile, she thought it was a veritable palace.

After the serving girl told them what food the inn had to offer, Aidan told Briana to ask for what she liked.

"Then that would be what she said."

The serving girl, who had been eyeing Briana's gown, lifted her gaze. "You want all of it?"

"Aye."

Aidan sensed that Briana had never before eaten in an inn. Before the serving girl could point that out to Briana or anyone else in this room, Aidan told her to bring an ample portion of each dish that they had.

As the girl walked away, Briana leaned toward Aidan. "Why did she look at you so queerly?"

"She's most likely wondering why a mere captain would be dining with a lady as lovely as you."

Briana giggled, then softly moaned as the food was quickly brought to their table. Her gaze darted from the herring to the pollack and eel, then to the cakes of bread, cans of butter, cabbage, and boiled bacon.

"For what do you wait?" Aidan asked.

Her gaze lifted to his, then returned to the food. She seemed about to weep, but that quickly passed as she tasted the fish, then the boiled bacon, and after that everything else.

Never before had Aidan seen a woman eat with such raw pleasure. Oddly enough, it reminded him of her delightful abandon when they kissed.

As he was reliving those pleasant moments, her chewing finally slowed. Swallowing fast, she lifted her gaze to his. "Am I eating your share?" She looked at the meager portions he had taken and had yet to eat. "Do you lack funds to pay for more?"

Before Aidan could answer, she pushed to her feet. "I shall offer to work for the innkeeper's good wife so that you might also fill your belly."

Aidan caught her wrist before she could go too far. "Please be so kind as to return to your seat."

Briana looked over her shoulder to him. "Come now, Aidan, you mustn't let your pride stand in the way of your hunger."

Indeed. "My hunger is not for food alone," he said, keeping his voice low.

Despite this, or perhaps because of this, Briana's

cheeks turned a bright pink. ". . . That may be, but your belly must be attended to. Release me, so that I may speak to the innkeeper."

"I would prefer you speak to me," he said, "a man that surely has adequate funds to pay for more of this fare if *you* should require it. And please don't thank me for my kindness—simply prepare for those moments when I shall again seek your kiss."

Her throat was now as pink as her cheeks. "Very well, Captain, but might I also eat during that preparation?"

He suppressed a smile. "If you must."

Briana had no other choice. Though her passion for this man was very nearly out of control, her hunger was unfortunately far worse.

She slipped one delicious morsel after another into her mouth, finally whimpering in delight.

And Aidan surely noticed. "When was the last time you had your fill, Briana?"

If she were to respond truthfully, then her answer would be *never.* She had been born hungry and had remained that way even to this moment. Not that she was about to tell Aidan that, for she had her pride.

"Why, that would have been just yesterday," she lied. "The truth of it is, I cannot stomach another bite now." She pushed her plates to him.

He pushed them right back. "Best you finish it all, as I did not order this to be wasted."

Briana glanced at the lovely food. ". . . I would surely not want to do that."

"Then eat," he said, his voice filled with tenderness.

She finished it all save for the boiled bacon and

cabbage on his plate. When he offered those items to her, Briana finally shook her head. "I am so filled, I am quite certain I will now break your horse's back."

Aidan laughed.

Briana smiled, but only briefly. "Might we now go to see about my ring?"

The Kennedy cottage was not easy to locate what with the darkness now fully upon them and Briana slumbering so peacefully against Aidan's chest.

He looked down at her so frequently and was so lost in his desire for her, he kept missing those turns the serving girl suggested he take to get to the proper location.

At last, though, the dwelling was in sight.

"Briana," he whispered, "we have arrived."

She stirred briefly, mumbled what sounded like an oath, then snuggled into Aidan's chest as if that were the end of it.

As far as Aidan was concerned, she could have remained as she was for as long as she liked. Trouble was, he knew she wanted her ring so that she would be wed to the first man who had asked her name—as he had; and had held her hand—as he had; and had kissed her—as he had.

Aidan's heart started beating all too fast. Perhaps he shouldn't wake her at all.

As fortune would have it, Briana suddenly awakened on her own.

Yawning quite loudly, she finally asked, "Would that be the Kennedy cottage?"

". . . It would."

"For what do you wait?"

What else? The courage to face her enchanting smile that seemed so assured he would wed her . . . or to face those tears that would surely come if the ring were not here.

As fortune would have it, Aidan was soon faced with the prospect of her tears.

They welled in Briana's eyes as she stared at the young man who had opened the door. "What do you mean, you're not the Kennedy I seek?"

"The serving girl must have misunderstood our request," Aidan said.

Briana frowned. "Or *she* would be the one this fellow fancies and intends to wed."

"Please, Miss," the young man quickly said, his voice quite low, "me wife might hear—"

"Your wife has already heard." A woman who was twice this lad's weight and of a mean disposition came to the door. She took one look at Aidan, then turned her frown on Briana. "Would you be making eyes at me husband?"

"With me here?" Aidan asked.

"I want me—my ring!" Briana cried.

The woman looked perplexed. "And what ring is that?"

"The one your husband give to the serving girl!"

The woman's frown became deadly. She looked at her husband.

"I fear we have the wrong Kennedy," Aidan said, before blood was spilled. "You wouldn't be Hugh Kennedy by any chance, would you now?"

"No," the man cried, "me name's Liam!"

"And lucky for you that it is," his wife said, then turned to Briana and Aidan. "The Kennedy you would be seeking is me husband's cousin."

Briana pushed to her toes, trying to see over the woman's fleshy shoulder. "And he resides here?" she asked.

"Until I threw him out," the woman said. "He's now moved on to another relative in the next town."

Aidan named it.

"That would be the one," she said, then slammed the door in their faces.

Briana's eyes were downcast, her spirit low as Aidan led her back to his horse and helped her to mount.

"Briana," he said at last, "all is not—"

"It *is* a lost cause," she muttered, "and best forgotten."

Aidan thought, not so long as her lovely face wore such sorrow.

But when he started to speak, she again interrupted. "Would you be so kind as to take me back to town so that I might go home?"

So this was the end of their adventure, he thought, then tried to imagine taking her home and riding away. In that moment, Aidan's heart so quickly ached, he had to rest his hand on the horse's rump to steady himself.

When he could trust his voice, he asked, ". . . If I leave you for a moment, will you be all right?"

Briana finally looked at him. "Leave me? Why? To go where?"

"I became lost coming here and do not wish to become lost in going back. I want only to ask for some directions from Mr. Kennedy." Before Briana could question that lie, Aidan returned to the door and knocked hard.

As fortune would have it, Mrs. Kennedy answered and was fully prepared to give Aidan a bad time until he offered her some coins.

She eyed them greedily, but suspiciously. "And what do you want for this sum?"

"Only for you to pretend to converse with me."

"Is that right?" She arched one of her hairy brows, then peered around his shoulder to Briana. "Wanting to make the young lady jealous, are you?"

He wanted to see her smile and needed this deception to accomplish that goal. "Just go along, all right?"

The woman finally did.

When Aidan returned to his horse, he saw that Briana had been weeping.

Though his heart went out to her, he kept that from his voice. "No need to cry."

She muttered something that sounded very much like an oath.

Suppressing a smile, Aidan mounted, slipped his arm about her waist, then wheeled his horse around. When he headed back toward the inn where they had eaten, Briana finally looked over her shoulder to him.

". . . Where would you be going?"

"To the inn to spend the night."

"What?"

"We must, dear girl."

She frowned. "And why must we?"

"Because my estate is surely on the other side of the moon which makes it too far to ride to this night."

Briana's frown paused, then deepened even more. "Aidan, I have already told you, I want only to go back to the town where I reside and go to me own—"

"Without your ring?"

"Of course without me ring!" she cried. "It is always just out of reach, it is a lost cause, it is—"

"Proper to say *my* ring," he corrected her, then lied, "and the ring would now be in the possession of the young lady Hugh Kennedy fancies and intends to wed—though she won't have it for very long."

Briana stared at him. "What do you mean? What's this about?"

What else? He wanted to see her smile. To that end, Aidan intended to secure one of those rings for Briana even if he had to make the blasted thing himself. Of course, time was not on his side, so he continued to lie. "The girl in question resides in the village near my estate. She and her family would be one of my tenants, in fact. Therefore, she cannot say no to my request that she return your ring. That was the matter I was speaking to Mrs. Kennedy about just now. She has promised to send word to the girl to deliver the ring to my residence."

"Will it be there when we arrive?"

How could it? Even so, Aidan was certain one of his servants could surely find a substitute once he gave the order. "I think not, as we are closer to my residence at this moment than the girl is from where she resides. But take heart, your wait for the ring will be quite short."

"Oh Aidan, you are a wonder."

He was a liar, but felt no guilt . . . her smile warmed him to his very core. "Are you happy now?"

She nodded. "Quite sleepy, too."

"We shall be back in town shortly."

They arrived at the inn more quickly than they had at the Kennedy cottage. Even so, only one room was available for the night.

Seeing Briana's blush, Aidan made quick work of paying for the lodging and leading the way to their room guided by a rushlight. But once the door was opened and the light inside, Briana held back.

"Go on," he said, briefly glancing at the spartan furnishings that seemed adequately clean, "it's not that terrible."

"It's quite lovely," Briana said, without even taking a look. "Have a pleasant night."

Aidan caught her wrist before she could leave his side. "What would you be doing?"

"Acting as a lady should," she said, giving him a frown that said he was daft to ask. "It's not proper for the two of us to share a room." She looked about, then pointed to the shadowed hall. "I shall sleep out here."

"On the floor?"

"Won't be bothering me. I have surely done it many times before."

He frowned. "But your gown."

She suddenly remembered it, and very nearly moaned.

Now, he had her. She would have to join him in this—

"Give me your coat," she said, interrupting his thoughts.

Aidan looked down at it, then back to her. "My coat?"

"Aye. I shall wrap it about the gown and in that way protect it."

"You shan't harm your gown for you're sleeping in there."

"No, I am—" Her words abruptly paused as Aidan lifted her into his arms and carried her into the room.

"Aidan, put me down."

"In time." He kicked the door closed, then brought her to the bed.

Briana's heart was beating so wildly she feared it would burst through her chest. "Now, look here," she said, though her voice sounded more excited than afraid. "I am not a fancy wo—"

"Nor am I anything but a gentleman," he interrupted, lowering her to the straw mattress. "You will stay where you are for the remainder of this night even if I'm forced to secure you to this bed."

Her face quickly burned. ". . . And where do *you* plan to sleep?"

"On the floor next to the door, because," he said, speaking above her, "it would hardly be proper for me to allow you to sleep unprotected in this room."

He secured the door, took off his coat, rolled it into a kind of pillow, then shoved it beneath his head as he lay on the floor with his back to her.

Given that position, his linen shirt hugged his broad shoulders and strong back, while his breeches and boots were so snug, they surely revealed every muscle in his impressive form.

Briana's heart flooded with desire, while the rest of her felt quite selfish and ashamed. She thought of the battles Aidan had bravely fought to conquer Ireland's many enemies. He had surely slept on the hard ground, and now fared no better with a hard wooden floor as his bed.

"Aidan, you cannot sleep on the—"

"I can," he growled, "if you would just hold your tongue."

Briana made a sour face to his sour tone. "Might I at least offer you a pleasant good night?"

He lifted his head and looked over his shoulder to her. "You might, but I warn you, Briana MacCullen, you say anything more than that, and I shall surely join you in that bed."

Her cheeks burned even more. "Good night, Aidan."

He regarded her for a very long moment, then finally spoke in a soft voice, "Good night, Briana." Once more, he rested his head against his jacket.

As sleepy as Briana had been only a short time before, she was as alert now. She watched Aidan's shoulders rise and fall with his strained breathing. She pretended not to hear the many oaths he muttered as he attempted to get comfortable on an uncomfortable floor. She allowed her gaze to caress his full length that was exciting for its strength and power, but even more so for the gentleness that was always afforded her.

She recalled those moments on Aidan's horse when

his male heat and protection had so surely lulled her to sleep. She remembered his many kisses, with one being more exciting than the last.

She wanted him to share this bed with her, but she also craved his respect—she required his love.

She watched until he, at last, fell to sleep and the light started to die.

Turning on her right side so that she remained facing him, Briana pressed her face into the pillow and whispered, "Take care, Aidan O'Rourke, for the first man to sleep in the same room as me, will also be the one who will wed me."

Five

Come morning, Aidan awoke not on the floor, but in the bed. And yet, that wasn't the worst of it. Beneath the worn blanket, he wore naught but his breeches, and surely knew nothing of what had brought him to this moment.

Swallowing hard, he considered what he should do . . . not that it mattered, of course, as he had apparently done far too much already.

With that in mind, he at last found the courage to feel behind himself, but Briana was not in this bed with him.

Good Lord, where was she? Good Lord, what had he done?

Aidan pushed to a sitting position and was about to swing his legs over the side of the bed, when he heard a rustle of taffeta to the side.

Swinging his head in that direction, he saw that Briana was fully clothed and at the window. Turning to him, she casually regarded his naked chest . . . as if she were quite familiar with it.

Good Lord, what had he done?

"Did you sleep well?" she asked, giving him one of her dimpled smiles.

Aidan feared he might never sleep again, for he knew not what had transpired last night. If he had ravished her, why was she still smiling? Unless she had enjoyed being ravished, which seemed unlikely given her previous reluctance to share this room with him.

"Why am I here?" he asked, pointing to the bed. "And why are you there?"

She arched one slender brow as her voice teased, "It's hardly proper for both of us to be using the bed."

So they hadn't used it . . . or had they? Aidan still wasn't sure. "What happened to my neckcloth, shirt, and boots?"

She pointed.

Aidan saw that his neckcloth and shirt had been freshly laundered and someone had also blacked his boots. He next noticed that there was now a washbasin and soap, not to mention several cakes of bread, a can of butter, and a wedge of cheese.

"You did all this?" he asked.

"Aye."

"How?"

"How else? I done give my requests to the inn-keeper's good wife. When she demanded payment before delivering one crumb, I proudly told her of the battles you have surely won against Ireland's many enemies." Briana frowned. "The woman was not impressed." She lifted her shoulders in a gentle shrug. "So, I then told her that you were my protector. Even with that, she was not fully impressed."

Perhaps not, but that surely got Aidan to laughing. "And what did you do then?"

"Why, I attempted to find some coins in your coat to pay the greedy woman. Sadly, though, I found nothing and guessed those coins were still on your person." Her gaze drifted to his chest. When she spoke, again, her voice was quite distracted. ". . . After that, I did what was required. I helped put her kitchen in good order and—"

"You *what?*"

Briana lifted her gaze to his. "No need to shout, Aidan."

"I believe there is," he said. "You helped put that woman's kitchen in good order? What about your gown? What about your—"

"Allow me to finish and I will tell you."

Aidan arched one brow to her suddenly ladylike manner, when only the day before she might have used her cudgel to ensure his silence and good behavior. "Go on."

"Thank you," she said quite daintily, then continued. "I helped her in other matters besides the kitchen, and during all of that labor, I wore a dress she was kind enough to supply. As you can see, this gown is quite—"

"That hardly addresses your working for the innkeeper's good-greedy wife." He frowned. "You worried about your gown, but not yourself, Briana. Did you scrub your hands raw while you assisted her? Come now, show me."

She hid her hands behind herself.

It was just as Aidan thought; she had scrubbed the flesh from them.

"Will you show me," he said, "or will you force me to look on my own?"

"I am considering your demand," she said, then added, "or might it be a request . . . would you be asking for my hand, Aidan?"

Just like that, he felt the blood draining from his face.

Briana seemed not to notice as she rocked back and forth on her heels. "I await your reply, Aidan."

He could see that. Trouble was, there was no reply he could give. He hardly wanted to see her tears if he gave her a negative response . . . and that only left the other—for him to ask for her hand in blessed and eternal wedlock.

"I—I—I—" he began, and continued, unable to say anything but that one word.

"Aidan," she finally interrupted, using a tone reserved for an idiot child, "are you going to thank me or not for being so kind as to provide for you?"

That was not the question he had expected, nor that she would toy with him. Despite his relief that she expected no more than his gratitude, he was also disturbed that she wanted no more than his gratitude.

It seemed he was losing his mind.

". . . I thank you," he said at last, "but I am still confused as to how I came to be in this bed, and in this condition. Surely, you didn't carry me here." Surely, she hadn't undressed him.

Her peal of laughter quickly filled the room and Aidan's heart. Again, he was overcome by both an overwhelming passion and tenderness for her.

"No, I did not carry you," she said. "You come on your very own."

He did?

Seeing his distress, Briana gave him the full story. "You slumbered for a bit, then awoke swearing and complaining of your sore shoulders and back. When I next heard a *clunk—clunk,* I knew you had taken off your boots. After that, you pulled off your neckcloth and shirt, rose to your stockinged feet, walked yourself to the bed, and without so much as a 'by your leave' dropped yourself onto the mattress and commenced snoring."

Indeed. ". . . And what did you do then?"

She crossed her arms over her chest and arched a brow as a lady might. "What else? I got up and left you to the bed."

"You slept on the floor all—"

"No. I scrubbed the greedy-good wife's kitchen and—"

"All night?" he interrupted again, then promptly left the bed. "Come, you must sleep."

"We must eat. And then we must journey to your estate for my ring. Because of our night here, perhaps the girl will have delivered it by the time we arrive."

Not likely, thought Aidan, though he wasn't about to say such a thing.

He washed and dressed as quickly as he was able, but declined the food she had provided for breakfast.

Briana looked skeptical. "I secured enough for the both of us . . . there would be no need for you to give me your share as you attempted last night."

"That may be, but I'm simply not hungry," Aidan lied,

then suggested they take the food with them to be eaten somewhere between here and their destination.

"And further delay our arrival? I hardly believe that would be necessary."

On the contrary, it was essential considering there was no ring as yet, though Aidan wasn't about to admit it. So he lied. "The journey is quite long and fraught with any number of perils." The least of which was hunger, and the greatest of which was the state of his heart.

With the back of her head against Aidan's broad shoulder and her gaze on the lovely countryside, Briana had never known such happiness.

Sighing deeply, she asked, "Where are the perils you spoke of? Come now, point them out."

Aidan's chest rumbled as he cleared his throat. "We are, for the moment, quite safe."

From thieves and ruffians, surely. But what of love?

Lifting his hand from her waist, Briana pressed her lips to Aidan's knuckles, then ran her tongue between his fingers.

In that moment, he was as besotted as she, for he reined in his horse and tightened his arm about her waist. "Take care," he warned her now as she was always warning him, "as you tempt me far too much."

Briana turned her face to his and kept her tone innocent. "At the moment, Aidan, you tempt me not at—"

That was as far as she got, for Aidan kissed her not only with passion, but an unexpected tenderness that brought quick tears to Briana's eyes.

So moved was she, that the very moment their kiss

was at an end, Briana pressed her face to his shoulder as she struggled not to weep.

". . . You all right?" Aidan asked.

She was in love, which was another matter entirely. At last, Briana answered with a nod, for she could not yet trust herself to speak.

Aidan didn't press for more. He gently stroked her hair, offering comfort, until the horse snorted loudly, wanting to be on its way.

"Best we go," Aidan murmured.

"We will stop again, will we not?" she asked.

His chest rumbled with his gentle laugh. "That we shall."

And so it went during their journey. They rode for a bit and stopped to kiss for far longer, until at last Aidan's belly rumbled louder than Briana's had the night before.

Tearing her mouth from his, Briana insisted that he eat.

"Later," he said, "for now, your lips are all that I require." He lowered his mouth to reclaim hers and failed miserably. As a woman, Briana was far nimbler than he in dodging kisses.

"Come now," she said to his frustrated growl, then gently touched his bristly cheek with her fingertips, "give me the reins. I shall see to the horse so that you may eat."

Aidan promptly laughed, then directed the horse to a stand of trees near a lovely pond. "We shall rest here. No arguments, mind you."

Argue with this place? Why, it was surely paradise.

Scores of swans glided effortlessly across the pond's

glassy surface. Plump, white clouds dotted the seam-
less blue sky, but did naught to restrict the sun. The
air was warm and welcoming, as was Aidan's arm.
Slipping it about Briana's waist, he guided her to the
spot he liked best, then put a blanket on the ground.

"Did you sleep on that blanket during your many
battles?" Briana asked.

"Aye—but only when it was safe to sleep."

That surely settled the matter. Briana was doubly
resolved that he should know only comfort and happiness. "You will be safe here, I intend to see to that."
Looking about, she chose a stout limb that had been
broken off one of the trees, perhaps by another woman
who chose to protect her man. "With this in my hand,
you can be assured of an uninterrupted slumber."

"You mean to strike me with it until I swoon?"

Briana laughed at the thought of him swooning like
a mere woman. "I mean to strike anyone who would
be daft enough to intrude."

Aidan arched one brow, but there was a smile tugging at his lips. "I think not." He took the limb from
her, casually tossed it aside, then pulled Briana into
his arms. "I hardly intend to sleep while I am here."

Indeed. "Then you shall be safe to eat," she said,
nimbly escaping his embrace.

Aidan again arched a brow, but this time there was
no smile to accompany it.

"Come now, eat," she said, carefully laying out the
food they had brought along.

Swearing beneath his breath, Aidan sank to the blanket, tore off a piece of bread, shoved it into his mouth,
chewed, then stopped.

"You all right?" Briana asked.

"I am not," he said, then finished chewing and quickly swallowed. "This bread is surely the best I've ever tasted, and yet you saw fit to keep it from me until now."

"You claimed to require naught but my lips."

Aidan gave her a sly grin, then greedily ate the first cake, before grabbing a second. "I must ask the innkeeper's greedy-good wife to tell Cook what sorcery went into this, for surely only magic could produce such a heavenly taste."

"Or a girl by the name of Briana MacCullen."

Aidan's mouth paused around the next cake of bread. "You made this?"

"I did." She narrowed her eyes. "Did you not know I am apprenticed to the town's baker?"

All at once, Aidan recalled the flour that had been streaked over her dress, hair, face, and hands. "Yes, of course," he lied, "I guessed that from the beginning."

Her laughter briefly filled the warm air. "You did not. You thought me a complete simpleton, what with the flour I had on me—myself."

"I thought you were lovely," he said.

Her cheeks turned pink. "I want you to know, I have never been as careless with flour as I was yesterday. I take my trade quite seriously, I do."

The taste of her heavenly bread had already told Aidan that. ". . . Will your master be expecting your skills on this fine day?"

"He will, but I have my Claddagh ring to recover."

Ah yes, the ring that was forever out of reach, would finally be replaced with another, and would return Briana's hope of being wed. Because of this, Aidan avoided the subject entirely. "Tell me, have you always wanted to be a baker?"

She gently shook her head. "My true desire was to be a butter carver. I always dreamed that a lovely lady or fine gentleman would see the imprints I had made, such as a gentleman's coat of arms or some other lovely design, and enjoy my work before eating it."

Aidan couldn't help but smile. "Then why don't you study that trade?"

Briana waved her hand as if he were foolish to even ask. "One from my station in life cannot hope to attain such a lofty position. 'Twas no more than a foolish dream." Lowering her gaze, she brushed the crumbs from the blanket.

Seeing the shame in her eyes, Aidan quickly said, "Baking's an honorable trade."

"It is . . . and I like it well enough," she said, her gaze still lowered, "but even if it suited me not at all, it was one of my mother's dying wishes that I become a baker, with the other being that I would wed, of course."

Aidan coughed, then swallowed hard to force down the bread in his throat.

". . . You all right?" Briana asked, keeping her gaze lowered.

He was fine, or would be, once the subject was changed. "You speak often of your mother." But what of the other half of that pair, the man who had obviously given the woman her Claddagh ring? "What sort of a man was your father?"

Briana's gaze jumped to his, then lowered once more.

"What are you doing?" Aidan asked as she suddenly pushed to her feet.

"I believe the swans want a bit of my bread. And why not? I'm surely filled, and have been since we met."

Aidan smiled, but Briana hardly saw it as she was already hurrying to the pond. After a moment, Aidan followed.

She briefly glanced to the side as he joined her.

"That fellow over there needs more of this than the others," said she, then threw a bit of the bread.

It hit the *fellow* on its neck.

"Oh my," Briana said.

Aidan suppressed a laugh. "I fear your baking skills far outweigh your throwing skills."

She arched one brow, then threw another piece that bounced off another swan's head.

Aidan laughed.

"My father never come around much," she said.

His laughter quickly died. "What?"

Briana glanced in his direction, but her gaze remained on his captain's coat. "He was away a lot," she said.

Aidan looked down to his uniform. ". . . He was in the army?"

She was momentarily silent, then met his gaze. "Not as a captain like you."

Before Aidan could speak, or question the brief shame in her eyes, Briana had already turned and was walking around the pond to throw bits of bread at the rest of these startled swans.

Though the creatures scurried away from her, Briana surely followed. She was even prepared to join them in the pond if only to avoid another of Aidan's unexpected questions about her mother and father.

To tell him the truth now would cause him to bolt from her, and she hardly wanted that.

As it was, he asked nothing more, but simply watched as she circled the pond, then returned to their blanket.

They ate in strained silence after that until the food was finished.

". . . Best we go," Briana finally said.

"As you wish."

They conversed not at all during the remainder of this journey. At last, though, Aidan lifted his hand and pointed to the left. "My residence is near at hand."

To him, perhaps, but Briana saw only a vast expanse of land, with much of it planted in wheat.

They passed acre after acre before they were close enough to get a wee glimpse of his home.

Even from this distance, Briana saw that it was of gray stone and surely as large as a castle.

Wanting to see more, she straightened.

"What is it?" Aidan asked.

"You have so much."

"That may be," he quickly said, "but I'm a fair landlord."

Briana looked over her shoulder to him. "I have no doubt of that as you are a fair and honest man."

Aidan's gaze drifted away as he thought of the ring, and how he continued to lie about it. Now that they were at journey's end, he had to secure someone else's heirloom for Briana as she would surely not accept any further delays.

She was already twisting this way and that while also craning her neck so that she could see more than the distance allowed. When that didn't accomplish her goal, she placed her hand on Aidan's upper thigh, using it to push herself higher.

Whether she succeeded, he knew not at all. His gaze had already shot down to her small fingers so effortlessly arousing each part of him. ". . . Briana."

"What?"

"Do be still," he very nearly groaned, his voice strained with passion, "or we may never arrive!"

Glancing over her shoulder to him, Briana offered an enchanting smile, but did keep still.

Aidan, on the other hand, continued to breathe hard, then harder still as they approached, for he saw his housekeeper, Mrs. O'Leary, and several of his other servants coming outside to greet him.

Good Lord, he had forgotten about them. However was he going to explain Briana? Worse yet, however was he going to explain to one or all that he needed a blasted Claddagh ring?

"Is that stout woman your aunt?" Briana asked.

Aidan suddenly wanted to laugh, though he hardly dared. "No. Mrs. O'Leary keeps my house in order and my servants to their tasks."

Briana nodded, and asked no more as Aidan reined in his horse.

"Welcome home, Captain," Mrs. O'Leary said, speaking for the rest.

He nodded as the women curtsied and the men gave a brief bow. After that, all eyes flew to Briana.

Aidan hurriedly dismounted, then assisted her. "Mrs. O'Leary," he said, turning to the housekeeper, "this would be Miss Briana MacCullen . . ." Aidan briefly paused, then blurted, "the sister of a dear friend of mine who was lost on the battlefield, which rendered Miss MacCullen homeless. She will be staying with us for the time being."

Briana looked at him, as did everyone else.

Aidan cleared his throat, then made his voice stern. "Welcome her."

"Welcome hom—, that is, welcome, Miss," the housekeeper said for the rest, then curtsied.

Briana was about to do the very same, when Aidan again cleared his throat, making it sound far worse than the time before. Briana froze in mid-curtsy and looked at him.

He quickly shook his head.

She slowly straightened.

"Mrs. O'Leary, how I have missed you!" Aidan said, then promptly hugged the startled housekeeper, and whispered, "Go along with whatever I say."

"Aye, Cap—that is, I have missed you also, Captain."

"Indeed," he said, then again whispered, "whatever I ask in the coming moments, your answer to me will always be *no,* is that understood?"

She nodded.

"Well then," he said, at last releasing her and stepping back. "Has the girl yet arrived?"

Mrs. O'Leary opened her mouth to say no, but then paused and looked at Briana.

"The girl from the village," Aidan explained.

"One of the captain's many tenants," Briana added.

Mrs. O'Leary looked from one to the other and shook her head so quickly, her cheeks jiggled. "No."

Briana's shoulders slumped.

"Take heart," Aidan said to Briana, cursing himself for this deception and what looked to be her coming tears, "the girl will surely arrive."

"Not if the ring means more to her than your position," Briana countered. "Not if it was her mother's dying wish, as it was my very own mother's, that her daughter would someday be wed."

The servants exchanged quick glances.

Before matters got completely out of hand, Aidan said, "Mrs. O'Leary shall take special care to watch for the girl." He looked at his housekeeper. "Will you not?"

"No."

Briana gave the woman a frown, then looked at Aidan.

He tugged at the neckcloth about his throat, but that did little to facilitate his breathing. "As I stated during our journey, we were always closer to this residence than the girl, but to make certain she arrives, I shall send one of my men out to hurry her along."

Briana pointed to one of the younger men on the right. "That one looks sturdy enough for the journey."

Aidan continued to tug at his neckcloth. "Indeed. The moment your needs have been seen to, I shall give my orders."

Briana quietly regarded him, then leaned close. "What needs of mine are to be seen to?"

Aidan smiled. "Because of me, you lost the chance to sleep last night."

Briana's cheeks turned a bright pink. Her gaze slid to the servants, who seemed to be leaning closer so they might overhear. Clearing her throat, Briana grabbed Aidan's sleeve and led him away from the rest. "Resting sounds quite lovely," she said, keeping her voice low, "but what I would truly fancy is a bath."

"It's yours." He looked over his shoulder. "Mrs. O'Leary."

"Aye, Captain." She hurried to his side.

"Might you have a bath drawn for Miss Mac-Cullen?"

"No."

Briana frowned.

Aidan pressed his fingers to the inside corners of his eyes. "Perhaps you misunderstood," he said, then inhaled deeply and hissed, *"have a bath drawn for Miss MacCullen."*

"Aye, Captain! Molly!" Mrs. O'Leary snapped to one of the younger servants, then told the girl to see to Briana's bath.

"Yes ma'am!" the girl said, then spoke to Briana. "Please follow me, Miss."

Briana didn't budge. "How lovely your hair is," she said. "Why, it's the very same color as the captain's endless fields of wheat."

Molly's round face turned a bright red. ". . . Thank you, Miss." She leaned forward slightly and said in a lowered tone. "Your gown is surely the loveliest I have ever seen."

Briana smiled. "It was made for Mrs. Sweeney, a true lady if ever there was one as her mood is often quite sour and will surely be even worse now, for once the captain saw this gown, he purchased it for—"

"Might you see to that *bath?*" Aidan said to Molly in his sharpest tone.

The girl's face drained of color. "Aye, Captain. Come with me," she said to Briana, taking her charge's hand and pulling her inside.

Once they were out of earshot, Aidan told Mrs. O'Leary what room Briana should have.

The old woman's eyes widened slightly, though she dared not question that request or the others he had.

At last, Aidan said, "I need a Claddagh ring and I need it now." He looked from his housekeeper to the other servants. "I will pay whatever is required. And the one who gets it for me will be amply rewarded."

Not only did Briana get that bath, but her hair was also scrubbed until it was good and clean. After she was rubbed dry, a lovely nightgown that had been carefully stored in a nearby chest was pulled over her head. As Molly tied the ribbons that ran down the front, she whispered "This belonged to Mrs. O'Rourke, it did."

Briana's gaze shot up from those darling ribbons. ". . . The captain was once wed?"

"Oh my, no," Molly said. "This was his mother's, the very same as this room."

Oh my. Briana's gaze darted about the lovely space. "Does he know?" she whispered.

"Aye. He lived here, he did, when his mother was—"

"No—*no*," Briana quickly interrupted, then kept her voice lowered. "Does he know I am here and that I wear this?" She fingered the delicate folds of the ancient gown.

"He should," Molly said, "as he was the one that told Mrs. O'Leary to put you in here and to give you this."

Did he now?

"Then he doesn't fancy anyone?" Briana suddenly asked.

Molly's face and throat turned pink. "Aye, he does."

Briana's heart fell.

"Oh, Miss," Molly quickly said, "it would be *you* the captain fancies."

"You're quite certain of this?"

"Aye. The look he give you outside was never give to another, I can tell you that."

Briana smiled, until she caught her reflection in the mirror. How lovely the nightgown was, how lovely Molly's words, but what of the real truth? Briana thought herself far too plain to capture any man's interest, in particular, the captain's.

And that set her to wondering . . . what if his attention to her was only a gentleman's kindness? What if his kisses and passion were only a soldier's loneliness?

What if he had her put in here because this was the room given to all his female guests?

Briana could have asked Molly, of course, but didn't rightly want to know the brutal truth. Instead, she stewed over the matter even after Molly had taken her leave.

As luck would have it, the very moment Briana was fully convinced of her own inadequacies and Aidan's pity, there was a gentle rap on her door.

"Might I come in?" Aidan asked.

Briana faced the mirror. Given that she had not turned into a beauty or a true lady within the last hour, she quickly glanced away.

". . . Briana?" Aidan called, his voice tinged with worry. "All is not lost with your ring. If you will only allow me to come in to tell you—"

"In a moment," she interrupted as she quickly looked about. Wrapping a blanket around herself, she moved to a part of the room that was the greatest distance from the door and fully in shadows. Taking a deep breath, she said at last, "You may enter."

Aidan did, making certain to close the door behind himself.

Briana's gaze darted from that to his freshly washed hair, shaved faced, and the new set of clothes he wore. Her heart quickly fluttered for he was even more handsome than she recalled.

Aidan, on the other hand, glanced at the bed and seemed puzzled that she wasn't in it. He looked about and finally saw her, though it did little to relieve the concern on his face, especially when he noticed the blanket she had wrapped about herself.

"You're chilled?" he asked, then spoke before she could answer. "I shall lay a fire for—" His words paused as he noticed the blaze Molly had already set. Aidan glanced over his shoulder to Briana. "You're chilled?"

In truth, she had never been as hot.

"Blast," he said to himself. "This room always was far too drafty and—"

"It belonged to your mother."

His ramblings paused. He nodded. "Does it not suit you?"

"Did it suit the others?" she asked.

Aidan glanced to the side, then returned his gaze to her. "What others?"

Briana wasn't quite certain how to answer that. ". . . Your other guests who have stayed—"

"No one has ever stayed in this room but my mother and now you."

Briana's heart soared, but only briefly. ". . . Won't she mind?"

Aidan frowned. "I did not hear you. Why do you whisper? Why do you hide?"

She surely did not wish to be overheard by the servants or his mother's spirit. And she surely did not wish to remind him that she was no great beauty or lady.

Seeing that he understood none of this, Briana held back a sigh and went to him. Pushing to her toes, she whispered in his ear, "Won't she mind?"

Aidan was momentarily silent, then turned his face to hers. His gaze drifted to her lips; his voice was quite distracted as he asked, ". . . Won't who mind?"

Briana's heart quickened to his rumbling voice and

clean male scent. "Why, your dear mother, of course. Won't she mind me being in here, and in this?"

Aidan's gaze finally moved lower. He inhaled deeply, then swallowed hard. ". . . she was often chilled in here and also wore a blan—"

"Not that," Briana murmured, her gaze on his mouth. "This." She opened the blanket to show him the nightgown.

Aidan's gaze dropped to those darling little bows, but not for long. His attention was now fixed on her tightened nipples pressed against the thin fabric. He moistened his lips and swallowed even harder than before. ". . . If she were here, she would be honored to know you."

Briana surely doubted that, but could see that Aidan believed it. She paused before closing the blanket about herself. "It would be me who is honored, for the woman who slept in this lovely room was surely a noble lady."

Aidan's gaze lifted to hers. "That she was, but now there would be an angel in here with her son."

Briana's fingers played with the edge of the blanket that was making her far too hot. "A plain one, to be sure."

"You think me plain?" he asked.

Briana's eyes widened, until she saw that he was teasing. Smiling, she cooed, "Why, I think you will do quite nicely, Captain."

Laughing, he pulled her into his arms, then paused to see her response.

Briana's heart beat all too quickly as she finally

loosened her grip on the blanket, then slipped her arms about his neck.

Aidan briefly glanced down as the blanket dropped from her shoulders. Easing her still closer, he lifted his gaze to hers. ". . . You are a beauty," he said, then kissed her.

Briana's breath caught; she drove her fingers through his hair, using it as an anchor so that he might not lift his mouth from hers.

He did not. His kiss deepened as he boldly moved his hand from her waist and covered her left breast.

It was the most intimate move he had ever made with her, and Briana not only allowed it, she surely welcomed it.

With that, Aidan could hardly tolerate any fabric separating him from her flesh. He pulled at those satin ribbons, unfastening them. Slipping his hand inside the nightgown's opening, his skin at last touched hers.

A soft moan escaped Briana's throat as his long fingers gently squeezed her breast. She trembled with pleasure as his thumb flicked over her nipple, tightening it even more. Her breathing grew quickly strained, her mind surely reeled when he suddenly pulled his mouth from hers so that he might fasten it on her nipple instead.

He suckled and stroked this small part of her until Briana felt that pleasure to the very ends of her hair and to the coiling tension between her legs. When she was certain they would no longer support her, Aidan effortlessly lifted her into his arms and carried her to the featherbed.

It was as soft as a cloud beneath her, while the man above her was all hard muscle and strained breathing.

Aidan's clothes flew in every direction as he quickly disrobed. And then he relieved Briana of the nightgown so that he might regard her naked flesh.

With any other man, Briana would have felt awkward. With this man, she felt no shame in being naked and vulnerable. She lifted her arms above her head; she spread her legs, allowing him to gaze at her naked flesh as she gazed at his.

In the firelight, Aidan's skin was golden, his chest heavily furred as was that part just above his stiffened shaft. The muscles in his powerful arms and thighs were corded with a need that was as great as her own.

And yet, his voice was quite soft as he said, "Never have I seen a woman more lovely than you."

Briana smiled to his kindness, then blushed like the virgin she was as he spread her legs still further and moved between them as a man should do with a woman.

"How I have longed for this moment," he murmured. "How I want you."

"And I you," she said.

That seemed to please him beyond anything else. He even took a moment to tenderly kiss her before touching her opening.

As his fingers stroked, then explored this part of her, Briana's heart pounded out of control; every bit of her flesh tingled. There was no stopping now, and yet, she still whispered, "Take care, Aidan."

"I shall," he assured, "I will be more than gentle with—"

"I have no doubt of that," she interrupted, then cupped his face in her hands so that he might see her, so that he might hear that what she most needed was his respect and his love. "My fear is not for my flesh. You must take care with your passion, Aidan, for the first man to bed me will be the man who will wed me."

He heard the warning, of course, as he had heard all of the others, but what did it matter when her small hands were cupping his face and her lovely body was so heated and moist beneath his? At this moment, nothing could have run him off. At this moment, Aidan felt no fear, only wonder.

"A ghrá mo chroí," he murmured. *Love of my heart.* For she was that, and he wanted her.

Briana's gaze instantly softened; she yielded all the more.

If she had been any other woman, Aidan knew he would have now taken his pleasure—and quickly, too—but she was Briana MacCullen, the bonesetter's daughter . . . the love of his heart. With her, Aidan enjoyed a patience he never knew he owned. He wanted to act the part of her teacher, so that she might learn the wonders of the flesh.

To that end, he kissed the satiny skin on her throat and suckled her tightened nipples, inhaling deeply of her sweet, womanly scent. He stroked her nether lips until they grew moist and even plumper beneath his skilled touch. He next tasted her there, teasing this most intimate part of her flesh with his tongue.

In times past, those other women he bedded had either stiffened or shrieked at so bold an act.

Not so Briana. She fully delivered herself to him, even lifting her hips so that his tongue could more easily reach her.

How she enchanted him, and that made him want her all the more.

At last, her whimpers turned to wanton moans and finally to a cry of delight. Aidan smiled at the pleasure he had given her, while his heart quickened. It was time for him to know her as fully as any man can know a woman.

As Briana's chest continued to heave with her strained breathing, Aidan lifted himself to her. In that moment, their gazes touched. Briana's was still glazed with passion and the knowledge of what was to come.

Aidan gently smiled, then eased himself inside of her, ever mindful of her virginal state. When, at last, he saw that the pain of her deflowering was minimal and had quickly passed, he gave himself fully and accepted all that she had to give.

Six

Love of my heart.

Those words echoed through all of Aidan's dreams.

Come morning, they were still in his thoughts as he awoke with Briana by his side. He looked at her in renewed wonder even though her flesh had been his all of the night.

Now, she slumbered. Her dark hair streamed over the pillow and mattress; she lay on her belly, her arms above her head, her lovely legs spread wide with his seed still glistening on the inside of her thighs.

Love of my heart.

She was that, thought Aidan, and far more. She was a bonesetter's daughter and a baker's apprentice; she was honest and guileless, good-hearted and proud.

She wanted her Claddagh ring. She needed to be wed.

You must take care with your passion, Aidan, she had said, *for the first man to bed me will be the man who will wed me.*

It was her mother's dying wish. It was Briana's one desire.

Even so, it had nothing to do with love, for Aidan

already knew that Briana owned his heart . . . he would never cherish another as he did her.

But loving a woman—no, needing a woman so very badly that her mere presence made the day worthwhile, was not, to his way of thinking, a reason to be wed.

One wedded a woman not out of love or passion, but for heirs. One wedded a woman not because of her enchanting smile or her lovely green eyes or her indomitable spirit and pride, but because her dowry was substantial and her clan made honorable allies.

Over the years, Aidan had met countless young women who had all of that and beauty besides. Even so, he had considered none of them for very long. They were passing fancies, and, if luck was with him, willing bedmates.

He was simply not the marrying kind. He was a soldier. He was an adventurer. Even now, he felt the need to move.

Leaving the bed as quietly as he was able, Aidan pulled on his breeches and went to the fireplace, though not for warmth. All that remained of last night's blaze were three embers that left the room far too chilled.

Blast, he thought. He should not have allowed the fire to die out. He should not have allowed Briana to sleep in such a drafty room. He should not have given her his mother's nightgown. He should not have followed her from that inn, nor offered to assist her in getting that Claddagh ring, nor lied to get her here.

He should not have fallen in love.

Take care with your passion, Aidan.

Too late for that now as his desire was for her and

her alone . . . he knew in his heart it would always be that way.

Love of my heart. She would always be that, too . . . but also a wife?

Aidan slowly shook his head, then paused, and looked back to the bed.

Briana was sitting in the center of it and had been for the last few moments. She was about to avert her gaze, to pretend she had not seen the regret on Aidan's face, but she had.

Love of my heart, he had called her yesterday. *Regret,* his eyes said now, for pleasure had been had and a future between them had been doomed from the start. They were from two different worlds—he was a captain and a gentleman, she was only Briana MacCullen, a fool in search of enduring love. But his love for her was as out of reach as the Claddagh ring . . . and it was now time for her to leave.

Blinking back tears, Briana pulled the sheet to her chin to hide her nudity and a bit of her shame. She next forced a smile and said in her lightest tone, " 'Twas quite a night, was it not, Captain?"

Aidan turned to face her, but said nothing at all.

His eyes, though, told Briana all she needed to know, for now there was even more regret in them.

At last, she forced a laugh. With the sheet about her, Briana left the bed to put even more distance between them. "Fear not, Captain, you are in no peril from me. Being what I am and what you are, our night together was mine to give and surely yours to enjoy."

"Briana, please," he said at last.

"Please what?" she offered in retort, her voice quite

saucy, even though tears continued to fill her eyes. "I thought I pleased you very well last night, as one from me lowly station is expected to—"

"Briana, I must insist—"

"And I must have me say!" she finally cried, her voice breaking.

Aidan sighed deeply. "Go on. I will listen."

Of course he would, he was a gentleman . . . and she was a fool. Even so, Briana was determined to leave this estate with her head held high. To that end, she needed to make her confession. If she did not, someone else would surely tell him the truth.

"Those in town did not lie," she began, "for they know me true heritage. Me mother was not a bonesetter as I told you. Oh, she set bones all right, but only for her sisters who needed them set, and not because they had accidents as you thought. They were just as me mother was—all of them fancy women. All of them feeding and clothing themselves by seeing to the pleasure of the men in town.

"Trouble was," Briana quickly said, seeing that he was about to speak, "some of them men hardly liked paying what was owed, and when me aunts insisted on their money, as was their right, one of them got her thumb broke, another got her arm twisted until it snapped, and still another got—"

At last, Aidan interrupted, "Briana, you don't have to tell me any of this."

"But I do," she said, as tears finally rolled down her cheeks. "I need you to know that you owe me nothing, Captain, nothing at all. I give what I did from me heart, not because I wanted something else. I may be the daughter of a fancy woman, but I have tried to better meself. I once told you I could read. Though you surely know I lied, I want you to know I always hoped to acquire the skill, but there was no time for that, nor school. I had to do what I could to feed meself and me brother, so I took kitchen work and such. And now, I am learning to be a baker. If Fate is kind to me, I might someday find a way to become a butter carver, and you will see me work when you and the woman you wed have a grand feast in this—"

"Briana, will you please stop this!"

"Stop what? The truth?" she cried, though her voice remained soft. "I want you to know it from me, not others, for they will surely tell you what I am when they learn I have been here. Have you not guessed that me mother never got a Claddagh ring from me father as they were never wed? To this day, I have never even met the man. A town husband was often sent to me father to make the man pay for me and Conor's support, not that we saw much of it. Why do you think Seamus Fahey and Mrs. Walsh laughed so when I claimed the Claddagh ring was an heirloom? Them and everyone else in town know I had found it in the belly of a fish . . . them and everyone else in town know I was naught but a hopeless fool."

"You are no fool!" Aidan quickly said.

No? Then why was she here offering everything she had, with him keeping his respect and love? Briana lowered her face and finally wept.

Aidan crossed the room to her, but she quickly stepped away. "Stay where you are, Captain O'Rourke. I do not require your pity."

"It wouldn't be pity I wish to give, Brian—"

"*Miss* MacCullen to you," she interrupted in a proud tone that was choked with tears. "Me mother may never have been wed . . . I surely never will be, but you will treat me with respect for at least trying to better meself."

Aidan knew not what to say or do.

"I must leave," Briana said, then glanced about the room, and quickly cried, "Where is it?"

Aidan shook his head. "Where is—"

"Me dress, what else? I must have it so that I might leave this—"

"Not without your ring."

"Me ring?" she cried, then abruptly laughed. "Did you not hear me, Captain? I found the ring in the belly of a fish! A good omen, I thought, for a Claddagh ring must be got in a special way. How wrong I was. The ring was never mine. The ring will never be—"

"It *is* yours," Aidan countered, his voice hard, "and you shall have it once more. I will not allow you to leave this estate without it. I am master here and—"

"You are hardly master over me!" Briana snapped. "Nor are you me husband! I will leave when I choose!"

He arched one brow. "Not without your dress, you won't. And," he said, speaking above her, "my servants obey me, not you, and they will not allow you to leave without my consent."

Briana breathed hard, then turned her back to him. "You may force me to stay," she hissed, "but be certain of one thing, Captain. You will *never* again share me bed nor me passion."

"Briana," Aidan said, his voice quickly pleading, "will you please listen to—"

"No! If you are a gentleman, you will leave a girl to her shame!"

Aidan briefly closed his eyes, then turned on his heel and left the room, making certain to close the door gently behind himself. After a moment, he heard Briana returning to the bed, then trying to muffle her sobs.

What have you done? he thought, then cursed himself for causing her tears, for bringing her even a moment of sorrow or shame that she hardly deserved.

What her parents were, or had been, troubled Aidan not at all, for Briana was nobler than any lady he had ever known.

Resting his hand on the door, he whispered, *"A ghrá mo chroí."*

She was the love of his heart. She was his to protect and to cherish. Aidan knew that now, and vowed to set things straight.

Briana cried herself to sleep and awoke to find Molly gently stroking her hair.

"Are you also a prisoner or my warder?" Briana quickly asked.

The girl blushed crimson. "I am your maid, Miss."

"You will address me as Briana," she corrected, "as our station is quite the same. In fact, you might very well be superior to me."

"Oh no, Miss. You must eat, Miss."

Briana glanced at the bread, cheese, cold meat, and

wine Molly had brought. "That is hardly what I want."
She looked at the girl. "Where is me dress?"

Beads of sweat began to appear on Molly's forehead,
though Briana could hardly imagine why. This room
was quite cool since the girl had yet to lay another
fire. "Molly," Briana said, "did you throw the dress
out for the dogs to play with?"

"No, Miss!" The girl gave her a queer look.
"Whyever do you think I would do such a horrid
thing?"

Because Aidan had ordered it done? Briana knew
he wanted her here until he could deliver the blasted
Claddagh ring. Only what could that matter now when
she'd never have him?

Briana's heart ached anew, but that only increased
her shame and hardened her resolve. She would go
through life without Aidan O'Rourke and never lie
with another man. And if she had conceived last night,
she would raise Aidan's child alone. She would make
certain that child learned to read, she would send that
child to school, she would raise that child to be a gentleman or a lady despite its mother's lowly station, and
she would recall the man who had created that child
with her. She would love him until her very last breath
even though he hardly loved her in return. Because of
that, she could not remain here a moment longer.

Sighing deeply, Briana finally leaned close to Molly
and whispered, "You must help me to escape."

The girl shifted nervously on the bed.

"Come now," Briana said, "take off your dress so
that I may wear it to es—"

"The captain would have me head," Molly said as

she nimbly escaped Briana, then pointed to the food. "You must eat. I am not to leave until you do."

"Throw it out the window, for all I care," Briana said.

Molly began to cry. "If you refuse to eat, I will lose me work, and me poor mother and father will have nowhere to live and nothing to—"

"I am eating!" Briana said, then shoved the cake of bread into her mouth.

Molly's tears quickly dried, while Briana frowned at the foul-tasting bread. "Your cook has much to learn."

"Is Miss MacCullen eating?" Mrs. O'Leary called from the hallway.

"Aye, she is, ma'am!" Molly shouted, then looked at Briana with a plea in her eyes.

Briana lowered her gaze as she ate only a bit of the bread and some cheese, but quickly finished all of the wine. At last, sleep returned to claim her.

When Briana next awoke, Molly was no longer in the room, though Mrs. O'Leary was.

The older woman glanced up from her knitting, then gave Briana a startled but pleading smile.

Briana eyed the newest food this woman had delivered. "Must I now eat to save your work?"

"Oh no, Miss. Would you care for a bath?"

Briana brought her knees up to her chest and held the sheet to her throat. "I want me dress. Where is it?"

Mrs. O'Leary began to sweat as Molly once had. Of course, the room was now quite warm as a new fire had been laid. ". . . I must ask the captain about that."

"Do so now. I wish to leave."

"Oh no, Miss. Not without your claddagh—"

"Did you not hear me? I wish only to leave!"

Mrs. O'Leary's knitting fell to the floor as she jumped from her chair and ran to the door. "I shall see about your dress."

To Briana's way of thinking, Mrs. O'Leary must have been looking for that dress on the other side of the moon, as she did not return for the remainder of that night. She sent Molly, instead. The girl pleaded with Briana to take a bath and allow her to change the bed linens.

Once Briana was washed, another servant came into the room with a length of ribbon in her hand.

"Miss," this woman said, then curtsied.

Without thinking, Briana curtsied in return. "Who are you?"

"The seamstress, Miss. I've come to measure you."

"For what?"

"Why, your new dress."

"What became of me other dress, the one I come in?"

The woman and Molly exchanged a quick glance.

Briana frowned. "Take off your dress, I shall wear—"

"Oh no, Miss. You shall have a new one."

"That will take *days* to—"

"It will be quite lovely," she said, "now hold out your arm."

Briana crossed them over her chest.

"If you behave like that," the woman said, "your dress will surely take even longer to make."

Clenching her teeth, Briana allowed herself to be measured.

After that, one day ran into the other, with Briana caring little whether it was morning or night. She forced herself to eat, she lost herself in sleep, she was measured and remeasured, but not once did Aidan come to see her, nor did anyone speak of her ring.

At last, Briana wondered if Aidan was keeping her here to see if she had conceived. Perhaps he wanted an heir even though he did not want her.

She was sighing to that truth when she heard carriage wheels clattering over the path. Once they stopped, others took their place, each growing louder and closer.

Was Aidan having a gathering?

Had he invited a young lady he fancied?

Briana buried her face in her hands and was about to weep, when her door was flung open.

Dropping her hands, Briana stared at Mrs. O'Leary, Molly, and especially the seamstress, for she had three gowns hanging over one arm.

"You must quickly bathe and dress," Mrs. O'Leary said to Briana, then spoke to Molly. "Go on, girl, help her."

As Molly approached, and still other servants arrived to draw the bath, Briana backed away. "What is this?"

"The captain wishes to see you below stairs," Mrs. O'Leary said.

He did? Briana smiled, then frowned. "He has guests—don't lie to me, I heard the carriages arrive . . ." She paused briefly, listened hard, then continued, "They are still arriving."

"That is not your concern," Mrs. O'Leary said, "the captain wanting to see you is." She gave Molly a look that got the girl moving.

Before Briana could protest, she was forced into the bath, scrubbed better than she had ever been before, promptly dried, then all but forgotten as the seamstress and Mrs. O'Leary argued over which gown Briana should wear.

"The captain fancies the pale green or the darker green," Mrs. O'Leary said.

"Aye, but the ivory one is far more fitting."

"For what?" Briana asked. "I can hardly return to town in any of those gowns." Surely, Aidan knew that. So what was his plan? Did he intend to avoid guilt over their one misspent night by giving her a gown? Did he hope she would sell it and live off the proceeds?

Or was he, at last, troubled by her lowly station? Did he fear she would leave this grand estate looking like the girl she surely was and shame him in front of his guests? That, more than anything else, caused Briana to proffer her own demands. "You," she said to the seamstress, "give those gowns to Molly for I shall wear her—"

"No!" all three of the servants chorused.

At last, Briana was pushed into the pale green dress. "It does *not* fit," she hissed.

"It does!" the seamstress quickly countered.

"Then why is it not tight on the top and loose at the waist?" Briana asked.

"Because it fits you properly," Mrs. O'Leary said, then took a bit of ribbon and lace and gave it to the servant who was brushing Briana's hair.

Within seconds, it seemed, that hair was done up in ribbon and lace.

Mrs. O'Leary smiled. "You look lovely."

Molly nodded, then started to cry.

All at once, Briana was heartsick. "Me ring has finally been brought here, has it not?"

A tear rolled down Mrs. O'Leary's cheek as she nodded.

Briana held back a sigh and her own tears. Even though she had insisted on leaving, she was sadder than she had ever been. After today, she would never again see Captain Aidan O'Rourke. He would wed another . . . he would love another.

"Come now," Mrs. O'Leary finally said, then gently took Briana's hand. "You mustn't keep the captain waiting."

Briana slowly shook her head, then followed Mrs. O'Leary out of the room only to run back and hug Molly quite hard. "I shall miss you," Briana whispered.

The girl instantly stopped weeping, then laughed.

"Molly!" Mrs. O'Leary snapped.

"Sorry, ma'am." Molly looked at Briana. "Sorry, Miss." She bobbed a curtsy and ran snickering from the room.

Briana frowned, then followed Mrs. O'Leary

through the hall, down the stairs, and through another hall. It wasn't until they reached a set of double doors, that Briana's eyes filled with tears.

"You look quite lovely," Mrs. O'Leary whispered.

"I feel quite sad."

"Oh no," the older woman said, "you mustn't feel like that. Chin up, head high, and don't forget to smile."

Briana stared at the woman, then over her shoulder as the doors were suddenly pulled opened, revealing a large room with dozens of candles burning in countless chandeliers. But that wasn't the sum of it. There were also people in there—scores and scores of people.

Briana's eyes widened to that and the small shove Mrs. O'Leary gave her. As Briana finally started moving on her own, she stared at a man to the right. Though it seemed impossible, he was the very same shopkeeper whose shin she had accidentally hit with her cudgel.

Not only that, but behind him was the gentleman whose toes she had accidentally stepped on, and next to him was Mr. Rooney? Aye, it *was* Mr. Rooney wearing fine clothes and a powdered wig, just like all the other gentlemen that were here, while the ladies were all dressed as ladies should be.

Even Mrs. O'Donnell, the town seamstress, wore a new dress, and eyed Briana's gown with envy despite its poor fit. Briana was about to greet the woman, when she saw Mrs. Walsh to the side, then Mrs. Sweeney, *and* everyone else from town who had always looked down on her.

Only now, all of the men were graciously bowing, while the women bobbed a curtsy.

Briana was about to bob one right back, but was stopped by loud throat clearing.

She looked over her shoulder and nearly swooned when she saw Aidan.

He was at her side in a moment, his arm slipping about her waist. "You all right?" he asked.

She was not. She was in love with this red-headed giant of a man who wore a snowy white neckcloth, a new captain's coat and breeches, and shiny boots.

"Aidan," she finally said, grabbing his coat to keep from slipping out of his arms to the floor, "why are these people here?"

"Why else? I ordered them here so they might know of my love for you." He looked up. "Hear that?" he said to one and all. "I *love* this woman!"

"Aye, Captain!" all of them said.

Briana was now certain she would swoon.

Aidan's arm tightened about her waist. "You all right?" he asked.

She was not. She was surely dreaming or perhaps had even died and was in Heaven. Even so, she had to ask, ". . . Did you say you love me?"

"Aye. I learned nearly too late that I cannot live without you." He raised his voice so all could hear. "I am also begging you to please be my wife. Will you?" he asked, his voice lowered so only she could hear. "Will you allow me to put this ring on your finger?"

Briana's gaze lowered even as her eyes widened. "That could not be me—my Claddagh ring?" She whispered, "The one from the fish?"

Aidan grinned. " 'Tis your lost ring, my love. That was what took so long. I was forced to use a cudgel on the poor servant who had it, but then I am no more than a brute that scares the truth out of those beneath me."

Briana laughed, then cried, "Aidan, do you indeed wish me to be your wife?"

"Aye, *a ghrá mo chroí.*"

Her eyes filled with tears. He spoke those words of love from the heart and in the presence of all.

". . . Aye," she said at last, "I will wed you, Aidan O'Rourke." Glancing over her shoulder to those who once looked down on her, Briana said, "Did you hear? I will be wed!" She turned back to Aidan. "I will share my life with the man I love."

All of the women nodded, and during the ceremony even Mrs. Walsh was moved to sentimental tears.

Aidan gave Briana a wink that had her smiling. At last, he took Briana's hand, then finally and forever slipped the Claddagh ring on her finger.

And why not? He was the first man to have asked her name; he was the first man to have held her hand with such gentleness; he was the first to have kissed and bedded her.

He was the only man she would ever love.

"The ring is now yours," he murmured, "but someday, it will belong to our daughter."

Our daughter, thought Briana, as Aidan kissed her. A child who would belong to them both. A girl who would be raised a lady, and who would know naught but happiness and love.

THE KEEPSAKE

Jill Henry

One

"Saw him, I did. Our new lord approaches the gates!" A stableboy yanked open the buttery door, his young voice echoing through Wild Wind Hall's bustling kitchen. "Regal, he is, and rides a stallion so black it gleams with the sun's light."

Maeve O'Brien looked up from her sweeping, not sure what to think. So, Connor Raeburn has returned to Ireland, has he, to manage one of his grandfather's estates?

She watched as a strange excitement shivered like a candle's flame through the room. Cook gave a dramatic cry. Half the kitchen maids dropped their work and raced to the door.

It had been a lifetime ago when young Lord Connor had come to visit his uncle who called this place home. Connor had been a boy, aye, and she but a spindly lass with curls and a charmed life.

Time had passed, and her world changed.

Would he recognize her? She hoped not. Shame settled like a wet mop in her chest, and she clutched her broom more tightly, the worn wood smooth against her palm.

The entire staff may be in an uproar with excitement over the new lord's arrival, but she had been dreading this day. Kindly old Shamus Raeburn had passed away two months hence, and still she grieved for him.

As difficult as it was accepting a new lord, did it have to be Connor Raeburn? Shame filled her, and her broom stilled. With any luck, he'd not be recognizing her in the homespun apron she wore over her plain brown muslin.

"Now he passes over the stone bridge!" The boy returned, popping through the doorway, aglow with the latest news.

The rest of the kitchen girls dashed from their work peeling potatoes or kneading breads and craned their necks out the back door for a look toward the court-yard.

"Come and see him, Maeve. Hurry!" young Ailis cried above the crush at the door. "Oh, he's a handsome one. A fairy must have kissed him in his sleep to have such a face!"

Maeve could imagine. She remembered the boy, bonny then in his carefree youth. Whatever changes manhood had brought him, she knew he'd be tall, broad of shoulder with a deep voice that could melt a lass's heart.

Maeve's chest warmed at the thought. She *did* want to join the other servants in the dooryard and see Connor Raeburn ride grandly by on his finest of stallions.

The clatter of many horses echoed in the courtyard. That had to be him, she guessed, and approaching fast.

"Oh, Maeve, quickly!" Ailis tore the broom from Maeve's hands and it fell with a clatter to the stones.

"Ailis! I'd best finish my sweeping—"

"What? And not greet the new Raeburn?" The girl gripped Maeve's wrist and pulled. "There is no end to this work, so what does it matter if you leave it?"

Maeve's shoes brushed over the hard cobblestones in the dooryard and, squinting against the sun, she squeezed into place in line, half hidden behind Cook's wide skirts. She peered between Ailis's shoulder and Cook's chin and saw the new lord.

Striking, he was, broad of shoulder and dark as night. Strong and bold, he reminded her of the heroes in tales told around the fire late, when the workday was done.

There was no hint of the boy she'd known in the man who looked with cold eyes on the servants standing beneath him. His coal black greatcoat caught the wind, shivering around the hard cut of his wide shoulders and the strength in his arms.

"Oh, look how handsome he is, and such fine shoulders," Patty the housemaid sighed.

"He looks finicky to me." Cook clucked her tongue. "Likely as not he'll want fancy English dishes served on the finest china."

His eyes are like stone. Maeve could not tear her gaze from the proud man, made as if fashioned from Grecian marble. Sadness tugged at her. The laughing boy full of mischief and humor was only a memory.

This stranger, this fierce-looking lord was a man who would not recognize her. And if by chance he did, he was far too fine to gaze upon a lowly kitchen maid and admit he once knew her by name.

Sorrow balled sharp and achy in her chest, and it

hurt to breathe. It was foolish, this wishing for what she could not put into words. It felt as if the past were truly dead, and all the beauty she'd once known turned to dust.

She saw the back of him now. His raven-black locks were restrained at his nape, giving him an untamed, dangerous look.

"A rogue he is, a pirate!" Cook was mortified.

As if he'd heard, Connor—Lord Raeburn—twisted in his fine saddle to look at the long line of servants stretching out behind him.

The back of Maeve's neck tingled. Could he see her? She bowed her head and spun away. The ring heavy on the string around her neck beat between her breasts as she ran.

Breathless, she ducked through the threshold and risked a glance back. The new lord was not looking her way—foolish to think he had been. He dismounted with masculine power and grace, a sight that made her heart skip a beat. For sure the fairies found him to their liking, for the sun parted between gray clouds at the moment his boots touched Wild Wind's soil, haloing him with gold and light.

Maeve dashed into the sanctuary of the buttery, breathing hard, wishing the past were as easy to escape. Thankful to be alone, she leaned against the narrow space between the shelves and the door. Her chest hurt as if a knife's blade had lodged deep between her ribs. Remembering hurt.

She lived her days one at a time without looking back, without a thought for all she'd lost. It was easier that way, when she was scrubbing floors or up late at night cleaning hearths, not to look back. For she would yearn to hear her mother's voice, or her father's hearty laugh, and what good could come from that? Wishing would not take her back in time, could not return the family she'd lost. Or give her a new one.

Still, a part of her could not stop wishing. She tugged at the string at her neck, drawing the ring from beneath her muslin shift. A heart-shaped sapphire, rare and rich, glittered like a promise made. Mama's Claddagh ring.

Maeve's fingers closed around the band of gold. She knew now why it hurt so deeply, seeing Connor grown into a harsh and distant man. It reminded her that nothing could be the same again. The last time she saw him as a carefree child had been the final summer her family was together. Looking at him made her remember that once she believed the world was kind. That she was once a little girl who spent her days looking for treasure on the beach or riding her beloved pony, always knowing she had a loving home to return to.

That had been the summer before her father's arrest.

"Do not lose heart, little one," Mama had said as she lay dying that winter, offering Maeve the family's heirloom Claddagh ring. "Always look to the treasures in life that are awaiting you."

Oh, Mama, what am I to do when the treasures are behind me? Maeve ran her fingertip across the stone. In the pure true-blue depths, she saw no answer to strengthen her.

She tucked the cherished ring beneath her shift and retrieved the broom from the stone floor. The past was gone as if it had never been, and that left her here. No longer the daughter of a wealthy Irish family, but a scullery maid of the lowest rank.

At least a small bit of fortune smiled down upon her—sure enough it was that she needn't worry about fine Connor Raeburn recognizing her among his servants and bringing up the past.

She'd swept the floor soundly and was starting on the new batch of pots to scrub when the others bustled into the kitchen, with gossip enough to carry them through the rest of the afternoon.

"Will you be requiring anything else this evening, my lord?"

The butler's presence jarred Connor from his daze. He blinked, breaking from his thoughts and focusing on the scene before him. He was in his uncle's library, a cozy, shelf-lined chamber where he'd spent many a rainy afternoon when he visited as a boy. And would spend many a night to come now that Shamus was gone. Sad it was, though he had not seen his uncle in over a decade, and he truly grieved the man.

"That will be all, Forbes."

The door clicked and, alone, Connor drained the fiery port from his goblet in one long swallow. The liquor rolled across his tongue and burned a pleasing trail down his throat. The smell of it brought to mind the pleasures of his former life. Being forcibly banished to the wilds of Ireland was bad enough, but without a decent club in sight? *Damn you, Grandfather. And you, Shamus, for vacating this estate.*

The candles flickered from one end of the library

to the other as if a breeze swept from north to south. A chill snaked down Connor's spine.

"Shamus, is that you?"

Just his luck, a mandatory internment on Irish soil *and* a restless spirit to endure. The hour was late and he was tired, so he lifted the empty glass. "Wager you are a bit surprised to see me here. You'll be pleased to know my father, your brother, proved the worse son. He had a weakness for gambling, drink and women. And so here I am."

The lamps flickered.

A violent bang like a gunshot echoed through the library. The candles sputtered and died; the lights vanished from the chamber as if one great breath had blown them out. Cold wind shot through Connor's chest like a bullet's impact, and the goblet slipped through his fingers.

A shutter cracked against the stone walls, and the window banged open—it was only the wind. Fumbling in the dark, and more than a little relieved, Connor fought his way across the room by feel. Rain cuffed his face as he wrestled the window closed, and the brutal wind died.

In the dark, lit only by the eerie dance of the hearth's orange-red flames, Connor untied his cravat and swiped the rainwater from his face. What else would go wrong this night?

The door exploded open, striking the wooden bookshelves. Light from the hallway sconces sliced into the library as the housekeeper bustled in, distressed, hands flying. "You scared me half to death, my lord! I thought for a moment you were the image of old Shamus come to visit us from his grave. What? Did Mays not repair that window? Hell's hounds to him, that lazy goat."

"Tomorrow will be soon enough to slay him." Connor had visions of the woman ordering a dozen workers into this private sanctuary. "The hour is late, and I wish to be alone."

"Then I shall send a maid with a light." The housekeeper marched from the room with military precision, leaving him alone again.

The firelight danced across the desk, exposing the quill, ink, and the sheets of parchment spread out atop the thick ledgers—no doubt the estate's books. Plainly, Forbes had done this, and his actions spoke clear enough. Grandfather expected an immediate report.

Rage tasted bitter on his tongue, and Connor washed it down with a full glass of port. It was unfortunate that when the goblet was emptied, the pungency remained—and the fury.

The library echoed with movements, a maid's whisper of a step as she lit candles against the storm's darkness. The raging winds muted the chink of crystal; a draft flickered the lights flaming to life one at a time.

Connor tossed the parchment aside, the stiff paper rustling as it slid to rest against the base of a lamp. The hell if he would come to heel so easily.

"Buck up, boy, and claim your place in this family," Grandfather had warned the day of Father's funeral, "or you shall regret it, as God is my witness."

Connor dropped into the chair. He needed more port. A decanter of it, if that's what it took to drive the sound of his mother's tears from his mind. Of that horrible day they had all learned about the insurmountable debt, when the solicitor barged into his Park Lane townhouse. The family wealth was gone. There was no allowance for his mother, no funds for his sister's debut and dowry.

The final blow came with the realization Father hadn't suffered a wound in a hunting accident. He'd taken his own life and left his son to manage the burden he could not face.

Connor didn't know what to believe in anymore, but he knew this for certain—money. That is what the world came down to. Those who had it and those who did not.

"My lord?" Forbes had returned to gesture toward the discarded parchment. "His Grace was clear in his wishes. He expects a message at once."

"To hell with his wishes. I dismissed you for the night."

"In order to write your missive. I have returned to fetch it. There is a rider waiting."

"To gallop all the way to England? This very night? Will he swim or wait for a ship?"

Forbes did not answer, but the quirk of his brow spoke his disapproval.

"Fine," he ground out. "Then you tell him this."

He scrawled two words across the creamy parchment.

"But, my lord, I cannot—" The butler's gaze widened with shock. "Highly inappropriate—"

"Yes, I am." Connor snared the thick ledger, shot around the corner of the desk, and nearly bumped into the servant replacing a broken candle.

She jumped back, as silent as shadow. He caught a glimpse of blue eyes, startling and true. Striding toward the door, he froze midway, glancing over his shoulder because there was something about that color, something that seemed familiar—

"I shall tell your grandfather you were far too exhausted from the journey to write." Forbes's gaze darkened. "Next time, I will make no excuse for your disrespect."

Anger punched through him. Trapped, that's what he was, with his grandfather's thumb on his throat. "When you see him, tell the old man I'll not be ridden like a broken pony."

"But—"

"You're fired, Forbes."

"My lord, surely you cannot mean—"

"I want you gone before the hour strikes." Connor could hear the venom in his voice and the hatred in his words.

Had anger and greed driven him this far? And so fast? His shoulders drew tight, weighed down by responsibilities.

He was already becoming like the men in his family. Grandfather *would* be proud.

Connor was halfway to his chamber before he remembered the maid and her extraordinary blue eyes.

"Have the kindling and wood laid before you quit for the night." The housekeeper gave her last order as she mounted the back stairs.

Maeve continued sweeping the hearth. "Aye."

"Was that impertinence I heard in yer voice?" Mrs. Gallagher stormed back into the kitchen with a jangling of keys, with all the fury of a winter gale. "I hired you as a favor to my lord and no other reason. Now the dear old man is gone and the heartless Englishman in his place will give not a care if I sack you on the spot."

Heartless, aye. Maeve didn't doubt the housekeeper's statement for she'd watched how coldly Connor had treated his manservant.

"I shall see to the task, ma'am. You've my word on it."

"I could have hired me only niece, and I still can if I've the mind to." Mrs. Gallagher nodded once, as if she'd settled matters to her satisfaction. The door slammed behind her, echoing in the cavernous kitchen.

Alone, Maeve shivered. Shadows from the single flame writhed over her, magnifying her sense of loneliness and the howl of the spring storm. Every scrape of the tree limbs against the outside wall, every strike of the tumbling rain scoured her nerves. 'Twas a lonely world out there and cold.

Bootsteps rapped in the stone corridor, heavy and bold, hesitating in the darkness on the other side of the threshold. A man's step.

And she was alone. Ice tingled down her spine as a large shadow fell across the stones at her feet.

The steps silenced, and the shadow became a man with pirate's locks and shoulders as wide as the hearth. She knew it was Lord Connor Raeburn, the heir to the great duke, before she lifted her gaze from his shadow to see him standing in the threshold, more handsome than any one man had the right to be.

She curtsied and bowed her head to hide her face.

"You were the maid lighting the candles in the library." He did not sound bitter now and his voice rang deep like the storm. "I have not been in this country since I was a boy. There is something I must ask you."

Had he remembered her? It gave her a start, and she dared not lift her chin.

"There was a family named O'Brien on the neighboring estate. I wondered—" He tunneled his fingers through his untamed locks. "What has become of the family?"

"They are gone." She fought to keep the tremble from her voice, although her heart rent with the truth of it.

"Gone?"

"Aye." She fetched the candlestick from the table and curtsied again. "I've work to do, my lord."

She darted past him, surprised at how tall he stood and how broad. The candle shivered with the speed of her gait. She took the stairs two at a time, and the bucket clanged against her knee.

The parlor echoed the tap of her shoe and the rustle of her skirts as she knelt at the cold hearth. Vowing to keep her mind from the past, she plunked the pail onto the stone and lifted the shovel from its depths. Banishing images of her childhood from her thoughts, she grasped the little shovel and dug it deep into the ash. The scoop filled easily, and she coughed as soot dusted the air.

While she worked, she tried not to hear the creak of

the downstairs door and the following squeak of a loose floorboard beneath Lord Raeburn's finely polished boots. His confident step tapped on polished wood, whispered on fine carpet, and then silenced outside the threshold.

There was something about the woman, Connor considered from the shadows. She looked to be hardly more than a girl, truly, almost frail at the nape of her neck where black curls escaped her snowy cap. The girl he'd known had hair the same.

"Here's the thing," he began and startled her, for she dropped the shovel with a clang and curse. "I cannot remember the girl's name, but you remind me of her. How can that be? And yet the color of your eyes, so strikingly blue—"

"There are a great many lasses in Ireland with blue eyes, my lord."

"I know that." He sounded like a fool and felt like one too, conversing with a maid at this late hour. Alone, no less. Damaging to both of them. Biting back a curse, he stalked away, ready to turn his tired mind to the books awaiting him upstairs.

Something troubled him, made him plant his feet where he stood, forgetting what was sensible and expected. The maid kneeling before the hearth kept her chin bowed as she swept up the last of the ashes with the quick flick of her hand.

A dainty hand for a maid of her age. Slim and fine-boned.

An icy shiver snaked along the back of his neck. "Tell me what happened to the O'Brien family."

"Ruined and disgraced."

"And the daughter?"

"She left the manor never to return."

"What became of her?"

Maeve closed her eyes against the horrible memories, of how it felt to be penniless, and so young, and with her mother ill. "The girl died the day her father was hauled away."

"I see." He sounded shocked, then sad. He left then with the knell of his step echoing in the vast darkness.

The storm raged and the winds howled and the surf beat mightily against the nearby shore, as if accusing her. She told the truth. The girl she had been was no more. And never would be again.

Two

He had slept little that night, plagued by dreams he could not remember come morning, and his eyes burned in the sunlit breakfast room. A maid arrived with a tray to serve him, but she was not the maid from last night.

He thought of last night and the woman at the hearth as he broke his fast. A whole family gone. Ruined. Kindly Mr. O'Brien carted away in irons.

The poor man. Connor's stomach clenched in sympathy, and the tea tasted sour on his tongue. He rose, grabbed the decanter, and doused the cup with port. The O'Briens' story struck too close to what might have been his. Being controlled by Grandfather, as detestable as it was, was preferable to being disgraced. At least here there were horses to ride, which he vowed to do the instant he could get away.

He did not think of the O'Briens again until later in the day when he reined in his stallion, the best in the stables, and let the sea wind cool his face. The ridge of a stone fence peeked between low trees and, like a tapestry unraveling, he felt the vibrant colors of the landscape before him fade and become sweeter, younger as the present blurred with the past. If he listened closely enough he could almost hear the voices of long ago, of children playing and ponies snorting as they raced toward the fence—

That was it. Maeve was the girl's name.

"These mares will be moved closer to the foaling stable." The foreman's words broke the spell. "Is this to your liking, my lord?"

Connor blinked and the past was gone. Sad it was, how childhood vanished. Duty drove him now, and yet he could not turn his back on the memory. "I am well pleased. The horses appear in fine condition."

"They were the former lord's passion."

They could be mine as well. Back to business, Connor leaned back in the saddle, scanning the vast meadow and the magnificent horses—the horses Grandfather saw as a problem. Connor's first task was to find a solution, one that would, of course, please the old man. "The fields appear overgrazed."

"Shamus could never part with a beloved foal."

I can understand that. Fine-bred mares, sides heavy with foal, lumbered closer to study him with friendly gazes. A shame to sell them, but any of the estate profits were his to pocket. "The duke's buyer will be arriving presently. You are to show him all the horses."

"Aye, my lord."

Connor studied the fertile, rolling hills and lush meadows dotted by a good hundred brood mares and hardened his heart—as a true Raeburn should. *It is about money,* he reminded himself. *Profit, plain and simple.*

In the road far ahead, a flash of pink caught his attention. "What the hell?" He circled the stallion for a better look and groaned at the sight of two lady's hats and a froth of silk in an approaching phaeton.

"The Bardells have arrived, my lord."

"Who?"

"The neighbors, bringin' their daughter. On the hunt fer a man, she is."

Good God! Connor fought the urge to race the stallion into the next county.

Maeve lugged the heavy basin through the kitchen door, the rising steam scalding her skin between her wrist and her cuff. The blasted thing was heavy. Her thigh bumped the bottom of it and boiled water splashed the length of her skirt. She plucked the muslin from her thigh just in time.

A stroke of luck, for she could not afford a burn today, not with a maid out with quinsy and another promptly rendered unemployed at mid-morning, having been discovered hiding her morning sickness from the housekeeper.

There was a lot of firing going 'round, and it wouldn't be Maeve O'Brien who was next. She emptied the steaming water and returned to the kitchen.

"The salmon is dry!" Cook fussed above the clang of pots and the clatter of serving dishes. "What am I to do? And the oyster sauce is clumping. Clumping! Ailis, you did not stir as I told you!"

"I did me best!"

"He'll cast me out for sure," Cook fussed, foreseeing doom as she transferred the salmon to the service platter and added the sauce.

"It's perfection as always," Maeve told her as she nudged the basin onto the table. "The lord will be pleased."

"Sure and I'll be remembering your sweetness when I am begging on the streets." Cook patted Maeve's cheek. "Leave the scrubbing, deary, and fill this with sweetbreads."

Maeve took the platter and set to work. "Tell me I won't be serving."

"That will be up to the Gallagher. She's in a mood today. Like the storm last night, truth be told." Cook gasped. "Oh, the beef olives! They look tough as hide."

Used to the woman's dire ways, Maeve filled the platter and helped Ailis with the vegetable pudding.

"I heard you met the new lord last night," Ailis whispered low. "Alone. In the parlor."

"You *heard?*" Maeve swung around, nearly knocking the platter of salmon.

"Mrs. Gallagher has the sight of a crow, she has, always on the watch."

Maeve laid her hand over her heart and felt the reassuring shape of her mother's ring. If the housekeeper knew about last night, then it looked as if there *could* be another firing today—hers.

"With two maids gone, she'd not send you packing," Ailis tried to comfort.

"I did nothing wrong." Sure of it, Maeve held the serving dish for Cook as she emptied the peas from the kettle.

"Of course not," Cook soothed. "Hurry and follow

the maids. Something is smokin' in the ovens. Maeve, take the peas and hurry."

Maeve did as she was told, but dread filled her. Surely the Gallagher would not have her serve. The thought of seeing Lord Raeburn again was bad enough, but the people who took the manor from her family . . . With the bowl hot against her palms, she hurried after the others.

The long stairwell ahead of her was dark with a great light far above, like the steps into heaven, and Mrs. Gallagher at the top of it, dispensing judgment.

"The salmon first, Ailis, and set it by the lord. The chickens next. Who has the chickens?"

Maeve eased to the front when the housekeeper called for the vegetables.

"You." Her eyes narrowed. "I'll not have *you* serve. You shall clear. Go on, give me the bowl—and hurry."

Such an insult. Maeve felt her cheeks blush, but she held her chin firm as she passed Gallagher the bowl and swept into the dining room, where two housemaids juggled to clear the soup bowls in time.

Do not look at any of them, she told herself, and then it was easier to make her feet approach the elegant table where the Bardells sat, as refined and assured as could be. Mr. Bardell droned on about the good English influence on Ireland while Connor glowered at him, his eyes as dark as a winter storm.

He'd perfected the look of fury, she could not deny it, and he made it look fine and fashionable. She lifted the last china bowl from the table. With his black locks tamed at his nape, he looked like a menacing pirate in gentleman's clothing. All real man so that Mr. Bardell in his padded coat seemed feckless by comparison.

She breathed a sigh of relief as she followed the other maids from the dining room. The lord had not recognized her and, with any luck, neither had the Bardells.

"It is a *shame* what that girl has become." Mrs. Bardell spoke loudly enough to be heard in the corridor.

Maeve's foot missed the floor and the bowls began to tumble. She caught them with a clatter, spilling carrot soup on her apron. Her pulse thundered in her ears as she froze, knowing what she would hear and wishing she could do something to stop it.

"Get on with you," Mrs. Gallagher scolded. "Out of the way."

"What girl?" From the dining room, Connor sounded confused.

Maeve didn't move. She couldn't command her legs to work or her chest to breathe. Frozen, with every muscle clenched tight, she dreaded Mrs. Bardell's answer.

"The O'Brien girl. Maeve—is that her name, Felicity?"

"Yes, Mama."

Maeve felt her heart freeze. There was no longer any sense to it beating. Ailis stared at her, mouth agape, before she disappeared into the dining room. That terrible Mrs. Bardell couldn't keep the truth to herself. Oh no, she had to go spewing it about like prized gossip when she knew the harm it would do.

She would not stand here and listen. Maeve stumbled past the kitchen maids, staring at her as if she'd become a lake monster right before their eyes, and raced down the steps, bowls tumbling from her grip to crash to pieces behind her.

She ran, but she could not escape. The conversation from the dining room trailed after her.

"A scandal it was, how her father let money flow like water through his fingers. Couldn't hold onto it. A gambling man he was. Tell me you do not gamble, my lord."

"Habitually," came the droll response.

"Beware that you do not fall victim to the dangers as O'Brien did." Mrs. Bardell shook her head with great disapproval. "Else your heirs will be clearing tables and scrubbing pots as the poor O'Brien girl."

Enough with the woman's prattle. "What do you mean, scrubbing pots? What became of Maeve O'Brien? I was told she died."

"Died? Why no, you have been sorely misinformed." Mrs. Bardell leaned forward, as if thrilled at the prospect of repeating more scandal. "She is as alive as you and I."

"She did not die?" Connor's hands fisted. He was not aware he'd struck the table until he heard the crystal ring and the silver clatter. *The girl last night at the fire, the one with eyes of the purest of blue—*

"She was in this very room, my lord." Mrs. Bardell plumped up like a peacock. "Cleared the very bowl in front of me. A shame to see her in near to rags. And such a pretty thing she was. Could have made herself a good match if only she'd had a living relative. I am surprised you didn't know."

"I arrived only yesterday." Connor eyed the doorway where silent maids listened with wide-eyed curiosity. Maeve was not one of them. He shoved away from the table, fury drawing him up like a tensed bowstring. "Enjoy the meal."

"But, my lord—"

He marched through the room with such force, the crystal lamps chimed.

She lied. His fury grew with every step, pounding down the stairs. Servants dashed out of his way as he strode through the kitchens.

The cook whirled from her work with a gasp. "Oh, my dear lord, and surely it's the salmon!"

He scanned the crowded room. Kitchen maids whirled from their work whipping cream and setting out desserts. Maeve was not one of them.

"You leave the firing to me, my lord." Mrs. Gallagher burst red-faced into the room. "My fault she was serving at all. Embarrassing the lord in front of his guests. I will see to her."

See to her? "No, you will not."

A movement at the doorway caught his attention. A bucket clanged against stone, and he saw the heavy pail of water land in the threshold.

She could run, but she would not escape him. He ducked through the door.

"Maeve!" He cupped his hands to shout into the wind.

Only the whispering leaves answered.

"Maeve O'Brien!"

At the sound of her name, she merely ran harder down the maze-like garden path. Connor had not remembered at all. That horrid woman who'd taken over her mother's house—she's the one who told him.

Pain tore through her, sharp and new. She stopped, catching her breath, uncertain what to do. In addition to running out on her duties, she'd disrupted the lord's dinner party with one of the wealthiest families in the county. She'd not keep her position now.

"Maeve!" How forceful his voice, as if not even the mighty wind dare diminish it.

He sounds angry and full of contempt. She'd not come like a pup being called. Nor would she stand obediently while he fired her. She'd been given the boot before and survived—and she would survive again.

But it was fear gathering in a hard knot in her throat, making it hard to breathe as she skirted the rose arbors and dashed through the rows of hedges.

The crack of a twig told her he was on the other side of the hedgerow. Tracking her, was he? Well, she'd not be outsmarted by an Englishman. She spun as silently as she could and doubled back—

And tumbled straight into arms as hard as rock. Her cheek connected with the textured wool of a coat, and she breathed in the faint aroma of fine cigar smoke. His hands curved around her elbows, keeping her safe.

His dark hair twisted in the wind, too long and wild. Towering over her, he reminded her of a marauder at sea, and no decent nobleman she'd ever seen. His storm-dark gaze fastened on hers, and in this man cold and bitter she saw a glimpse of the friend she had once known.

"My lord, you've no need to say the words, as I am

heading to the attic to pack." She splayed both hands on his steely chest and gave a firm push.

"I want the truth from your lips." He held fast, his strength mighty and his gaze cold. "Last night, we were alone. You could have told me."

She shoved with all her might, but his fingers banded her wrists, his hold unbreakable and troubling. His touch was fire-hot and made tingles on her skin. It was like having the devil clutching her.

She stomped on his toe, but that did not work either.

He held her fast and firm, the arrogant dog. "You lied to me and I'll know the reason why."

"I told you the truth, or the heart of it, so let me go."

"You will stay on these grounds until I am through with you."

"Through with me?" She twisted, and he released her.

Stumbling back, she rubbed her wrist against her apron to rid her skin of the feel of him. It didn't work. Sensation scorched her arm as real as any flame. "Careful, my lord, not to anger a kitchen maid. We've access to a good many knives, and I am skilled in butchering *and* castrating."

He threw his head back and laughed, deep and loud, the wind whipping his black hair free from his nape, lashing his long locks wildly. "There's the girl I remember from my youth. So, Maeve O'Brien lives."

"Not as you think." She glanced over her shoulder toward the kitchen door, visible in the distance through the trimmed hedges. No doubt the housekeeper was plotting ways to have her sacked. "I ruined your dinner party."

"It was not my dinner party. Those people barged in uninvited to push their daughter on me. They believe I am enormously wealthy and would make a good match. They are mistaken." He tugged at the cravat binding his neck. "I should have yelled mightily when they first arrived and scared them off."

"Tread carefully, my lord. The Bardells have influence in this county."

"Good, then I will stay with you and leave them to their outrage." Trouble glittered in his eyes. His hard, sculpted mouth crooked into a one-sided grin. "I have a certain reputation to keep."

"As a blackguard?"

"I work hard at it." His half-grin became a real one, warming his lean, chiseled face. "Care for a walk along the shore? I would like the company."

"Of a maid and outcast?"

"As it happens, you are the right sort for me. Remember, I have a certain reputation," he repeated and winked.

Saucy! She laughed, she could not help it. "Are you preparing to fire me?"

"Certainly not. I would not harm you, Maeve."

Maybe he wasn't such a bad sort. She fell in stride beside him. "You will have to, like it or not, as the Gallagher will be satisfied with nothing less."

"A peer of the realm, is she?"

"Make jokes, but they'll not save my position. I would appreciate a good letter of recommendation. I've not had one before and it would be of great help."

"Before?"

"My father was taken to prison when I was but thirteen." The sadness came anyway, although she tried to keep it trapped in her heart. "My mother died shortly after."

"I am sorry. I did not know of your loss until now."

"How could you? You did not return." She wiped at the wetness in her eyes, put there by the brisk wind and not by sorrow.

The tended grass gave way to rocky soil and, like the gentleman he was, Connor cradled her arm in the palm of his hand. "My father forbade me from visiting Shamus when he discovered that I had spent considerable time riding ponies with you. He feared it would put unacceptable notions in my head if I kept company with commoners."

"I seem to remember you had enough notions of your own without my influence."

"As I do now."

How deep his voice, warm with humor, the ghost of someone she once knew. His touch felt like a brand on her soul as he helped her around a log washed up at high tide and over rocks that made her shoes slip and slide.

Surf battered the shore, and great mists hung like fog in the air. Connor's hand on burned her arm.

She'd no right to feel attraction to a lord—and this man was more stranger than friend. She withdrew from his touch and deliberately kept her distance.

He followed, gazing out at sea as if something called to him, almost as if she were not there. He did not speak as they walked the shore, listening to the gulls cry and the sea roar. Sunlight played on the water, blinding and magical. The tug of the ocean as it beat against the land made her feel free. The ring tied between her breasts warmed her skin, and she thought of her mother's words. Of the promise of better times that could never be.

Walking beside a fine gentleman who rode ponies with her when she was young could not change the rules of the world. Or the people in it.

Too soon, their walk along the surf brought them to the far gate. The manicured lawns were behind it, hedges clipped and orderly.

Instead of passing through the gate, Connor gazed a long time at the sea, his feet planted and his hands fisted on his hips, dark hair tangling over his wide shoulders. "My father lost his fortune waiting to inherit the dukedom and more pounds than even he could spend."

Nothing he could have said would have shocked her more. He looked powerful, privileged, as if he could command the ocean before him. As if hardship dared not touch him.

"That explains why you came to manage this estate." She laid her hand on his shoulder. How powerful he felt, as invincible as sun-warmed stone. "Did you lose your family home?"

"Sold it to pay the money men." He didn't flinch beneath her hand but remained solid and steadfast, as if nothing could ever discourage him. He looked every inch a man willing and able to fight for what was his. "My father was in deep with his creditors, and after his death I paid what I could. It was not enough. Grandfather rescued me."

"You are fortunate to have family able and willing to help."

"Help? Blackmail is more accurate. The old man finally has me where he wants me—behaving like a proper Raeburn. And behave I must, unless I want our name dragged through every parlor in London, my gentle mother and sweet sister working for hire, and me cast out on the streets."

"We must spare the streets from your influence."

"True."

She ached for him. "Your grandfather requires nothing more than managing this beautiful estate? Truly, it does not sound so terrible."

"No, it is worse, for a good and proper heir to the duke must be well married." When he turned to her, his gaze blazed black. "I'm to be wed to an heiress Grandfather has chosen."

"You do not seem happy about it."

"I have no liking for the woman, but she is wealthy and looking for at least a marquis. And since I am to be a duke one day, she is well satisfied." He shoved his hands in his pockets and kicked at a rock on the shore. The large pebble shot into the air, arcing beyond the first white breaks of the surf, and disappeared into the mist and foam.

She did not know what to say. Duty was duty.

"What am I to do with you, dear Maeve?"

"You have troubles enough of your own, and I am no more the girl of ten you remember than you are that boy of twelve. We are as good as strangers, and you owe me not one thing. But as my former employer, a solid letter would be of help."

The ocean thundered, and the tide swept the sand at their feet. He leaned closer, protecting her from the mist and wind. "Have you worked since you were thirteen?"

"I had no choice." Her voice wobbled, and she bit her bottom lip, as if waiting for the strength to steady it. "Mrs. Bardell took no pity on me, and Shamus had gone visiting to England, so I walked from one village to another until I found work."

He swore, knowing full well the dangers of a young girl alone in this world. "You could have been—" He couldn't stomach it, thinking of all that could have happened. "You were not hurt?"

"No, the innkeeper and his wife treated me well enough. I had my own cot in the corner of the kitchen where I worked. Luck was with me."

Her hand so gentle on his own was delicate and small-boned and did not look capable of hard labor. Yet she'd scrubbed floors and pots, cleaned hearths and packed water. If the stubborn lift of her chin meant anything, then she was proud of it, too.

They stood so close that the wind teased midnight curls from her maid's cap, and the fine wisps caught on his unshaven jaw. So gossamer fine and silky. She was no longer a child, but a woman grown with beauty enough. Her heart-shaped face, her jeweled eyes, her rosebud mouth and softly rounded chin. Beneath her loose shift, he noticed the unmistakable curve of firm breasts and fine hips.

He was a man; it was his sworn duty to notice a

beautiful woman, but if he felt more, he buried it deep. Maeve was vulnerable, and he was to be a married man.

"I will make you an offer, my friend," he told her.

"We are no longer friends." Her chin lifted again, all spark and pride. "You are only my former employer and the author of a generous letter of recommendation."

"Am I?"

"I swear you agreed to it." The lilt of her voice was like music, soft and true and magical.

He realized she was enchanting him, but he accompanied her to the gate in spite of it. "Is the letter so important? I have an arrangement in mind."

"An *arrangement?* You'll aid me in securing another position, then?" Hope brightened her. "It would be a great boon not to go without while I search for work."

"Go without?"

"I work for my room and board here, and little more. The few pounds beyond that buys clothing and shoes. What do you think, the world can live as you do, without care to where your food comes from or if you will have a safe place to rest?"

"I have pondered it more than you might guess." Thinking of his own sister, younger than Maeve but pretty and sweet, made sweat break out on his brow. She would never be forced to labor long days in a stranger's kitchen. Why would he allow a friend from his childhood to do the same? "You will not clean another hearth in my home. I shall give you a room of your own and an allowance."

"You wish to promote me?"

"Certainly not." His dark brows drew together. "I thought I made it clear. You'll not be working for me."

"Then what will I be doing?"

"Whatever pleases you, as a friend of the family."

Her chest tightened until it hurt to breathe, for she could not let herself believe what he was saying. "You and I are not *friends.*"

"We can be." He raked one hand through his untamed hair in a completely dashing way, like a man confident in what he was asking. Like a man used to having mistresses fall at his feet right and left.

The knave. She should have known that Connor as a lord was used to having whatever suited his fancy. The betrayal stung, and the anger, too. "I am sorry to decline your generous offer, but I will never be a kept woman."

"I did not think you would be."

"Sure, and I heard you plain and simple." It was hard to look at the cur and not want to hurl something at his head. But in his way, she knew, he had meant to be generous. "There are some people you cannot buy with that money of yours. Or rather, with your heiress's money, since for now you are nearly as poor as I am."

It took great courage to turn calmly and push open the iron gate. All she could feel was the earth beneath her feet as she stumbled across it and the shame building like a quick-bleeding wound in her chest. How could he do this?

"Maeve! Will you come back?"

"And why should I, after what you think of me." Chin down, she refused to look at him.

"Wait, Maeve, and let me finish. As beautiful as

you are, I am not in the market for a mistress. I only meant to help you. I expect nothing in return."

"No one does a good deed in this world without expecting some gain from it—not even you, my lord."

"Has life been so cruel to you, then?" He laid his hand to the side of her face, some strange emotion aching in his chest. "Your hardship can end here, I swear it."

"Life is its own hardship, and there is no shame in it. I'll earn my way and owe no one for it."

"Then I cannot help?"

She ran her thumb over his wide knuckles, noble and finely-made. There was decency in him, and it heartened her. She pressed her lips to his knuckles. His skin tasted salty and warm.

The world silenced and the ocean stilled as his thumb traced the bottom curve of her lip. Tender, his touch. She closed her eyes, awash with the luxury of it.

The last thing she was needing was luxuries. As difficult as it was, she released his hand, afraid of the heat building within her. Afraid the tightness in her chest and the quickening of her heart meant something forbidden and unwise.

"I must hurry," she lied, humiliation burning her face. She gathered her skirts and ran.

He called out to her, but she ran faster.

His words still burned like an ember within her, all his generosity, all his caring. It would be easy for her lonely heart to make something of his kindness.

How foolish that would be.

Three

Fire crackled in the hearth as Connor studied the latest entries. Shamus had managed these lands well enough, and at least that would please Grandfather.

Damn the old bastard.

Connor missed his home, his friends, his club. He missed his family. After his father's death, he moved Mother and his sister into his townhouse. Surprising how accustomed he had become to Mother's gentle fussing and Cassandra's chatter. He actually missed the sound of the excited conversation while he read the *Times,* as his sister went on about gowns and shoes and who said what to whom at the latest soiree. So much so, that he could barely tolerate the quiet echoing around him now.

A faint clatter rang loud in the stillness. Far down the hall shone a single, flickering light. No doubt a maid cleaning the hearth in a chamber. Maeve?

Her name made him remember the heat of her sensuous lips against his knuckles. His pulse quickened, and he abandoned his late-night work.

There she was, with her back to him, kneeling on the floor before the cold hearth. As she dunked a brush into a bucket of water and scrubbed, he saw the flash of her lye-reddened hands and remembered the delicate feel of them against his palms.

A gently born lady down on her luck. So proud she refused charity. What was it she had said? She would earn her way. She would rely on no one.

Hell, he almost believed she honestly meant it.

Ashes hung in the air, making her cough as she bent into her work, breathing hard. When she straightened, leaning back on her heels, she swiped the damp from her face. Her sleeve came away streaked with ashes.

"Change your mind?" he asked.

"Heavens!" The brush thunked to the floor, and she whirled onto her feet, her hands to her throat. "It's you. You scared five years off my life."

"I rather thought you heard me."

"If I had, I would not be shaking. I guess my mind was off somewhere."

"Reconsidering my offer yet?" He tugged a handkerchief from his pocket and wiped a smear of ash from her forehead. "This could be your chamber. Your bed."

"Interesting how you should mention *that* piece of furniture." She saw the grime on his handkerchief and wiped her forehead with the cuff of her other sleeve. Unfortunately, it was dirty, too, and left a larger streak.

"I had a mistress once. Enjoyable until it came to our parting. Then I would have been better off to have taken a wife for all the noise she made—and demands." Amusement glinted in his eyes. "I learned my lesson. If sex is what I want, I pay for it as a business transaction."

She laughed and blushed, too, for she could read how clearly he was teasing her. "You *are* a rake, but I'm inclined to think you are not quite so very bad."

"Me, bad?" He shouldn't take pleasure in teasing her. "I should hope so. I have spent many a year defying authority at every opportunity."

"And building a reputation to match?" Trouble twitched at her mouth, lush and soft.

Infinitely soft. Wrong of him to notice, so he turned his attention to safer subjects. "The housekeeper has you working late. Shall I speak to her?"

"Not on my behalf." Maeve swirled to the floor and submerged her brush in the soapy water. "I've extra duties, as one maid is ill, another gone, and Gallagher is furious at me, so here I am without complaint."

She seized the brush and set to her work, her slim arms reaching and bending as she scrubbed. "I'm well pleased, for I can keep a roof over my head."

"You shall always have that, I promise you." He cleared his throat because his words sounded tender—how could that be? "You cannot be content with this work."

"What does contentment have to do with it? You have your duty, and I have mine. They are simply different duties."

He could feel her sadness. Or, maybe it was his. "True. I am far from pleased to be taken from the people I know and banished on this damned island. No offense."

"None taken." She reached for the bucket.

He caught hold of the metal handle and moved it for her. On one knee, he was closer to her and watched the candlelight brush the side of her lovely face. His fingers ached to caress where the light curved over her chin and her full, rosy lips.

"You must miss your home." She clutched her dripping brush, leaning close so he could smell the starch in her clothes and her skin's warm scent. "Your friends. Your interests."

"My decadent pursuits," he could not help adding.

"Why am I not surprised?" She rolled her eyes. "You always were an unruly boy, I remember, in and out of one kind of trouble or another."

"And you right along beside me."

"Me? Why, I was a good and proper lass. Always behaving as befitted my station. Any fault I had was in the company I kept."

"Meaning me?"

"Aye. You are twice the rogue now, I'd wager, so I will be wise and keep my distance."

"Wise, yes. But I am alone without family or friends, save for you." He caught hold of her hand, soapy and wet, and if his pulse soared, he ignored it. "Take pity on me. Accompany me to the stables."

"The Gallagher will toss me out with the morning rubbish if I do. Besides, I have work." She shrugged one slim shoulder beneath her plain, ill-fitting frock.

He hated that, how poorly she was dressed when, as a wealthy man's daughter, she had worn far better.

She did not seem to mind as she rubbed a towel over the sparkling stones to dry them. "That is one hearth clean."

One? There were others? The library clock bonged the time. Twelve midnight. The housekeeper had

Maeve working this late, and with more tasks ahead? He pitied her—and admired her, too, for she had not grown bitter with the years.

It had been a long while since he'd found anything in a young woman to admire, and so it was easy to take Maeve's hand.

"If Gallagher finds fault with you, then I will remind her who is in charge of the manor. Come, I have something to show you."

"Sure, but is it something I want to see?" She sparkled, even in the shadowed light, like a rare, perfect gem.

"Keep your thoughts from the gutter, my lady. I am attempting to be a gentleman, and it is not a simple task for me." He winked and blew out the candle, taking her slim arm in his. "I remember your father was a horseman."

"Aye, and it was the racing that ruined him, as he had a weakness for it." The sparkle dimmed. "Why are you asking?"

"Wait and see."

At the back door he slipped his warmest overcoat over her shoulders. Her nearness affected him. He wanted to explain it away as loneliness, but he knew sexual attraction when he felt it.

The moon gleamed like a rare pearl, lighting their path to the stables.

Maeve tipped her head back, held out her arms, and spun in a circle, gazing at the stars. "How wondrous it all is. I've not had the leisure to enjoy the night sky in a long while."

He loved the lilt of her voice, musical as birdsong.

Charmed, he tugged open the heavy half-door. A horse nickered from the shadowed aisle, and Maeve slid away from his side, her movements whisper-soft.

Connor found a lantern with little trouble and lit the wick. A tongue of flame chased away the dark, revealing Maeve leaning over a stall door, stroking a mare's soft nose.

"What a beautiful new babe you have," Maeve praised. "A fine colt, too. Come see me, young fellow."

A beautiful woman, with a tender heart. Connor slung a saddle over his shoulder, spellbound by her charm, her grace, and her simple country elegance. It was a shame that her maid's cap hid her bounty of ebony curls from his sight. As he passed her, he tugged out a pin and caught the cap as it tumbled.

"What are you about, you rogue?"

"It was falling off, so I thought I would come to your rescue," he alibied as he tucked the scrap of cloth into her apron pocket. "Since your hair is coming down as well, I shall loose the ribbon—"

"Scoundrel! Get your hands off me!"

"What has the world come to when a gentleman cannot aid a pretty girl?" At last the stubborn pins came loose, and her locks cascaded, satiny curls that brushed his knuckles.

Desire pulsed thick and urgent in his veins. He breathed in the scent of her—soft, warm woman and roses. He fought the urge to wind his fingers through her hair, tip her face to his and ravish her full, lush mouth.

"Fetched a saddle, did you?" Maeve asked, all innocence, unaware of his state.

Thank God for the dark. "I wanted to ride with you."

His words took on a meaning that made him growl with frustration. Had he no decency? She trusted him like family, looked to him as an older brother. He could at least control his baser appetites in her presence.

"You wish to take me riding? Me, a kitchen maid?" She ran her fingers smartly across his chest. Playful, hot little taps that made him ache for her.

There was no denying his physical attraction, although he tried to fight it. "Since you are off duty, you are not a maid until tomorrow morning arrives."

"Flawed reasoning, but you are a nobleman and it's to be expected. Have you become such a dandy that you need a saddle?" She stole the bridle from him and swished into the shadows, leaving him alone in the aisle.

Alone and desiring. This was surely the worst idea he'd had in a decade, bringing a pretty little maid to the stables with him. And not just any maid. He had never in his entire life been affected so quickly by a woman. Where was his willpower? His cold, heartless glare, the one that had sent more than one husband-hunting female running for the comfort of her mother's arms.

He leaned against the door jamb, uncertain if he dared to follow Maeve into the stable yard. His pulse thrummed in his veins, and with the way the moonlight tossed shimmering pewter over the meadows, it was a night of magic. Or was the magic Maeve?

"Will you sell all Shamus's horses?" her musical voice asked through the shadows.

He cleared his throat, fought to rid this hunger for her rising in his blood and almost succeeded. "How did you know? Wait. Forbes."

"Where there are servants, there is gossip, my lord."

"I'm Connor to you. That is one thing that must not change between us."

"Connor or not, you *are* the lord of the manor, and I am a servant."

"I can remedy that." Tenderness filled him, strange and unusual. He could not say for certain if it was only sexual attraction that drew him from the shadows. "You could have easier work with better pay. Say the word."

"I will not, so promise to put an end to this. There, the bridle is secure." As she climbed the wood fence, moonlight found her and caressed the ample fullness of her breasts, the nip of her slim waist, and the length of her lovely thighs.

He was a blackguard of the worst sort to notice.

"What a devil you are," she accused.

"I told you I was."

"I am speaking to the horse, although I am sure you are quite the devil, too." Wherever she moved, starlight found her and she gleamed like fine platinum. "Your mount is ready. Think you are man enough to ride this one?"

Too much man, as it were. He hung the saddle on the top railing. "Bareback, is it?"

"You say that with a question. I have been forgetting. You're a nobleman, and cling to rules and conventions."

"You confuse me with others of my kind. I live for danger."

"Then where is the proof?" She handed him the reins.

"I never back down from a worthy challenge." His fingers brushed hers as he took the leather straps in hand. Sensation scorched his skin. He mounted easily and, keeping the reins tight, wheeled the animal in a small circle to maintain a certain distance from Maeve.

What he ought to do was leave her right where she stood, for what could come of this attraction? Nothing, and yet he could not summon the willpower to gallop away. She watched him ride, her black curls tangling in the wind.

"Enjoy your midnight run." She swung onto the top rail, all innocence and sensuality.

He could hardly miss the soft sway of her breasts or the firm curve of her thigh beneath that plain, tantalizing fabric. He could not help it—he sidled the stallion to the fence. "I had not planned to ride alone."

"Fine. I suppose I could choose a mare to—"

"I cannot wait." The devil drove him to it, for he snared her by the waist and settled her firm bottom on his thighs.

Maeve gasped with surprise as the world tilted and she found herself hard against Connor's chest. What a man he was, lean and hot. She could not help but notice, and it was not decent. Not at all. His arms hugged her as intimately as any lover would, and with his muscular thighs hard beneath hers—

"This is scandalous and you know it, my lord."

"Connor, remember? And what of scandal? You and I have ridden together in these fields many times before this."

"Yes, but we were children then, and everything is changed. We cannot be friends."

"So you say."

"I did not make the rules, Connor, or I'd have made a kinder world."

"As would I."

His lips were in her hair, brushing the crown of her head as he spoke. "If you are going to be my friend, you shall have to become accustomed to breaking a few rules."

"Or my neck, if you cannot manage this stallion."

"You are safe as a kitten with me, sweet Maeve." Tender his voice, like an old friend's should be.

Then why was the salty scent of his skin and of the port clinging to his coat fogging her senses?

Shame balled in her chest. The horse leaped, Connor whooped like a young boy racing the wind and they were off, hammering through the night with Connor's hand solid at her waist.

He was temptation, all six feet of him, and she could feel every inch. From the top of her head to the soles of her feet, he pressed against her. The horse's gait made her thighs rock against his. She could feel his arousal—it was not insignificant. All her senses narrowed to that one place.

Oh, but she was a bad lass, noticing such a thing. He was heat and male perfection, and heaven help her, she couldn't stop noticing. Heat coiled low within her, a keen aching for what could never be.

A desire grew within her, one she could not stop as the night deepened around them and the stars swirled above. All she knew was the feel of Connor against her, surrounding her, holding her safe as the stallion reached out in a full gallop.

At the knoll of a hill, Connor drew the horse to a skidding halt. The animal trumpeted, sides heaving, and Connor's fingers curled around her hipbone, holding her tight against him. The sea spread out below like hammered pewter, reflecting the shine of stars and moon. The brilliance could not begin to match her happiness.

Connor broke the silence. "What I would sacrifice to continue riding forever."

"I know that feeling, that wish. But you would soon discover you can never leave your troubles behind."

"Still, it's a worthy thought. Enough to keep me going."

"Being controlled by your grandfather must trouble you greatly."

"I despise it." He sounded harsh, he knew, but it was the truth, and the fury drove him like the wind over the sea. "He has used my misfortune to place a noose around my neck. He has used my mother and sister as blackmail."

"What does he want from you?"

"To make me a true Raeburn. Commanding, controlling, cruel. What every duke should be." He ground out the words, fighting anger. "He swears he'll not die until I have become what he wants."

"He controls mortality, too, and the hearts of men?"

"Honestly, it is absurd, but I believe he is stubborn enough to make good on his threat. He has also vowed to spend every penny of his fortune so I inherit nothing. I have come to realize how important wealth is."

"The difference between disgrace and respect?"

He winced. "I am sorry, Maeve. I have brought up old wounds."

"Wounds no longer, only scars."

Affection ached within him for this incredible woman, tucked in his arms, warm as sin, as welcome as homecoming, and he brushed her tangled curls. Gossamer soft against his fingers. Lust coursed through him.

Damn! He swung to the ground, thankful for the cool breeze and the dark night.

Her hand caught his arm, hot as fire and pure temptation. "You were wrong to bring me here, Connor. You and I can not be friends. I've a reputation, too, and my livelihood depends on it."

"I see. Have I angered you?"

"Not as long as the stars burn in the sky above."

How wide and luminous her eyes. Physical desire beat through him like the surf on the shore. He could not help himself, the cad that he was. Trembling with need, moving swiftly so he dared not think, he cupped her chin with his hand and claimed her with a kiss.

She was sweet fire, and he wanted more of her. More of her petal-soft lips hesitant beneath his. More of the tiny sigh she made as he traced his tongue over the seam of her mouth, begging entrance. Her fingers splayed on his chest, as if not sure whether to push

Take 4 FREE Books!

We created our convenient Home Subscription Service so you'll be sure to have the hottest new romances delivered each month right to your doorstep — usually before they are available in book stores. Just to show you how convenient Zebra Home Subscription Service is, we would like to send you 4 Kensington Choice Historical Romances as a FREE gift. You receive a gift worth up to $23.96 — absolutely FREE. There's no extra charge for shipping and handling. There's no obligation to buy anything - ever!

Save Up To 30% On Home Delivery!

Accept your FREE gift and each month we'll deliver 4 brand new titles as soon as they are published. They'll be yours to examine FREE for 10 days. Then if you decide to keep the books, you'll pay the preferred subscriber's price. That's all 4 books for a savings of up to 30% off the cover price! Just add the cost of shipping and handling. Remember, you are under no obligation to buy any of these books at any time! If you are not delighted with them, simply return them and owe nothing. But if you enjoy Kensington Choice Historical Romances as much as we think you will, pay the special preferred subscriber rate and save over $7.00 off the bookstore price!

We have 4 FREE BOOKS for you as your introduction to KENSINGTON CHOICE!

To get your FREE BOOKS,
worth up to $23.96, mail the card below
or call TOLL-FREE 1-800-770-1963
Visit our website at www.kensingtonbooks.com.

Take 4 Kensington Choice Historical Romances FREE!

YES! Please send me my 4 FREE KENSINGTON CHOICE HISTORICAL ROMANCES (without obligation to purchase other books). Unless you hear from me after I receive my 4 FREE BOOKS, you may send me 4 new novels – as soon as they are published – to preview each month FREE for 10 days. If I am not satisfied, I may return them and owe nothing. Otherwise, I will pay the money-saving preferred subscriber's price plus shipping and handling. That's a savings of over $7.00 each month. I may return any shipment within 10 days and owe nothing, and I may cancel any time I wish. In any case the 4 FREE books will be mine to keep.

Name _____

Address _____ Apt No _____

City _____ State _____ Zip _____

Telephone ( ) _____ Signature _____

(If under 18, parent or guardian must sign)

KN032A

Terms, offer, and prices subject to change. Orders subject to acceptance by Kensington Choice Book Club. Offer valid in the U.S. only.

PLACE
STAMP
HERE

‖‖‖

KENSINGTON CHOICE
Zebra Home Subscription Service, Inc.
P.O. Box 5214
Clifton NJ 07015-5214

him away or to bring him closer. Taking advantage, he curved his hand around her nape, cradling her head, holding her mouth to his.

She returned his kiss hesitantly, uncertainly parting her lips at the insistent press of his tongue. He plunged into her warmth, boldly taking what she so gently offered. Her fingers curled, fisting his shirt.

Liked his brazen kiss, did she? He was happy to give her more. Nibbling at her lips, then laving his tongue along the sensitive edges of hers. She tasted like star shine, pure and sparkling. He could not get enough of her. Thundering need blinded him. He found the ribbon at her collar and gave it a tug.

She tore away, breathing hard.

"My lord." Her hands flew to her swollen mouth, covering her lips as if ashamed.

The ardor in his veins drained away. He was aware of the cool breeze on his heated face and the heartache stark on her face, sad in her eyes.

"Maeve." It broke him that he'd harmed her. "You must forgive me, because you know I am a bad, weak man."

Her eyes crinkled in the corners, as if she were trying to give him a smile, but her hand remained, hiding her mouth. "There's a rider on the road below. I think he is calling you."

"At this late hour?" He paced to the edge of the rise and spied a rider halted in the middle of the dark road, gazing up at them. Connor recognized the look of the thin man and the perfect tilt of hat and shoulders.

Forbes. Connor cursed the butler for daring to defy his authority.

"Mount up, Maeve, and ride home. I have a war to fight and win." Connor held out his hand, waiting for her to take it. A strange emotion warmed his chest and he did not know what to call it. "Will you forgive the kiss?"

"I am far too likely to forgive you anything, you charming scoundrel." She placed her hand against his palm. "I'll walk to the manor and leave you this fine stallion. You fight your battle on horseback."

"And leave you to walk home in the dark? Alone? I am a rogue, but I'm a gentleman as well." He snared the fallen reins and knelt to offer her a foot up.

"You've your grandfather's man to deal with, and I've my reputation to keep." Softly spoken, she lifted her chin and withdrew into the shadows. "It will be wise if you and I forget this night happened. The past is gone, and racing through the hills as we used to do will not return it to us."

"Maeve? Come back here."

He was lost and searching, she knew, and she didn't blame him. Only a man, he was, and used to taking what he wanted without much thought to the consequences, as it befitted his station.

But not hers.

With the memory of his kiss a flaming brand on her lips, she fled into the night.

Four

Connor was in a foul mood and let the door slam behind him to prove it. He took satisfaction in the crisp beat of his boots against the polished floors as he mounted the stairs and stormed down the corridor. He thundered through library doors, ready to grab the bloody spy by the collar and toss him out by the scruff of his neck.

"My lord, I bring news from your grandfather." Forbes spoke quickly, fear registering in his beady eyes as he backed against the edge of the desk.

"Impossible, and you know it. Grandfather is in London."

"His Grace is currently in Ireland and intends to arrive within the hour."

"What? That cannot be. He would never leave while Parliament is in session unless—" Pain pulsed in Connor's temple until his vision blurred. The bastard *was* coming to ensure the marriage offer to the heiress was made and accepted.

Forbes apparently had not the sense to remain silent. "I have been dispatched to ensure all is in readiness for his arrival. A warm bed, a stout whiskey, and a maid to rub his feet."

"The wretch can sleep on the floor for all I care, for the hell he is inflicting on me." Marriage! It sickened him. Grandfather had stolen more than his independence. He was no longer free to choose whom to love.

Maeve's kiss burned on his lips.

Forbes had been the very reason that kiss had been interrupted. Connor rounded on the unfaithful butler. "One word against a certain young woman, and you shall see that I am a Raeburn through and through, and you'll be sorry for it."

"I'll speak not one word." Forbes paled and vanished from the room.

Fierce, Connor slammed the door in his wake. The crack reverberated off the polished cherry shelves and hundreds of leather bound volumes lining the high-ceilinged room. He cursed his grandfather's meddling spy for interfering tonight.

Maeve. The fire of her kiss still burned in his veins. How could that be? She aroused him fast and furious, to the very edge of control. Had she not pulled away and ended their kiss, he would have been happy to disrobe her on the spot and introduce her to the pleasures of lovemaking.

Connor slammed his fist against the wall, driven beyond reason. Think, man! Think what that would have done to her. What future had a kitchen maid who dallied with her employer?

Gallagher bustled into the library, her starched apron tied crookedly. "My lord, I've two maids at work, and you've me promise that all will be ready for His Grace's arrival."

"I hardly care if the old jackass sleeps on the front steps." He stalked into the corridor, determined to find Maeve. He owed her an apology. He owed her his respect. Where was she? No doubt she was working at this late hour.

There—the edge of a brown skirt and white apron flashed in the corridor ahead, as if she'd caught sight of him and ducked into the chamber.

He halted in the corridor, inexplicably lost at the sight of her. With her riotous curls pinned up properly beneath a fresh, starched white cap, Maeve turned her back to him and knelt to her work.

She did not look at him again.

Maeve eased the bed warmer between the fresh linens, trying to ignore the ruckus around her as the old duke, Connor's grandfather, barked orders from his seat by the blazing fire.

His joints ached something fierce and he let everyone know it, for he complained loudly enough. He was the same disagreeable man she'd met once as a child and been terrified. The years had turned his hair gray and drawn lines on his face, but he looked as brawny and strong as ever, still a formidable force.

Just like Connor. She winced, for the midnight flavor of his kiss lingered on her lips and the thrill of it in her blood. Could she not forget the man or his kiss?

Angry with herself, she worked harder, but the memory did not fade. Her face heated when Connor stalked into the room, in cold fury and so different from the man he'd been with her. Grandson and grandfather argued bitterly, their anger darkening the chamber like smoke from a smoldering fire.

If this is the man Connor is at heart, it will be easy not to yearn for another of his kisses. Stubbornly, she closed her heart to him, for she'd not let one magnificent embrace make her dream for what could never be.

Forget the man. That was the most sensible course. Sure and he could charm the gold from a leprechaun with the passion of that spectacular kiss, but what good could come from it? He regarded her as a childhood friend needing his protection.

Why, then, the kiss?

As she knelt at the hearth to add seasoned wood to the crackling fire, she could see Connor out of the corner of her eye. He glowered at his grandfather and did not seem to notice she was in the same chamber. She was invisible to him.

Like the servant she was and nothing more.

Why was she disappointed?

With the fire blazing good and strong, she ran to fetch the tea, grateful to be out of Connor's sight. When the housekeeper approached behind her on the stairs, Maeve wasn't surprised.

"Hold up there, lass," the Gallagher ordered, puffing to a halt in the brightly lit corridor, where the lamps illuminated the triumphant disdain on her face. "Leave the tea to me. I shall see to His Grace. It's two times I've caught you alone with Lord Raeburn. If yer thinkin' the shortest route to a better life is by marryin' into it, sure and you would be mistaken. He is to be married."

Humiliated, Maeve hung her head. "I've done not one thing wrong. You've my word on that."

"A lie. I saw you romping off to the stables with him." Gallagher's upper lip rose in distaste, as if she'd sniffed something terribly foul.

She would *not* be ashamed. But her chin crept lower. She *had* allowed the man to kiss her like a lover and, worse, had enjoyed it thoroughly.

Shame welled within her, cold and deep. What kind of woman was she? To think of a duke's heir as hers to kiss.

The housekeeper dug deep into her apron pockets and pushed several small notes into Maeve's hand. "There. I'm done with ya, thinkin' yerself so fine. Well, you've made your last mistake, lassie, and now me niece, a wholesome and proper girl, can have a job to help her family eat."

Maeve wadded the notes into her fist. This, she regretted. She'd liked working at Wild Wind Hall. And yet to have known Connor's kiss, it was worth it. Surely, it was.

Her first kiss, and likely to be her last, but she'd not trade it for anything.

"I want you gone by first light." Gallagher sniffed, already turning away. "And don't you go runnin' to the lord. He is a man of a certain reputation and used to dallying with little maids better'n you."

Maeve opened her fist to look at the wadded notes. Gallagher was right. If she went to him, Connor would offer her a room and an allowance, for that was his notion of help.

How long would it be until she was wanting to give him more than kisses? And when he was to be married to another far better.

It's your own fault and you know it, Maeve O'Brien. She knew where to squarely place the blame. She'd betrayed Connor by wanting the man in him and not the friend.

Now she must pay the price.

She took the main stairs so she could walk past the guest chamber where the duke's voice boomed loud enough to rattle the portraits in their frames on the walls. She glanced through the open door to see Connor one last time.

How incredible he was. The flames of the fire shone bright against the dark fabric of his fine trousers and coat. The golden lamplight caressed his strong profile and long, black locks like a lover's hand.

Hiding in the shadows, on the outside gazing in, she memorized the look of him. The stormy set of his gaze, the rigid line of his mouth. Remembering how those sculpted lips had softened for her and kissed her senseless. Longing filled her, sweet as any dawn.

She tore away, smothering a cry, and hurried down the hallway, wishing for what could never be.

The moment Maeve quit the chamber, Connor could breathe again. The rush in his ears faded away as the minutes ticked past. The beat of his pulse slowed.

Grandfather growled like the beast he was, and Connor paced the room, unable to think of anything but Maeve. She'd soon be breezing in through that door carrying a loaded tray, silently avoiding his gaze—as if she despised him.

And dammit, he could not blame her. He was the lowest, mangiest cur in existence and he owed her an apology.

The minutes seemed like hours, and he hungered for the sight of her.

Down the corridor came the tinkling of china. The heavy gait was not Maeve's soft one.

Gallagher bustled into the room, prattling to Grandfather with her falsetto cheer. What was there to be cheerful of? Connor burst into the hallway. The sconce lamps flickered in an empty corridor.

Where was she? His fist connected with the wall, and he swore. His knuckles were bruised, but the pain was nothing next to the pain within him.

"I grow weary of your temper, boy," Grandfather roared from the fireside.

"And I weary of your disposition, old man."

Grandfather harrumphed with satisfaction, for he was a surly cuss who loved a good argument.

Connor took the stairs two at a time, his pounding step matching his fury. His lips tingled, remembering the magic of Maeve's kiss. His blood thrummed thick and heavy. He kept dreaming of that ribbon at her throat and had he the opportunity he would have tugged it. He could see the bow falling away, the fabric parting to reveal firm, round breasts—

Curses! Maeve was not in the kitchen.

There was only the cook, staring at him with wide-eyed fear at the fire. "I knew it. The duke did not care for his tea."

"Not one thing in existence can satisfy His Grace. Where is Maeve?"

"I've not seen her. Likely as not she's gone to bed at this late hour, where I'm headed next."

Right. Connor fisted his hands, a lone figure in the shadows, caught between the dark and the light. It was late. He could not speak with Maeve now, not if she had retired for the night.

Morning, then. If his conscience—or the desire coursing through him—would let him sleep.

Although she had tried not to fear the coming of dawn, Maeve slept poorly and woke knowing it. Her head felt thick and her body exhausted when the cock's crow heralded the rising sun. To awaken was to know she must leave. Yet she could not delay the dawn.

Trying not to fear what this new day would bring, she tossed back the covers. Already, several of the other kitchen maids had dressed and were washing at the basin at the small table in the narrow corridor.

No one moved aside when she approached. They crowded her out on purpose.

So, they were too fine to be friendly with the likes of her. Dallying with Connor had its price. Well, fine, she left them to their rudeness and retrieved her mother's satchel from beneath her cot.

"Maeve, what are you about?" Young Alana climbed from her bed, still pale from her bout with the quinsy. "Yer not leavin'?"

"Sorry to say I am." Maeve tugged open her bureau drawer and proceeded to empty it. "Wipe that worry from your brow, for I am not sad at a new beginning. Only the farewell."

"Aye, I'll be missin' ya, Maeve."

"As will I miss you. Do what the Gallagher tells you and you shall be moved up to chambermaid in no time." She snapped the satchel shut, for there was nothing more of hers in the tiny, airless room. "Take care, my friend."

The crowd at the basin had departed, and Maeve washed quickly, grabbed her satchel, and took the back stairs to the dooryard.

The sounds of the workday beginning greeted her ears; she had never noticed before how she welcomed it, for this place had been her home and the sounds in it a comfort. Cows lowed in the stable yard as they were milked. The call of the stable boys and the clang of the pots through the open kitchen door rose on the breezes as Cook gave her morning instructions. The fresh, dewy air and the trill of birdsong followed her as she ventured out into the sunlit courtyard.

Connor would soon be awake with his responsibilities to face and his heiress to marry at summer's end. A part of her longed to say goodbye to him, if only to remember the gentle times of her childhood when he'd been her friend. The woman in her wanted to see the man, to remember his kiss and his touch, hot and tantalizing.

That was why she could not say her farewells to him.

The truth was that he'd kissed her, but he'd not

meant it. She'd not fool herself into thinking Lord Connor Raeburn was harboring a newfound love for her. Hadn't he apologized the moment their lips pulled apart? Refused to look at her after?

Maeve turned south, where the road ribboned through the dewy hills, and turned her back on the past and Connor Raeburn.

He'd not miss her, not truly.

But she would miss always him.

Connor tore awake, the remnant of a dream charging through his brain. A woman's ebony curls tumbling through his fingers. The thin fabric of her skirt rough against his thighs. His fingers tugging the garment to her waist, settling between her thighs—

Maeve. He'd been dreaming of Maeve.

Bloody hell! Would he never control this newfound need for her?

He ripped open the window. The fresh breeze cooled his face but could not disperse the images in his mind, seductive and real. He had to see her.

After dressing, he marched straight downstairs and trapped Gallagher in the corridor outside the breakfast room.

"Send Maeve O'Brien to me at once."

"She's no longer in service here. I can call another." Gallagher quirked an accusing brow. "I trust you'll not be ruining all the kitchen maids?"

"What? Honestly!" He only wanted Maeve. Blazing flames of anger cannoned through his skull. "You *fired* her?"

"Aye. I saw her go to the stables with you. I keep my maids respectable or out they go."

"Is that so?" he growled, and found satisfaction when the proud woman flinched. "Careful, Gallagher. I am lord here, and you would do well to remember that."

She could have come to him, yet she'd left without so much as a farewell. Tormented, he felt ready to burst apart. Who would take care of Maeve? Who would take her in? It drove him mad to think of her alone in the world. He shot out of the room.

"Where are you going in such a blasted hurry?" Grandfather demanded, shaking his cane. "Come back here at once! We have business to discuss."

"Later. You may tighten the noose at my neck *after* I return."

"With pleasure." Grandfather's eyes twinkled at the prospect.

Because he would not wait, Connor bridled a horse himself, to the objections of a stable boy, and galloped bareback across the courtyard.

A fine mist rolled in on the sea, dampening him as he raced toward the village. He shivered, but not from the fog. No, he felt cold to his bones by his narrow escape—Grandfather had come to discuss the marriage offer. The one Connor had not yet made.

He cared not what happened. It was not rational or responsible, he knew. Only Maeve's safety was important—at this moment. But he could not avoid Grandfather forever.

His cravat tightened until it choked. Tugging the fabric loose didn't seem to help. Like a condemned man unable to escape, Connor urged the horse faster until the village came into view, thatched roofs and cheerful storefronts and people strolling from one merchant to another.

He dismounted swiftly, tied the animal to an iron ring outside a row of shops, and studied the main street.

Surely Maeve had come here. The village was the only place to look for work within walking distance.

"Little Lord Raeburn? Sure and I knew it was you," a friendly voice called from a shop's threshold. "I remember when you were a mere boy with that same dark hair sticking straight up like a wild buccaneer. How you loved my apple tarts. Does the man you've grown to be still have a fancy for 'em?"

"Mrs. O'Toole. Good to see you again." And it was. "I have not forgotten your apple tarts."

"It's 'my lord' now, as I've been far too familiar." Mrs. O'Toole blushed and curtsied as he approached. "I can see that rascal of a boy in the man. You and the O'Brien girl were inseparable. Pity what happened to that family. Thing is, I just saw her, too—"

"Where?"

Mrs. O'Toole took her time gazing up and down the street as she wrapped a half dozen tarts in paper. "Headed that way, when I saw her through the window. Was up to me elbows in pie dough, as I remember it. Wait! You cannot leave without a sampling of my pastries."

Connor eyed the offered package and pulled a two-pound note from his pocket.

"The devil will have me fer chargin' you, my lord."

"Then get ready for battle." He winked at her, making her laugh, as he tossed the bank note on the counter. Tucking the package under his arm, he strode out to the busy street.

Asking as he went, he finally spied her through a doorway at the far end of the village, where pubs lined an uninhabited lane. What was she up to? His boots knelled like thunder on the cobblestones. He burst through the doorway. There she was, safe and unharmed.

He stood panting as she turned from her conversation with a rough-hewn woman. Her black curls tumbling forward could not hide the gentle shock on her face.

Her spine stiffened. "Lord Raeburn. I should not be surprised you frequent this part of the village."

"I followed you here, and you know it." He would not be distracted from his fury. "You do not belong here."

"I have rented a cot for the night, and don't you go glaring at me." She shouldered past him through the threshold. "Mrs. Kelly runs a reputable establishment."

"You could have come to me."

"Oh? And you rode all this way to tell me that? Rather, you came galloping after me like an enraged bull because your pride is wounded. You think much of yourself—the great nobleman dispensing aid to a helpless commoner. Or perhaps so little of me, too witless to take care of myself."

"Commoner? You are from a wealthy family."

"Look at me. I am currently of the working class.

Lower than that, as I've no trade as the baker or a seamstress does, and I shall do what I can to earn a living honorably."

She was quick for a female, dashing down the lane. No doubt it was pride that drove her, too, and his conscience gnawed at him. "I admire you for that, Maeve."

"How can a nobleman admire a commoner?"

"The way a friend admires a friend."

"And what of the kiss? No, don't answer, for my argument has been made." She skidded to a stop outside a seedy-looking pub, the carved wood sign proclaiming "Pot of Gold" in crooked lettering. "Excuse me."

He was angry enough that he let her go. What harm would come from it? No doubt she would go inside, see the place for what it was. And decide there were better options than serving fishermen ale and chowder.

In time, the door swung open, spilling her onto the street. High color showed on her cheeks. She walked past him as if he did not exist.

Tenderness for her warmed his chest. "Your pride is one thing, and I respect it. But being hungry without a safe place to sleep is another."

"Fine words from a man who has never wanted for anything," she countered easily, but he heard the fear as well.

There could not be many available positions in a village this small. "Could I lure you away from your fury at me with an apple tart?" He held out the package so she could see. "From Mrs. O'Toole's shop."

"I shall buy my own breakfast, thank you."

"Sweets taste better when shared with a friend. You know that."

She looked sideways at him, as if he were a very naughty boy and she a governess. Then she laughed, and the beauty sparkled in her like the rarest of sapphires. "You are relentless."

Victory. He liked the feel of it. He spotted a bench outside a stone-fronted pub and led her to it.

She flicked her hair over her shoulder as she sat. Without the covering of her apron, the skirt she wore barely hinted at her delectable thighs.

Heat pulsed in his groin as he noticed.

Determined to ignore his reaction, Connor unwrapped the pastries and offered her first choice. "I am pleased to see you have retained a weakness for Mrs. O'Toole's baking."

"Aye, and a shame it is. My mouth waters each time I pass her shop." She tore apart the tart. "This is tasty. I thank you for it."

"We used to ride our ponies along the shore to purchase sweets from Mrs. O'Toole. I had not remembered until now."

The brightness faded from her. "Surprised I am that you look backward at all. When you first came to Wild Wind, I didn't think you would recognize me."

"I did. The first night when you were cleaning the ashes. There was something about you, for I am not in the habit of chasing after the maids."

"What? I thought you were a terrible rogue?"

"It is an illusion I use to frighten away husband-hunting females." A strange warmth rose in his chest. A rare tenderness for her he could not explain. He was puzzled by it, so he spoke of easier things. "I am remembering a girl who could leap her pony over the tallest stone fence on the estate."

"And beat you."

They were not equals, but at least now she no longer worked for him. And since he was not the rake he pretended to be, could it hurt to accept what he was offering? "I am in need of your help, Connor."

"Why do you think I rode here as if the devil was chasing me?" A grin tugged at his well-cut mouth, and he played that handsome smile for all it was worth, charming her thoroughly, for he was skilled at it.

Maeve knew she'd regret it, but she did have a weakness for him. "I've one favor to ask of you. Come speak to the pub's owner, as he would hire me but he has never heard of me and I've no references."

"Maeve, I would like to give you more than that."

"I told you. I earn my way." She pressed a kiss to his cheek. "The innkeeper gave me the news just this morning, for Mr. Kelly fired his serving girl last night late. Perhaps you could tell him I work hard and that I'll not be dallying with the customers instead of seeing to my tasks. Please?"

"I would not disappoint you, Maeve." He cupped her cheek, her skin soft as a dream, and kissed her luscious mouth. Quick and light, but the kiss was enough to make his heart ache.

He wanted her. Only her.

He wanted to take her in his arms, hold her safe against his chest, and breathe in the beauty of her, all glittering honesty and sweet charm. He wanted to be with her, to be better for her.

A horse and cart clattered past on the cobblestones. Across the lane a woman tossed wash water from a second-story window to *splat* on the ground. A drunk stumbled out back of the tavern, singing a bawdy tune off-key. All as if to remind Connor they were not alone, and he could not have Maeve.

Pain knotted in his throat and would not budge. He handed her the pastries. "These will keep you busy until I return."

"I adore you for it."

She was like spring coming into his life that had always been winter. And always would be.

Having one more reason to despise his grandfather, Connor did not look back. Only ahead, as he opened the pub's door.

Five

Strong sunlight tumbled through the library's southern windows as Connor studied heiress Crystal Browning's flouncing handwriting. *"We shall travel the continent, as in the manner of Lady Emmaline Andrews, whose wedding trip lasted seven months."*

Seven months? Connor buried his face in his hands. His head throbbed as if he'd been struck with a mallet. Seven months of travel with a woman he could barely tolerate? He'd be ready to jump ship halfway across the channel.

His vision blurred as he scanned her remaining demands. A larger townhouse on Park Lane, for his was not adequate; an unlimited wardrobe allowance; jewelry to befit her new station. Condition after condition, each more frightening than the last. Only two children, she told him, as she planned not to submit to him in the marital bed for a third heir. Twice was enough.

A cane thudded to a rest at the doorway. "Have you written the formal marriage offer, boy? What keeps you from it?"

"I could not imagine." Connor tossed the parchment into the fire. Flames leaped brightly, consuming it greedily. He watched the parchment burn with great satisfaction.

"Was that Miss Browning's letter? Have you gone mad? Do you know how long I was forced to negotiate for her to agree to consider an offer from a blackguard such as you?"

"Then you marry her."

"*I* do not have but a few hundred pounds to my name and a mother to support, do I? Or a lovely sister needing a Season untouched by scandal." Grandfather eased into a wing-backed chair before the hearth and relaxed into the cushion like a king content in his throne.

Connor shoved to his feet, fighting rage and a thousand retorts, and yanked open the nearest window. The dappled sunshine and warm breeze soothed but nothing could rub away this fury. Trapped, that's what he was, as surely as if he'd landed in debtor's prison and the jailer tossed away the key.

His life stretched out before him in an endless parade of misery—and a screeching woman's voice. Crystal Browning was not known for her quiet manner. To have children with her, heirs for this fortune—

"Where are you off to?" Grandfather fumed. "I wish to see the marriage offer. Connor!"

Sweating and sickened, he found himself outside in the garden, drawing in great breaths of fresh air. He braced one hand against the manor's stone wall and let the gentle breeze calm him.

In time, the images of taking Crystal Browning to wife faded and the terror with it. He became aware of the dappled sunlight warming him, the leaves new green and fully opened. The roses rubbing their branches against his knees held tightly closed buds toward the sky. Birdsong made tender the air, and in the fields beyond a mare whinnied, calling her new foal to her side.

"There you are, my lord. His Grace requests that you return to the library." Forbes bowed formally and left quickly.

Connor glowered, bitterness crashing through him. To insure his family's continued place in Society, he must marry the heiress at summer's end as promised.

But not before.

Until then, he would not be kept on a short leash. Not belittled or ordered about like a climbing boy.

He was not in the prison of marriage. *Yet.*

The noon rush was done, and the midday dishes washed and dried. The pub was quiet except for the owner's chums seated in the back, and they'd remain for a long while and fetch their own pints.

"Enjoy the rest of the fine day, Maeve," the owner's wife called from the stove where she measured flour for her fish chowder. "Remember, you serve the dinner crowd tomorrow."

Returning the good-day wishes, Maeve let herself out into the alley. Why, even the shadows felt warm. Spring had truly taken hold, and the thought cheered her. A new place to live, a new job, and she liked both well enough. She'd not been this fortunate in some time.

At the end of the alley ahead, an ember glowed in

the shadows. A man was there, leaning against the building, smoking when in the middle of the day he ought to be occupied.

Wild Wind was a peaceful village but was known to have a few cutpurses. Maeve laid her hand over her apron pocket to still the jingling coins. Perhaps it would be wise to slip back through the pub's front door.

"Maeve! Hold up."

She skidded to a stop, for she recognized that pleasing voice. "Connor Raeburn, I'm not in the least surprised to see you lurking in the shade like the knave you are."

"Spoken like a woman who knows me well." He drew on his cigar. "I have been waiting for you."

"Whatever for? What wrong I have done? Or else I would not deserve this torture."

He chuckled, as deep and rich as the spicy smoke from his cigar. Lazily, he met her in the shadows. "As you no longer work for me and I am in need of a friend, I've come to beg you for mercy."

"I cannot imagine you begging for anything."

"You owe me a boon for the stellar recommendation I gave for you, and I have come to collect."

"Awfully sure of yourself, I see. No surprise there." She ought to tell him no, for she had errands and laundry to do.

But the shadows curled around him, highlighting the fine cut of his profile and the impressive line of his chest. And she was only a woman, after all, and could not find the strength to refuse him.

In truth, she wanted to be with him. "Fine, then. Tell me what has put that gleam in your eye."

Trouble, he was, for he tossed her the same dazzling smile that made her weak in the knees—so very weak.

"Come with me and you shall see." He offered her his arm, ever the dashing gentleman, and winked at her, always the attractive rogue.

"I have made a great blunder, I know it, agreeing to be seen with the likes of you," she protested, so he would laugh his low, vibrant chuckle that made her toes tingle. "I suppose I shall survive."

"Good, as I brought out the phaeton just for you." He gestured toward the lane where the alley's shadows gave way to glittering daylight and a polished vehicle drawn by two of the finest horses she'd ever seen.

"Your chariot, my lady." His hand felt familiar against hers as he helped her up—familiar, and stunning all the same.

Maybe it was her reaction, she realized, as he settled beside her. She dared not look at him, hoping that would keep the attraction she felt from taking a firm hold.

She was wrong. Connor seized the straps in his hands so fine and strong. How masculine they looked, but she would wager her first month's earnings that when he touched a woman, those hands of his would not be rough but gentle and hot as fire—

She shivered, bone-deep.

"Are you cold?" he asked, concerned. "I will give you my coat."

"I was too long in the shade, was all," she alibied

rather than admit the truth. He made her shiver down deep inside. She wanted—

Aye, she would do well not to think of what she wanted. "I will warm up in the sun soon enough. So, explain to me how going for a ride in your fine phaeton is doing *you* a great favor?"

"It is not the ride but the pleasant company."

She was not going to be fooled by the likes of him, even if his words made desire run thick in her veins. "Likely as not, it is your grandfather you're wanting away from."

"True, but I would rather run away with you at my side." He halted the horses to wait for a wagon piled high with thatch to move out of their way. "I have become enamored with you, Maeve."

"Me?" She'd not believe that either, but her foolish heart hoped it was true. "That seems unlikely."

He said nothing to that except for the flash of trouble in his eyes. The wagon moved out of the way and Connor deftly drove them through the rest of the village.

He'd become enamored with her? No, she *could* not let herself believe it. She stared hard at the road ahead, as they left the village behind.

Presently, he broke the silence. "How do you like the pub?"

"The work is hard, but the company I keep is far more pleasing."

"Miss the formidable Gallagher, do you?"

"Oh, no." Maeve stared straight ahead to keep her gaze from adoring him. "It's *you* I do not miss in the slightest. Dragging me from my work, making improper advances, and costing me my position."

"I did all that, did I? Well, it is good to know I have accomplished something during my stay here." He held the reins in one hand and laid his free arm across the back of the seat.

They turned a sharp corner, and she gasped at the sight before her. Trees in full blossom lined the country road for as far as she could see. Branches arched over them in bouquets of white and pink.

Connor halted the team beneath the blossom-heavy limbs, but the beauty of the trees paled next to Maeve's pure loveliness.

"A lovely sign it is," she breathed, her cheeks rosy with pleasure. "I wager you'll make peace with your grandfather and be the happier for it."

"And what of you? What happy ending would you wish for?"

"More sights like this." She held up her hand as a petal tugged loose from the branch overhead and drifted away.

"That's no answer," he chided gently because her response was of consequence to him. "What are your dreams?"

She blushed, looking away. Her shoulders shook just a little.

Something in his chest twisted tight, and he hurt for her. "Why are you crying?"

"I'm not crying." She sighed heavily, a sad sound. "I've merely learned that wishes never come true, so what is the use of dreaming?"

She reached inside her collar and drew out a blue ribbon, frayed at the edges. A circlet of gold winked and a gem shot blue fire in the dappled light.

"This was my mother's, given to me on her death bed." She cradled the ring in her palm. "I have managed to keep it all these years."

"That is a valuable stone. You could live comfortably off its sale."

"I suppose you would see it that way. I'd not trade this ring for any amount of bank notes." Her chin shot up, all pride, all strength.

He was not fooled. "I have never known anyone like you, my Maeve. I used to believe everyone could be bought or sold, conscience and integrity, for the right price. Now that I have come to know you better, I see how cynical I've become. The problem is not with the world, but within me."

"What? Lord Raeburn is imperfect?"

"You knew all along, is that it?"

She nodded, shadows and light, and he felt a great rending in his chest. As if the hard, crusty shell around his heart had broken wide open. As if love, new and fragile, blossomed there.

She pressed the ring to her lips, tenderly, and he envied the gold band that kiss. "This is a Claddagh ring. Have you heard of them?"

He shrugged—he had not. He leaned closer, wanting to listen to her speak. For now, for the rest of his days.

"It is a tradition for the mother to hand her ring to her firstborn daughter, often on her wedding day. This ring has been in my family for over a hundred years."

"It's exquisite." Because it was an excuse to touch her, he ran his thumb over the sapphire set between gold-crafted hands and a crown above, and his fingers brushed hers.

She touched each part of the ring. "Hand, heart, and soul."

"Soul mates." He'd heard the term before and not believed it. Never before had he wanted to. The back of his neck prickled because he finally understood. "You will wear this as your wedding ring."

"If I marry."

"You sound uncertain. You have no wish to wed? If anyone believes in true love, it must be you."

"I did, once. I also believed in fairy tales, leprechauns, and gold at the end of every rainbow." She tried to catch another tumbling blossom and missed. "I was a child then. It took growing up to learn there is nothing at the end of a rainbow. Not even dreams. But I would like to marry. I've simply not had the opportunity."

The breeze gusted, sending hundreds of tiny pink petals to fill the air like bits of colored snow.

"This is enough to make me believe in magic—for this one moment." Maeve held her hands upward, tilting her face to let the petals brush her.

She was beauty, pure and true, and it made his heart hurt, like eyes did when the sun became too bright. That is what she was to him, sun to his shadow. As the petals clung to her hair and circled around her like angel's wings, his heart hurt even more.

It was tenderness he felt. Tenderness and something deeper. It came from far within him and this new emotion changed him. Made him different than he had ever been before.

Maeve stood, making the phaeton rock as she held her arms high. "Enchanting, isn't it? Oh, Connor, it feels as if the trees waited for an audience just to bloom. I've never seen the like."

"Nor have I." Bold with this new emotion blazing within, he brushed petals from her soft cheek. His thumb found her mouth and traced the rosebud arch of her upper lip.

"You are magic to me," he told her, for it was the plain truth, and claimed her with a kiss.

They met like fire and fate, and Maeve could not resist. His kiss tasted like sun-warmed satin. Felt like the greatest of pleasures. His arms held her as she melted against him, lost. So helplessly lost.

"You are my love," he murmured.

He was her dream. Right or wrong. Nibbling at his bottom lip and playfully sucking, she kissed him in return. His hands swept along her arms, over her back and across her shoulders, leaving her breathless and thrilled. His fingers hesitated at the upper swell of her breast. She felt hot and achy, and fought the urge to press her flesh into his hands. She wanted him. So completely she shook with it.

He broke the kiss. Desire thudded through the center of her, like thick melted butter, hot like flame. His gaze met hers, and it felt as if something deep in her heart connected with his. Could he tell how much she wanted him? Her face turned hot, craving his lips to her mouth, his hand to her breast, and more.

So much more.

"This is a matter of consequence," he told her, not scolding as she expected, but tenderly, with great affection. "We could be together completely, if you wish.

Or I could hold and kiss you and no more. It is your choice, Maeve."

Her heart broke apart, tumbling down in tiny pieces, like the blossoms drifting on the breeze. Leaving the core of her soul exposed and vulnerable. She was safe in his hands—and in his love.

"There is nothing I want more than this. I wish to be with you. To love you wholly." She placed her hand in his and her trust there as well.

On the grass just out of sight of the road, he spread his coat on the dappled grass for her. Like a fairy tale, she knelt and let him take her into his arms.

His kisses were like fire and rain and his touch like sunset as he urged her onto her back. Since she did not want to be lying alone, she drew him over her, surprised by his hard weight and pleased by it, too, for the ache between her thighs grew keen. Like a hunger she could never appease, a thirst she could never quench. Blinded by it, she tugged at the wooden buttons on her bodice.

Eagerly, he pushed the fabric aside. "You are just as I knew you would be—extraordinary."

At the first touch of his fingertips, her nipples pebbled tight. What pleasure. She sighed, surrendering to the kneading caress of his fingers. Unable to lie still, she rained tender kisses across his brow, smoothed her hands over the width of his substantial shoulders and the hard plane of his wide back.

On a moan, he drew her taut, swollen nipple into his mouth and suckled. Ecstasy twisted from breast to womb, coiling ever tighter until she cried out from the thrill of it.

"Ah, sweet Maeve, you torture me." He flicked her sensitized nipple with his tongue. The way his eyes flashed and the dimple cut into his cheek, he didn't look tortured.

He looked like a man in love.

How could that be? A man as fine as he. Could he truly love her?

Incredible, she thought as he kissed her again. Hot and wild, this time, and then with tender affection.

He unhooked her shoes and peeled off her stockings like the master he was, bless him. He stroked her everywhere, the soles of her feet, the backs of her knees and the insides of her thighs. Dazzling, clever caresses, and she was aflame, thrashing and moaning and not at all ashamed of it. His touch parted her, opening her gently to the pressure of his fingertips and then his entire palm. He knelt down, kissing her deeply, introducing her to a pleasure as bright and blinding as the sun.

"Oh, Connor." She clutched his shoulders at the unbearable sensations. Every muscle in her body felt clamped tight. She gasped, feeling ready to break apart as she arched her back, lifted her hips, and struggled for what she'd never known. One thing she was sure of—she wanted him. *Now.*

As if he read her thoughts, he rose over her, his hands planted on either side of her shoulders, his knees spreading apart her thighs. His hard shaft nudged against her, and the blunt, smooth pressure of him there, where she was wet and achy, made her wild. She wanted more of him, and he responded. His hard thickness eased into her, and she gasped at the tearing pain.

Her fingers dug into his shoulders, holding on as the discomfort remained.

He stopped, waiting. "I can withdraw if you wish."

He gazed at her with passion and kissed her with tenderness. She loved this man. Her heart opened wider with the power of it.

"No. I want all of you, Connor. All you have to give me."

"Oh, yes, my love." He kissed her again and filled her deep.

The pain sharpened then ebbed away, and there was only the hard, hot feel of him buried within her. To her delight, he moved, withdrawing and thrusting deep, rocking into her.

"Oh, Connor." There was no word for it, this sensation of being joined with him. She could feel him pulse within her, feel the beat of his heart and the draw of his breath. Mindless, her body moved to his, as he thrust over and over again. She buried her face in his shoulder, holding him tight, rising up to meet him.

His back tensed beneath her hands and he pounded harder, faster. Feeling the pulse of his release began her own, and the coiled tightness in her exploded, again and again in waves, white-hot and consuming.

Finally, she was aware of his kiss on her face. Loving kisses so tender, her soul ached with the beauty of them. Blindly, she found Connor's mouth with her own.

Trembling with the power of their lovemaking, she couldn't let him go. Not until he grew iron hard within her, and he loved her all over again.

Lost in their lovemaking, they did not notice the

dark figure lurking behind the trees. Having seen enough, he sneaked soundlessly down the road until he was far from their sight.

"The sun is beginning to set." When Maeve spoke, her gently lilting voice vibrated through him. "I suppose our day together must come to an end."

How wistful she sounded. Connor smiled to himself, lifting his head from her breasts where he rested. He liked knowing that he'd satisfied her well. "The day is far from over. There is the evening to come. Then the night."

"A lovely notion, but we must part sometime." Her fingers smoothed through his hair, cradling him to her breasts.

Contentment rolled through him, and he caught her hand to kiss her palm. He loved her feel, her scent, everything about her.

The breeze gusted, tossing blossom petals onto them and spreading gooseflesh over Maeve's silken skin. Her rosy nipples peaked, and he felt compelled to warm them with his mouth and hands.

"You tempt me far too much, but I like it. I do." She shivered again, and this time he wagered it was not from the cold. "What of your duties, my handsome lord? You'll not accomplish them pleasuring me."

"A pity, since pleasuring you is all I want to do." He had found his heaven, and he refused to let it end. "We could dress and drive to the next village. I can buy us a supper basket from the inn, and we'll eat together on the shore, if you wish it."

"Alone?" Her kiss-swollen mouth curled into the most amazing smile. "Sure and you're planning more of this, but I must return soon before someone begins to wonder why I drove off in a phaeton with the likes of you, you knave."

"You seem to like me well enough." He stirred, hardening, as he trailed a hand along her thigh. She was wet from him, and no doubt as ready as he for more loving.

A part of him wanted to keep her here forever, to hold this moment and never let it pass. But he knew she was right. "As you wish. We will return you to the village, but I want your promise to go driving with me again."

"I doubt *driving* is what you wish to do." She laughed at him, merry and beguiling. "The look on your face! Do not worry, my love. Since you obviously need the practice, I will oblige you."

"Me? Need practice?" He chuckled, rolling from the soft haven of her breasts and handed her the pile of her clothing. "Since you're willing, I shall accept your brilliant offer."

He kissed her thoroughly.

Shaking bits of grass and crushed pink petals from his trousers, he could not help watching Maeve dress. Finely made. He could not find a flaw on her. She'd always been beautiful, but now, after being quite thoroughly loved, she was beyond beauty. She was like magic, precious and rare, and he wanted her more than life.

"Where is my mother's ring?" Kneeling on the

ground, she frantically searched through the grass. "I cannot see it. Connor, please help me."

"One moment." He felt his coat pockets, withdrew the valuable ring, and placed it in her hand.

"You are my champion." She came to him, bringing all her light, and allowed him to slip the ribbon around her neck. "My mother never stopped believing in the good of the world."

"She sounds amazing." Connor cupped Maeve's face gently.

"As you are."

He pulled her to him, his arms banding her tight and held her, simply held her, his always-and-forever love.

"Mother said there would be treasures awaiting me in this life," Maeve dared to confess. "Now I know for sure she was right."

For now, for as long as she could, Maeve would accept this gift of his love and celebrate this rare magic of one heart finding another.

All was right with the world as they drove away in the phaeton, holding hands.

Six

Maeve's shoulders burned as she hauled the tray heavy with bowls of fish chowder and plates of thick bread across the crowded pub. She hardly minded the hard work because the truth be known, she couldn't stop thinking about Connor. How he had returned her home that day, like a gentleman, his tender love for her unmistakable. She would be seeing him at evening's end when her work was done. Oh, to be in his arms again!

A local musician played a jig on his fiddle above the shouts and calls of pleased patrons. Hands clapped, feet stomped, and cheers rose as the music ended.

Maeve reached the table, emptied the bowls around it, and laid down the thick bread slices to words of appreciation. The fishermen were polite enough for having a few pints in them. Since she knew they would leave plenty of pence on the table when they were done, she gave them a smile and a crock of fresh butter.

"Lass, a table, if you please," called out an unfamiliar voice.

How cold and heartless. She whirled, nearly dropping her tray at the sight of the man in the threshold.

She recognized the spotless coat, the pole-straight spine, and the long face of disapproval. Disbelief numbed her as the fiddler began another wild tune.

"Forbes." She'd only seen him once, the night Connor had returned to Wild Wind. Foreboding slithered down her spine.

"Cook and the kitchen maids send their greetings." He pushed past a pair of fishermen as if they didn't exist and offered her a cold but charming smile. "A table by the fire would be best, where I can warm myself while I enjoy the *entertainment.*"

He didn't fool her one whit, but she found a table for him and wiped the chair before he was seated. "The ale is simple but stout, so I am told. The chowder today is potato and it is tasty, that I do know."

"All I require is refreshment." Lording it over her, Forbes managed a frosty grin. "And a moment of your time."

"I've work to do and no time for chatter," she answered handily, although her tray began to shake. He noticed, damn him, for his grin became sly and he relaxed into his chair. She spun away, distributing ale and chowder as she went.

How she hated making her way back to him, sitting so sure of himself near the fire. Orange flames danced in the hearth, flashing eerie light over him. Like a messenger of the demon, he seemed, dressed all in black, so sparse and bony.

"Your pint." She set the tankard before him. He frightened her and she was glad to turn quickly, with more pints needing to be delivered.

His hand banded her wrist. "Run while you can,

little maid. In time, the fishermen will leave, the pub will empty, and your work will end. I shall still be here. Waiting."

Dismay felt like lead in her stomach. She slipped her tray on an empty table and grabbed a chair next to Forbes. "What is it that you're wanting?"

"It is not what I want, but what the duke wishes." Forbes pulled a folded length of parchment from his coat pocket. "His Grace wishes for you to consider a generous proposal."

The duke? Connor's grandfather? Maeve's hands turned numb and she couldn't feel the bundle as she took it.

This could not be about Connor. How would the duke know of their love? She'd told no one, and surely Connor had not.

"You've ambition, but Connor will marry for the good of his family. Offering him your considerable charms in the grass pleased him, no doubt, but surely you know you're not good enough to keep him."

"How did you—" Her jaw dropped, horror stealing her breath. "You followed us."

"It was not difficult." Forbes gestured toward the parchment. "You need not worry. I found little interest in what I saw. I have no taste for common women, I assure you. Now read the offer. You can read?"

Fury flashed like lightning. She tossed the parchment at him and bounded to her feet. "Tell your duke that Maeve O'Brien is not for sale."

"But you will be." Forbes's threat sliced through her rage. "Is that what you want? Another scandal? To be shamed again? You would lose your job and your room. What of Connor? What would you cost him?"

"I require nothing from him."

"You would ruin his life. Cause him to lose the life he deserves *and* his inheritance. Is that what you wish for him?"

Ignoring the calls from the fishermen at the back, she snatched the letter from the table, unfolded it, and nearly choked at the thick collection of bank notes staring back at her.

"One thousand pounds, and more to follow," Forbes informed her. "Enough to help you start your new life."

"What new life?"

"With the fisherman you are to marry." Forbes leaned close, frightening the flame from the candle-wicks. "The duke has found you a man to wed so you are neatly out of sight and Connor will get on with marrying his heiress."

"What if I'm of no mind to marry a stranger?"

"Then you'll be kept from Lord Connor in one manner or another. You cannot win, little maid. His Grace has the power to ruin you and destroy Connor."

The enormity of her mistake hit her like a falling brick. "I have made no demands."

"Lord Connor cannot be with you. He has made a marriage offer and received acceptance, and he is as good as married. If you love him, you will let him go."

She did love Connor, deep and true. She knew they could never be together as man and wife.

Her heart shattered, and her dreams with it. Her hands shook as she stuffed the letter and money into her apron pocket. From the way Forbes glared at her, she knew she could not refuse this offer. Only heartache would come from it. Her reputation ruined, Connor's future destroyed—and his family with it.

She knew that kind of pain.

"A carriage will be awaiting you within the hour." Forbes tossed a shilling on the table. "Good evening, Miss O'Brien."

He sauntered past, tipping his hat as if they'd had the most pleasant of conversations. Rage shook through her like a gale, and she felt near to bursting apart from it. No, she could not do it!

What other choice did she have?

She had an hour, only that. To pack her few possessions, to say goodbye to the Kellys who'd hired her. It was not time enough, but she had to see Connor. She could not give him up without saying goodbye.

Connor stared out the library window, the smell of ink and melting candle wax reminding him of the work he must do. A stack of correspondence waited on the corner of his desk, but every time he reached for a letter, he saw Maeve's lovely face, tasted the passion of her kisses, and relived the thrill of making love to her. Desire beat through him, as hard and quick as a blow to the chest, and left him breathless.

He wanted her. Now.

The tick of the clock drove the hands slowly toward midnight. Not fast enough, for she would not be finished with her work until one. And then—

Then he would love her until dawn turned the clouds gold, and it was a new day to share at her side.

He'd take her to the neighboring village and the market fair there. Buy her a remembrance of their love, maybe a gold chain to replace the frayed ribbon for her Claddagh ring.

"Have you gone daft, boy?" Grandfather smacked the door open with his cane. "Staring off into thin air like a half-wit."

"A better occupation than striking objects and frightening the servants." Connor leaned back in the comfortable chair, crossed his ankles, and enjoyed matching wits with his grandfather. "Shouldn't a crotchety old fellow like you be asleep at his hour?"

"I will not rest until I know you are man enough to inherit my title. Have you written the letter to the Browning girl?"

"Your scowl hardly intimidates me, so you're wasting the effort." Connor sipped the port, letting his grandsire get off a bit of rage first before he waved the parchment in the air. "It's a pity you can no longer use my sister to manipulate me. Cassandra has received an offer."

"Of marriage? So soon?"

"She is a sweet girl, and the Viscount of Abberly is a fair match. I know him well enough to say he is worthy of her."

Grandfather scowled. "And the sum he expects?"

"I shall take it out of the proceeds from the estate. There will be enough to provide a fine dowry." Connor felt free, nearly giddy. He was pleased for his sister, of course, but this was also a good turn of events for him. "You did say the profits were mine."

"Be mindful not to sell the furniture out from under me." Grandfather scowled. "Back to the Browning fortune."

"I have the entire summer."

"We struck a bargain, you and I, and by God, you will keep your end of it." Grandfather waved his cane for emphasis. "Shall I write the offer myself?"

Connor couldn't work up a good anger. Everything had changed—what he wanted, what he expected, what he knew was possible. All because of Maeve.

The clock struck, and it was time to be off. He could not wait to see her.

"We shall discuss this in the morning, Grandfather." Connor tossed back the last of the port, uncrossed his ankles, and stood. He was taller than his grandsire, which gave him pleasure as he glared down at the tough old bird. "Sleep well."

"Where are you off to? Defy me, boy, and I will make you sorry!"

"Honestly." He had enough threats to let this one worry him. Connor took the stairs two at a time, in a hurry, for he couldn't wait. Maeve would soon be in his arms.

The courtyard was dark and fresh with the scents of full spring. A mare nickered in the meadows, and the breeze smelled of the ocean, and it hit him then. He was content here. For the first time in his life, he was happy. He could keep half the horses, and try his hand at training and breeding them. There was always a demand for good hunters.

As he made his way to the stables, he felt a rare sense of joy, one he wanted to hold onto. Yes, he would keep the horses, Mother could have his Park Lane townhouse, and as for his heiress—

A footstep padded in the darkness behind him. Before he could demand to know who was there, she stepped out of the shadows, as lovely as a dream, as welcome as heaven.

"Maeve!" He opened his arms and she flew into them. Holding her tight, he felt complete. Nothing could trouble him as long as he held her.

Love for her blazed, inferno-strong within him. He pressed a kiss to her hair, and cradled the back of her head with one hand. She curled against him, fitted to him like a lover should be with her firm breasts hot against his chest and the curve of her hip pressed to his. He kissed her full on the mouth, taking his time to lave his tongue across hers until she moaned at the pleasure.

"I was on my way to you," he confessed, no longer frantic now that he held her. "The days since we were last together have been too long."

"True." She pressed a kiss to his palm. How could she find the strength to say what she must? Maeve faltered, overcome by her love for him. How could she walk away?

"I had plans to take you to the shore. We can stay here if you wish." He looked at her with love, invincible and true. "Grandfather has retired for the night. The manor is ours."

She wanted nothing more than to have the right to

kiss the heat of his skin, to hold him intimately within her, to fall asleep in his arms—

The weight in her pocket made it clear what she had to do.

Her heart broke all over again. "No, Connor, I will not be staying with you tonight."

"I had plans to greet the dawn with you."

How tenderly he gazed at her, as if she were the most precious of all things to him.

She could not do it.

She *had* to. He was to marry another. The offer had been made and accepted and could not be honorably broken.

Their time together was over.

She loved him, so she found the words. For his sake, she took a step away and steadied her voice. For his reputation, his honor, and his future, she found courage. "An amazing thing has happened. I have received a proposal."

"Of *marriage?*" Hurt reflected in his eyes. "You're to be *married? To whom?*"

"A fisherman in a nearby village." Her pulse beat too fast, and she felt unsteady. "It is a good arrangement, and so I've accepted. I have always wished to marry."

"I will not allow it. *No.*" Anger contorted his shadowed face, but could not disguise the pain in his eyes. His jaw tightened until muscles stood out in his neck. "This is my grandfather's doing. Has he threatened you? He has, and you agreed to leave so I can get on with the blasted marriage—"

"No, Connor." She hated seeing him hurt and would

not be the cause of more anger in his family. "This is my decision. Truly." And it was.

"How could that be?" He took her hands in his. "No, I do not believe it."

Pain tore through her more fiercely than a knife's blade. "You have your duties and your wife. We can never be together. You know this."

"If there were a solution—"

"No." How wonderful he was, ready to fight for her, and she loved him more for it. "We have separate paths in life, different destinations."

"It need not be." He kissed her, urgently, magically. "Stay with me, Maeve. I love you truly. Only you."

She kissed him in return, with all the tender love in her heart. "You are my one true love, the very treasure my mother promised I would find one day. Never forget that."

"Do not do this. I forbid it."

She tugged the ribbon over her head, the circlet of gold shimmering in the faint starlight. "I want you to have this—"

"It was your mother's."

"Aye, and so you know how precious you are to me." She placed the ring in his big hand and curled his fingers around it. "Whenever you look at this, remember that once a young maid met a dashing nobleman, and together they found a true and rare love. Although they could never be together, he would always be in her heart, and she in his."

"No, Maeve—"

"Connor." She interrupted with one last kiss. "This

has to be. You know it. Please put aside your anger and love me one last time."

Tears mingled with kisses as he gathered her in his arms. There was no time for lingering as he laid her on his coat in the garden and she held out her arms to him. They came together in the reverence of the night, tenderly, memorizing every touch, every taste, every sensation.

Afterwards, Maeve could not look at him as she pulled her garments to rights. Untying the rented livery horse from the post, she mounted without looking back. She turned the mare's nose toward the gates.

"Remember me." It was all she could ask—the only thing. "You will be in my heart always."

"Mine as well."

She kicked the mare into a gallop and passed through the gates.

Her last image was of Connor in the shadows, his head bowed, his hands fisted. His heart breaking.

Seven

Connor wanted to race after Maeve, rip her from the horse and never let her go. He loved her with everything he had—all his heart, his dreams, his soul.

And he'd lost her.

He felt as if his heart were dying. He did not care about duty and responsibility. Or the loyalty he owed his grandfather. This is what noblemen did—they married for practical reasons, they provided heirs for the family name, they did not marry kitchen maids and throw away a life of leisure and privilege—

But the truth was this: he did not want a life of ease.

All he wanted was Maeve.

Her Claddagh ring bit into his palm, he held it so tightly. He closed his eyes, torn between his duty and his heart. Responsibility and passion.

The sound of Maeve's horse on the road gradually faded into silence.

She was gone. Forever.

Christ, it hurt, losing her like this. Rage cannoned through him at the injustice of it. Rage at her, for being able to ride off and choose a future with another man. How could she do that? Leave him for a better offer?

And yet, what could you have given her? Not marriage, that was for certain. If he *did* walk away from his heiress, he had a London townhouse and a few hundred pounds to his name. His sister was provided for, and as for Mother . . . He could not leave her alone to fend for herself.

How could he leave Maeve to do the same? Maeve, who had become his entire heart?

He cried out, his anguish echoing in the darkness. The vast night stretched out before him, empty and alone. Like all the nights to come without her.

Her scent clung to his skin, his clothes. Wanting what he could not have, a man bound by duty, he turned his back on his grand estate and ran. He ran to the sea's edge and watched the tide crash into the shore, relentlessly, tirelessly. No answer came to him as he watched the stars wheel around the firmament.

When dawn chased the stars from the sky, all he had was the ring in his hand. A band of gold, unending, a symbol of her infinite love for him.

She did not love this man she was to marry. But she would lie at night with him, have children with him, share her life with him.

Bitterness rubbed out the blinding light of Maeve's love. Soon, Connor would be as he was before, a man without heart.

As his father had been.

A new day's light greeted Maeve as she climbed from the carriage. Her eyes hurt from lack of sleep and not from sorrow, she told herself, even if it was a lie. Unsteady, she squinted at the cottage in front of her.

Newly blossoming flowers sprinkled color on either side of the cobblestone walk. Wild roses promised generous blooms soon to come. Windows on either side of the stout door reflected the rising sun's light and gave the place a smiling look.

"They are expecting you." The coachman pressed the satchel and a thick letter into Maeve's numb hands. "That is all what His Grace promised ya. Good luck, lassie."

She bobbed a curtsey, too dazed to speak. This humble cottage, cozy and pleasant, was to be her new home.

For a brief instant, the weight of the envelope—with the promised nine thousand pounds, no doubt—reminded her that she could flee. She had the means, but not the heart. Wherever she went, she could not escape her grief or a life without Connor.

Besides, she'd always hoped to marry some day. Now, she had the chance.

Needing courage, she reached for her mother's ring, only to remember it was gone. Connor had what was of value to her now. Heartless, she made her feet shuffle forward toward the pretty porch.

A door flew open, and a gray-haired woman emerged. Her face was kindly, and there was a dash of pity there, too, glinting in her green eyes.

"So, you've come to wed my boy, just as it was promised." Her greeting was warm, as she took Maeve's hand. "Ack, look at ya. Near to freezin' to death. Come inside, love, for I've set tea water to boil.

We'll share a cup and a hearty breakfast and take the time to come to know one another. Will that do?"

Kindness. Maeve had not expected it. Her throat ached with too many emotions, too many regrets. She allowed her new mother-in-law to guide her into the house, where flames snapped merrily in a clean hearth.

"We're simple but happy, as you will soon see. Come, take the chair closest to the fire."

This would not be so bad a life, Maeve decided later as she dried the dishes for Mrs. Riley. Sean was a good man, even with the limp so no girl would have him; and it was not so much of a limp, the older woman promised. He'd be along, after his boat came in from the sea. Tomorrow, they would have the wedding.

"This is for you." Maeve remembered the envelope. "My dowry, I suppose."

"You keep it, dear, or give it to my Sean." Mrs. Riley held up one hand. "That you're a good girl with a good heart, why, that's worth more than all the bank notes in existence. I could not wish for more for my dear son."

At least she would no longer be alone.

It would not be such a bad life—for a life without Connor.

"Where have you been, boy?" Grandfather growled from the library desk. "The broker is here to take the horses, and I must find the list you made."

"He may as well take all of them. Every last bloody one. I will not be keeping any of them." Connor tasted bile at the thought—and at the sight of his grandfather looking so satisfied. So pleased.

"Sell all the horses?" His cane hit the floor and he rose with great vigor. "That's the spirit! Horses are a drain on the pocketbook, and sheep, there's a more sensible use of the land. Well chosen."

"Damn it all. Must it always come down to money with you? There ought to be more to life than accumulating pounds and worrying what people think."

"What are you going on about now?" Grandfather shook his head, disapproval furrowing his brow. "Duty. Stability. Position. Wealth. These are the important aspects of life. You know that."

Connor leafed through the correspondence on his desk and found the list, not that it mattered now. He had no passion, no dreams. Every horse in the fields, every brood mare in the stables, was to be sold. It was the sensible decision for a man with a wedding to prepare for. An heiress to marry.

Reality hit him like a sucker punch. Dizzy, he sank into the chair. He didn't want Crystal's money. He would never be able to stomach her for his wife. Marrying her would be a lie, an illusion that went against everything he believed in. He knew what it was to love.

He could not truly be alive without Maeve.

He pulled his hand from his pocket and there, cradled in his palm, was Maeve's ring, a golden band of two hands, one heart.

"Since we are speaking of wealth," Grandfather's cane struck the desk, "as soon as the Browning family accepts your formal offer, the chit's fortune is yours to spend as you wish. Why wait a moment longer?"

Why, indeed?

"Five hundred thousand pounds *is* an enormous fortune." He had to admit it would give him everything he'd ever wanted—freedom from his grandfather, comfort for his mother, and a life of leisure and privilege.

Five hundred thousand pounds could even buy happiness. Marrying the heiress was the right thing to do.

Connor stared at the ring, then curled his fingers around it.

Remember me, Maeve had asked him.

Yet he had his duty.

In one hand he took the quill, ready to face his responsibilities. If he wrote the offer, then he would have all any Englishman could want in life.

In the other hand, he held Maeve's ring. If he chose her, he would forsake his family, lose his home and his comfortable income.

"Splendid! The broker has arrived." Grandfather's cane tapped a happy rhythm across the library. "He shall be so pleased we intend to sell them all. You will do my title justice when you do inherit. I am proud of you, Connor."

"Grandfather, wait." He looked at the quill, then at the ring. The sapphire caught the light, gleaming as blue as Maeve's eyes. As true as Maeve's heart. "What of love?"

"Love? Who needs it, I say. It ends in heartbreak and bad consequences all around." Grandfather looked sad—briefly—then scowled, in control again. "Love is as close to torture as English law allows, and no wise man marries for it."

"Have you never loved?"

"Me? Why, a long time ago, and she married another who had more blunt and a better title, for I was not then a duke." Grandfather hid his face, clomping into the hallway. He paused, his shoulders slumped. "Get on with the marriage, boy, and secure your future with your heiress. That's the wisest course."

Alone, Connor dropped into the chair, the quill in one hand, the ring in the other.

"A lovely bride you make," Mrs. Riley praised in the little room beneath the thatch roof. "You're a gem, you are. Let me weave the last of these flowers into your hair. Turn so I can finish."

Maeve obeyed, fighting to hide the devastation she felt. The dress Mrs. Riley had lent her was as beautiful as the spring day. And the bonnet she'd purchased herself in the market this morning was a pleasing match. She stared at her new shoes peeking from beneath her skirt hem.

Sean had quietly insisted she use some of her dowry for her own needs. He was a kind man. He would earnestly try to make her happy.

She had so much. And yet for one tiny instant, she dared to dream what it would be like to marry for love.

I'll not think of him, she vowed, or she'd never be able to make it through the day. Connor was her heart. Nothing would ever change that.

And Mama, after all, had been right. Something great had happened to her. The most beautiful, shining love—the only real treasure in this life. Treasured memories Maeve would cherish forever.

"There, you look like a princess with your hair down and the flowers braided into it." Mrs. Riley beamed, a woman easy to love. "Your groom will be the proudest man. Come, Sean is making himself useful at the church and has already hitched the cart for us. Heavens, your hands are as cold as ice, lassie. There is nothing to be frightened of."

Her throat too tight to speak, Maeve could only nod. She was glad for Mrs. Riley's hand in hers, keeping her steady on the stairs. She felt so numb she could not feel the wood beneath her feet.

The promise of summer blew on the temperate midday breezes. The sky shone as blue as promises—the perfect day for a wedding. Spring flowers bowed to her as she passed, nodding in the gentle breeze. It was a beautiful world, she reminded herself.

Maybe, in giving up one rare treasure, she might find others. She would have a mother. A husband. And children to come.

There was much to hearten her as the donkey plodded along the rutted road. It would be all right. Soon the stone steeple of the little church, the thatched roofs of homes and businesses came into sight. The shouts of children playing in the streets rang cheerfully on the wind.

When the donkey halted and the cart groaned to a stop, there was no more waiting. The church door was open and her groom was inside.

"Go on and meet your man," Mrs. Riley called to her, tethering the donkey.

Maeve couldn't seem to make her new shoes move toward the church steps. Finally, she was inside out of the sun, her gait echoing in the tiny vestibule. Was the church empty? Sean had said he would be waiting here for her, ready to make her his wife.

But there was no one in the sanctuary. Golden sunlight shot through the single glass window to gleam on polished wooden pews.

Something blue glinted on the front bench. Gold sparkled. What could it be? It looked like a ring.

Her ring. The one she'd given to Connor.

Her fingers trembled so she nearly dropped it. The gold was warm against her fingertips, and the sapphire twinkled joyfully. What did this mean?

Bootsteps knelled in the aisle behind her. She recognized that gait—steady, authoritative, confident.

Connor.

"I hear you are to be married today." He stalked closer, all man and might. "I thought you might need a ring."

Looking at him made her heart stop. It could not be. This had to be a dream, even to see him again. "You came to see me married?"

"No, my sweet Maeve. I love you true. If there is to be a wedding today, then let it be ours."

She could not believe him, but sincerity shone in his eyes and rumbled in his voice. His touch felt like a promise kept as he slipped the Claddagh ring on her finger. The sapphire flashed and the gold gleamed and made her want to believe—

"But what of your heiress? You've offered for her and she accepted."

"No, only words were exchanged, but no agreement formally reached." He cupped her chin, so tenderly, so very tenderly. "I am free to marry you, if you will have me. As I have broken away from my grandfather, I have no way to provide for you. I figure I can land on my feet. I always have."

"And give up your wealth? Connor, I do not understand." Her head was spinning, her heart tumbling, but the chance to love him forever was here in her hands.

She held him tight, so incredibly tight. "You would leave your riches for me?"

"All I will ever want in this life is you, Maeve. You are my treasure."

"As you are mine." Tears welled in her eyes. Joy filled her soul-deep. "But what of your mother?"

"She will always have a home with us. She's a true gentlewoman, through and through. You shall love her, you have my word on it. She's as kind as Mrs. Riley, who was good enough to come to my aid this morning."

He had planned this. He followed her from Wild Wind to make her his wife. His *wife*. She was truly going to spend the rest of her life with him.

"I love you so much, Connor," she choked, holding onto him so tightly. "I know I will love your mother, too."

"Then will you have me as I am, a common man, with only my heart to give you?"

Yes, her heart answered. "I will have you for my husband, Connor Raeburn. To have and to hold forever."

Like a dream come true, she let him guide her down the aisle, where a minister waited. *She was about to become Connor's wife.*

A clatter at the back of the church shattered her joy. A cane smacked against the wooden floor in time to an old man's angry step. Maeve's dreams died at the sight of the duke.

"Wait! How dare you begin this ceremony!" He looked like a general preparing for war as he marched down the aisle. The fire snapping in his eyes was for Connor and Connor alone. "What do you think you are about? Tossing your life away, your fortune, your inheritance?"

"What do you care, as you've vowed to turn your back on my sister and spend every pence of your fortune if I did not come to heel." Connor's control shattered and he fought it, for he would not let his anger or Grandfather's ruin his wedding day. "You are not welcome here. There's the door. May you enjoy squandering your wealth all by yourself."

He turned his back on his grandsire and he hated doing it, but only Maeve mattered.

Only Maeve.

"Begin," he told the minister and brought Maeve's beautiful hand to his lips. The kiss was tender, and he hoped she could feel how much he loved her. How he would cherish her for the rest of his days.

"Hold!" Grandfather's cane smacked against a pew, cutting off the minister's attempt to speak. "I have something to say to my grandson and by God, he will listen, or there will be no wedding this day."

Connor's neck tingled. "What did you say?"

"I said, you will not marry the girl until you listen." Grandfather's stance didn't seem quite so rigid. "I have reconsidered. You may stay on at the estate and manage it for me. And when I pass from this earth, you shall have my title *and* my fortune."

"I am no longer interested." Connor felt his anger ebb, unsure what his grandsire was about this time. "I have heard you, so sit and be quiet while I marry my true love, or leave. The choice is yours."

"Fine." Grandfather tapped an angry rhythm to the nearest bench. "My boy, you may have more character than I first thought. She's no heiress, but I suppose love is worth something."

That sly old fox! Connor faced his bride, wiped happy tears from her eyes, and repeated the vows that made them man and wife.

Epilogue

"I seen 'em, I did!" A stable boy raced ahead of the carriage, his high voice echoing in the courtyard of Wild Wind Hall. "The new lady arrives!"

Seated beside her husband, Maeve struggled not to laugh. "Does young Byron know it is only me?"

"I suppose he does, since Grandfather returned here to manage things for the duration of our honeymoon." Amusement glittered in Connor's eyes. He was still a rogue in spirit, but constant of heart.

"You love him, you cannot fool me." She squeezed his arm, so glad to be his bride.

"I will always love you more, my precious wife, as I intend to prove to you the moment we are alone." He kissed her cheek and winked, bringing to mind this morning when he was far too familiar with her in their private rooms by the sea.

Desire spilled into her blood, making her hotter than any flame. "I shall hold you to that promise, my lord."

"Good, for I am a man of my word." He winked again. "Lucky for you."

Aye, lucky for her.

There was a commotion in the courtyard. Maeve leaned forward to see better over the horses—

No, it could not be. The servants had formed one long line from kitchen dooryard to the manor steps. A cheer rose up as she passed. There was Cook, waving her cap and whistling. And the maids Ailis and Alana, curtsying as the carriage rolled by.

"They are glad to see you," Maeve told her husband.

Connor laughed, rich and deep and easy. "No, my dear bride. They cheer for you."

"Me?"

"They like happy endings, I assume." He halted the horses in front of the grand steps.

The door opened wide, and a woman emerged. She had a gentle smile and an obvious grace that left Maeve speechless. The duke pushed ahead of the woman and approached the phaeton. Leaning lightly on his cane, the old man held out his hand.

"My granddaughter. Welcome." He helped her to the ground with the strength of a much younger man.

"Move aside, Edward," the woman ordered kindly and wrapped Maeve in a generous hug. "I cannot believe my rake of a son has married! And well done, too. What a beautiful girl you are. Come, daughter, we shall leave these two men to discuss the horses—"

"Horses?" Maeve dared to glance at the duke, who was scowling as if he were in the worst temper, but his eyes were twinkling.

Connor's jaw snapped tight. "I thought you said it was a fine idea to sell the lot of them. Horses are a drain on the pocketbook."

"I could not get the best price—the damn broker tried to cheat me, so I kept the better mares."

Connor laughed and took Maeve by the arm, a possessive and passionate touch that said he would be hers forever.

As she would be his.

"You will have to become acquainted with Maeve later, Mother, for I have made a promise to my bride I intend to keep."

Like a dream, her husband escorted her into the manor's main foyer, where light sparkled on polished floors and smiled off the fine glass lamps.

Her home now. Where one day their children would chase down the staircase shouting in play, and laughter would fill these great, still rooms.

There would be little boys with Connor's dazzling grin, and little girls with his dimpled chin. She and Connor passing each day of their lives here, in their home, happy and in love.

Joy blossomed inside her, more brilliant than the best summer day, more infinite than the sea and the sky. What a beautiful life it was, waiting for them. She couldn't wait to begin.

Connor led her upstairs and closed their chamber door.

FOR THE LOVE
OF AILEEN

Elizabeth Keys

One

Crisp salt air whisked in from the bay, stinging expectation across Aileen Joyce's cheeks, heightening her worries long before the herald's shouts echoed down from the point.

The black prow of a ship cleared the east granite promontory and sliced, sharp and clean, through the swells. Certainty pounded through Aileen, quickening her heartbeat and tightening the tension inside her. The approaching ship was Liam Ahearne's hooker making to port at last. It had to be.

Her mouth went dry as a thrill of fear raced through her stomach. She bit her lip and shaded her eyes, gaining sight of Liam's yellow pennant snapping at the top of the fleetmaster's mainmast.

"Oh, Miss Aileen, my uncle's come home at last." Aileen's maid, Jenna, tugged at her sleeve. "Surely that means he's found Master Rourke and brought him back to us."

Aileen nodded, unable to speak as hope leapt to collide with the dread clogging her throat.

Rourke McAfferty. Piercing blue eyes filled with recrimination and loathing. Shoulders rigid with grief and blame as he turned away. As he tore her tattered heart asunder.

So much had happened, so much time had passed since they'd last stood together near this very spot. What would his homecoming bring? Would she be able to escape her brother's schemes? Or would she fail and be mired forever in a life not of her choosing?

She swallowed hard, twice, and tightened her trembling fingers on the basket in her grasp. This was no time to let nerves flay her intentions to pieces. There was no other choice. At least none that she could bear to live with. Rourke would have to agree.

"Aye, Jenna." She nodded to the maid who still awaited her reaction. "I've never known your uncle to return with his nets empty when he's pledged to fill them."

The vessel's burgundy sails swelled as the ship leaned into the wind, cutting the edge of the channel at a rapid clip. Her heartbeat quickened still further as conviction swirled in her stomach. Only Rourke shaved the rim of the point just so as he made the turn for home. No doubt he had convinced the fleetmaster to give over the piloting of his ship.

She smiled despite her anxieties. Although the distance was too great for her to glimpse Rourke's proud stance or his dark hair whipping in the wind, it could be none other than the king of the Claddagh fishermen's second son turning the wheel for home.

Rourke.

His name pounded through her again like the surf. He'd answered his father's summons. For the tiniest moment the years of bitter silence and fathomless loneliness sluiced away and she basked again in the warmth of what had once been more than friendship between them. But only for a moment. Their bitter reunion beckoned, drawing nearer with each slice of bow through water. She could not let something that had died so long ago keep her from gaining her liberty. The spray from the waves broke high on the vessel's hull, making it sparkle with promise in the late afternoon sunlight.

"We must go and tell the household at once so they can make ready." Jenna's tug grew more insistent. "The king will be so pleased, poor soul. I only hope he is not too weak to know his son's come home at last."

Aileen glanced down at the berries they'd spent the afternoon picking, hoping to make a sweet compote to tempt the king's nonexistent appetite. Strawberries had always been one of his favorites. Since she had been forbidden entrance to the sickroom almost a month ago, she had been helping with the household chores as much as possible. Anything to keep herself busy and her thoughts from dwelling on the fate her brother, Eoghan, planned for her.

"We're nearly through with those." Jenna nodded to the lush bounty of their afternoon's labor. "I'll send me brothers back to fetch 'em. Surely Master Rourke deserves a grand homecoming no matter the circumstances?"

Aileen touched the blue and red kerchief covering her hair. Her plan and her worries would be ill begun if she greeted Rourke in the simple homespun-and-berry-stained apron of the village women. When he'd left without a backward glance five years ago she'd been little more than a girl, easily dismissed. She needed to present him with a full-grown woman. A woman who would not be gainsaid. Not by pride and not by honor. She was too familiar with the pain those noble virtues brought, though if the tales carried by the traveling merchants held true, perhaps neither quality would cause her a problem from Rourke anymore.

She shook off the thought, dropped her basket, and grabbed Jenna's hand. "Come on then. We'll have to hurry."

They set off down the hillside at a pace marking her as far more the young hoyden she'd once been than the lady she pretended to have become. Racing behind the churchyard and the rows of neatly thatched cottages, her breath burned in her chest as they reached the two-story stone edifice that served as home to the remainder of the Claddagh king's family. Aileen outdistanced Jenna by only a few paces and they both collapsed against the arched entry, panting for air and giggling with high exhilaration from their run.

The cool, gray stones of the outer walls offered respite. Claddagh Village might stand outside the traditional protection of Galway's walls, but this centuries-old granite enclosure was built to shelter the fishing community's people in time of storm or invasion. Yet even its enduring strength could afford her refuge for only a few days more. The truth scraped raw against Aileen's heart as the stalwart rocks grated against her shoulders.

She looked out across the harbor toward Liam Ahearne's boat. The crewmen were aloft, lowering the sails of the fleetmaster's ship as it glided toward the docks at the far end of the village. Rourke was nearly here. She fought back the wave of panic clenching her stomach.

"Hurry," she urged Jenna again as she pushed away from the wall. "We haven't much time."

The sun skimmed the hills as Master Ahearne's boat slid through the currents to close on Claddagh's docks. Having given over the wheel to the second mate, Rourke stood at the ship's bow, absorbing his first glimpse of home in five long years. The raw power of the wheel in his hands and the rise and fall of the deck beneath his feet had brought boiling back to the surface everything he'd thought was stowed away forever.

He had spent too much time away, immersed in any pursuit that would offer the tiniest hope of distraction from the pain and guilt that were his constant companions. Coming back was both a boon and a torment, reopening all of the old wounds even as the very place known as Claddagh offered to succor him.

The king's house rose black and silent within the purple shadows cast from the crest, just as it had when he'd sailed away five years ago. A lifetime ago. It had been a castle draped in mourning then for a life taken far too young. And all too soon the mourning flags would fly again. A banner fluttered in the shadows against the dark gray stones. Cold dread wrenched his gut. Was he already too late? Had he let his father down for the last time?

A firm hand clapped his shoulder and he winced from the wound not yet fully healed there. "Yer father awaits ye yet, lad. We made it home in time," Liam Ahearne's rough voice assured him.

Rourke would have to mask his anxiety more thoroughly. And any other wayward feelings. Especially from here on. No good could possibly come from wearing his regrets pinned to his sleeve. He'd learned that all too well in his time with the Green Dragon.

He turned and studied Liam Ahearne's gray-bearded, sea-weathered face. "How can you be so sure?"

"It took a mite longer than I had hoped to hunt ye down, lad. But I promised yer father I'd make landfall with ye afore it was too late." Liam nodded toward the king's house, a twinkle of compassion lighting his sea-green eyes. "His banner still hangs from yon parapet. I did not fail my king."

As Liam spoke, the banner fluttered high into the sunlight and Rourke spied the purple cloth. Purple. Not black. Da yet lived. Relief nearly stole the strength from his knees. One less failure to notch into his belt.

He took a deep breath of air laced with salt, fish, and the life he had left behind. Smoke curled above the thatched roofs clustered near the Claddagh waterfront. The church spire from St. Brendan's rose behind the homes of the fishermen who plied the waters of Galway Bay and the North Sound as their ancestors had done for centuries.

A small crowd gathered on the docks to greet them. Children, too young to remember their king having sons of his own, waved as did the wives and old men who joined them. Despite himself, Rourke peered into the crowd as the boat pulled in, telling himself he did not search for the tempting gleam of pale hair—shining like gold in the sun—that haunted him despite all attempts to rid his mind and soul of her image.

Through all the long trip with Liam overland from Dublin to Limerick then down the River Shannon to Kilkee and across the South Sound, he'd held back even the barest whisper of her name. Surely by now Aileen was settled elsewhere—anywhere—dandling her children from her matronly knee, her life among the Claddagh a fading memory at best.

He clenched his fists against the false waves of longing this homecoming coursed through him. He'd worked too hard to put her violet-gray eyes and tempting smile out of his thoughts to allow himself to be pulled back into the disastrous tangle of his desire for his brother's betrothed. He was here in answer to his father's summons. Here for the deathbed vigil and explanation he owed the old man. Surely that was enough to ask of him.

He had no more to offer Aileen than he had five years ago. Envy had cost him his brother and his soul. What kind of life could be founded on such bleak shores? Still, he could not stop his gaze from sweeping the crowd one last time as he returned their shouted greetings while a crewman tied the boat off.

"She's most likely up at the house, lad. She's been a great comfort to yer father through the years."

"Who?" Rourke jumped, feigning a defect of understanding as he grimaced again at his own lack of restraint. Since when had the right hand of the Green Dragon become so transparent?

"Miss Aileen." Liam chuckled, a dry sound that scoured Rourke. His fists balled at his side as the urge to pound his father's friend almost overcame him. Liam had been one of the few who knew his feelings five years ago. Before the tragedy that changed all their lives forever.

"Ye've had her name on the tip of yer tongue more times than not this past week. From the time her useless brother sent her here, all forlorn, orphaned skin-and-bones, the two of ye were practically inseparable. It's natural ye'd want to see her as well now that ye've come home."

Natural? There was nothing natural about his erstwhile feelings for his brother's betrothed. Lust for your brother's intended wife could only end in disaster. As it most certainly had during that dark storm five years ago that had washed Ranall out to sea and driven Rourke from home. A traitorous corner deep inside him shivered with longing at the knowledge she still dwelt in his father's house. He ground his teeth together and gripped the railing until his knuckles showed white, trying to strangle the seditious feeling.

"I am here to see my father." His gruff denial sounded hollow even to his own ears. He swung himself over onto the docks before Liam could point this out.

"What is taking so long?" Aileen's anxious whisper echoed through the great room's dark expanse.

If Rourke didn't put in an appearance soon, she wasn't sure she'd find the nerve to ask him anything. He'd come home to wait on his dying father, not dance attendance on her and her whims. Except her plan was no whim. It was as necessary as her next breath.

Aileen's satin skirts whipped behind her as she turned and paced back across the length of the hall toward the candle-lit hearth. Her heels clicked with sharp impatience against the stone floor before sinking into the lush confines of the Persian rug.

Of course you'll find the nerve, she scolded herself and steeled her spine. She turned at the hearth to cross the room again. There was no other choice. Eoghan's plan to secure his future at her expense was beyond intolerable. And by all accounts Rourke's life in Dublin had prepared him for far more debauchery than any proposal she offered.

Cold comfort there, but she clung to it.

She shivered as the mix of dread and anticipation collided in her stomach. Maybe it was the short, capped sleeves and daring décolletage of her lavender satin gown that set the gooseflesh on her arms. She smoothed her hands over the cool fabric, so different from the linen and homespun she usually wore. The high-cut gown, the elaborate hairstyle, and carefully applied lip color were essential to her plan.

The king's son deserves a grand homecoming despite the circumstances—that's what Jenna had said earlier. The gambler and rake Rourke had become would also get a welcome befitting his character.

She clenched her fingers—white with cold and the scrubbing she'd used to get the berry stains out—then gripped them tight and muffled a groan. Part of her wished he might never come down, that she might never have to face the task she'd assigned herself. The rest of her just wished she could get this night over with.

And a tiny, wistful part of her wished everything was far different and they could go back five years to the days when they could laugh and tell each other anything with impunity. When Rourke had taught her how to fish with a net and how to sail a skiff across the harbor. She shoved those memories aside. That friendship had died when he'd walked away after their fateful kiss. Walked away and never looked back at the faithless girl who betrayed his brother.

Guilt harrowed her afresh, a guilt she'd carried for five long years. She'd proven herself unworthy of the one son and driven the other from his home. Perhaps she should resign herself to the new marriage Eoghan proposed as punishment deserved.

Everything in her rebelled at the thought of a lifetime with the groom of her brother's choosing. His greed and cruelty were fabled throughout the province. The king himself had pronounced his disgust with her brother's intentions. Right before the old man had barred her from the sickroom, he'd promised to see her free of the proposal. And then he had looked at her with those deep sea-blue eyes so like his son's.

Opportunity does not often come more than once, Aileen. Let none pass you by.

She shivered again. In that moment it had almost been as if the old man could see straight into her soul. She'd clung to his words. And now she would grasp the opportunity presented by Rourke's return and pray that his father would forgive her for following his advice so thoroughly.

She bit back a sigh and swallowed as her glance at the clock above the hearth did little to allay her anxiety. There had been a time when discussing anything with Rourke would have been easier than taking her next breath. But that time had passed. Awaiting him like this was sheer torment.

Her betrothal ring dangled against her breasts as it had now for so many years. Two hands holding a heart-shaped emerald under a golden crown that had once belonged to Ranall and Rourke's mother. She would like nothing better than to hand it back to Rourke and put as much distance between them as possible. But the first thing she had to do was eliminate the distance altogether.

She smiled at the irony and sighed as she continued pacing. Perhaps a glass of sherry would bolster her sagging courage if Rourke delayed much longer.

Stopping at the windows, she looked out toward the harbor in the distance. Lights from the cottages dotted the shoreline. She would miss this place when she left, the home that had sheltered her since her parents' deaths so long ago.

Her heart twisted. Rourke was home, as he should have been all along. A cool draft puffed by from the window casing and she shivered.

The fine hairs at the back of her neck stiffened; she knew even before turning that Rourke had entered the room. Her breath hitched in her chest as fear lanced her spine and shivered over her skin. It was time to face him, face her past, and take a daring leap for the future.

She stayed immobile, staring out the window, betrayed by fear and the impossibility of it all. Now that the time had come, she seemed completely incapable of so much as turning around, let alone asking him to do something that by all rights should offend him to the very core of his honor. If his years of gaming and womanizing in Dublin had left him any.

"Aileen." His voice, so deep and rough—and achingly familiar—swept through her, leaving her feeling naked and raw.

Dismay held her immobile for the span of several more heartbeats. She had forgotten. Even in the deepest recesses of her memory, where she embraced every word, every gesture that had ever passed between them. How could she have so thoroughly forgotten what just the sound of Rourke McAfferty's voice saying her name could do to her?

Her knees seemed to have turned to mush. She gripped the cold slate of the windowsill and willed herself to stay on her feet. Now was not the time to allow her bones to melt nor lose all sense of her purpose in summoning him to the hall. There was very little time left to her. Very little protection left in this granite fortress that had become her home.

It was now or never.

Despite the breath locked in her chest, she turned to face him.

Two

Rourke caught back a groan of longing that welled from the very depths of his soul as Aileen finally turned to greet him. He had been shocked enough by the sight of the elegantly clad figure gazing out the window when he entered the hall. Looking across the shadowed room toward her, regret and dismay clashed within him as he took in the changes the years had wrought.

Somehow in his mind, Aileen had remained frozen in time. Frozen on a windswept hillside with her golden hair spilling over her shoulders and berries staining her lips as her laughter cascaded through him. Untried innocence shining in the sun of his memories—he'd steeled himself to deal with that Aileen. Yet here she stood now, the very embodiment of a sultry temptress. And he was at a loss.

Every nerve in his body tightened in traitorous response to the transformation. Dressed in lavender satin fit for a Dublin ballroom, the Aileen who turned to meet him was no longer the artless girl who harrowed his dreams, but a woman full-grown—remote and sophisticated. Pale, golden-blond tresses swept up into a sleek knot with tumbled curls that kissed her slender neck and soft cheeks. Her sweet face had haunted him for the past five years—arched brows, wide violet-gray eyes, and lips that begged a kiss to ravage his honor and his life—had ripened to full womanhood. But no winsome smile curved those soft lips, no welcoming sparkle lightened her gaze.

What had not changed was his reaction to her. Derision twisted within him, writhing like a snake. He had but to look at Aileen and the time and distance he'd worked so hard to place between them disappeared like mist in the sun. He wanted nothing more than to reach across the separations dividing them. To take her in his arms and hold her there. To claim her as his own.

He had been right to don the guise of a man without honor and principles, for he still possessed none where she was concerned.

"Hello, Rourke." Aileen's voice came low and husky, rasping over his raw nerves and delving neatly betwixt the barriers he had so carefully erected.

Her breasts rose above the impossibly low neckline of her gown, plump and full as she walked forward to greet him. The fabric of the gown clung to her hips and moved enticingly with her graceful pace; he could see now that it was far closer to a courtesan's dress than a debutante's. Where had Aileen gotten such a garment? And why?

She stopped a half-dozen paces away. Tantalizingly near and yet safely out of reach. Firelight flickered across her creamy skin and caught the gold ring glowing on the chain that dipped from her neck. The Claddagh ring. Hands for friendship, an emerald heart for love, and a golden crown for loyalty.

His mother's ring. Ranall's betrothal gift.

"Welcome back. I hope you have not found things too unfamiliar." Aileen held his gaze, but what lay behind her impersonal greeting remained unreadable in her eyes. "You have been missed."

You have been missed. A weak and watery description of the tortured moments he had spent over the last five years and the homecoming that was tilting his new universe even further off-kilter.

For an instant the desire to escape this folly, to escape her by turning and leaving her standing alone in the hall, arched inside him. He had been a fool to see her alone. A fool to think he could see her at all and not suffer the need to pull her into his arms and taste just how much she had missed him on those soft lips.

But he wanted to do more than taste her. That knowledge burned a hot path along his soul. He wanted to . . . With an effort, he shoved his unwanted lust aside, realizing she still awaited some comment from him.

He loosened his dry tongue from the roof of his mouth.

"Da has refused to let me enter his chamber tonight. This seems a long journey for nothing save frustration. How have you found him over the weeks since Liam left to fetch me here?"

She looked away at last. Glancing down at her clasped hands, she shook her head. A hint of the wisteria scent that had always been hers wafted to him across the rug between them. "I can tell you naught of Niall McAfferty's condition. Your father has denied all save Muire and Liam access since he first fell ill. Even me. Your father has changed a great deal since you left him to carry on by himself."

"Is that why you told Jenna you needed to see me? To heap recriminations at my feet?" He stiffened, ready for years of accusations over his escape, his neglect.

She shook her head, her golden hair and shimmering gown shining in the light. A figure from his past—more dream than reality, even now.

"Then why?" Why had he been summoned for this torture? He longed to escape. He longed to draw nearer.

Color washed her cheeks as her teeth worried at her lip. Whatever it was she wished to speak to him about, it had her knotted up inside. His interest tightened.

"I . . . I wanted to welcome you home." Rosy red washed her cheeks again as the words came halting and soft. "I mean . . . I needed to . . . oh, why does everything have to be so difficult?"

The last came in a rush of frustration. For an instant the worldly woman's mask fell and he saw a flash of the girl she had once been. Memories knifed him.

She turned away—a lady once more, the girl gone—tension rigid down her slender spine.

His gaze traveled from the few loose curls dancing at the back of her neck, down over her almost-bare shoulders. Desire tightened painfully inside him. Her skirts swayed and clung seductively as she paced to the windows and looked out over the harbor again.

At one time he would have thought nothing of crossing to her side.

Of inhaling her sweet scent and tracing his fingers over her shoulders.

She had been his friend.

She had been his torment.

She had belonged to his brother.

He ground his teeth together, remembering the feel of her in his arms, the taste of her mouth, and the fire she unleashed in his soul.

He shuddered as the urge to touch her nearly overcame him. He wasn't about to give in to temptation again, no matter the provocation. The one time he had indulged his craving sparked the worst tragedy in the history of his family.

She cast a half glance over her shoulder, a gesture he had forgotten, but which instantly tore memories free from their forced seclusion in his mind. He stifled yet another groan and armored himself with the steely determination that had seen him through the last five years.

"If you have nothing further, I'll bid you good night."

She jumped as he spoke and turned back to face him, her eyes widened. "No, please."

"I've had a long journey, Aileen. I have not arrived in the best of moods. Whatever it is you wish to say to me would be better approached on a full stomach in the light of day."

She paled and gripped her hands tighter together. Her lips pressed together in a thin line. A twinge of sympathy panged inside him. He squashed it. Her problem, whatever it might be, must be of her own making this time. As well as her own solution. He would have nothing to do with either, and, heaven willing, he would manage to keep his distance despite the ancient feelings roiling through him.

He inclined his head and bowed slightly. "Good night, Aileen."

He turned to make good his escape. To live to fight another day, as Garrett would say.

"Rourke."

Her one-word protest, his name alone, sank into his heart like a barbed hook and halted him before he had taken so much as a step. He blew out a quick and all-too-shaky breath. If his men could only see him now—the Green Dragon's right-hand man, a scion of command, paralyzed at the sound of his name on a woman's lips.

Derision snaked through him again. He straightened his shoulders and forced himself to face her. "What is it you want, Aileen?"

Determination etched her features as she advanced on him, her satin skirts whispering across the stone floor. "There are many things I want, Rourke. But what I mean to discuss with you now has nothing to do with that."

He arched a brow at her, fought to keep from stepping back as she halted in front of him. All too close. The soft scent of wisteria assailed him. He could almost taste her. He swallowed hard and held his ground as the demons dancing madly inside him made the detachment he craved impossible.

He met her gaze, those wide violet-gray eyes that haunted his soul.

"State your purpose and be done with it." He bit the words out.

She took a deep breath that threatened to spill her breasts from the low décolletage of her gown. The Claddagh ring glistened at their crest, taunting with its intimate caress of the skin he'd give his soul to touch and yet branding her for all time as untouchable. Not again. Never again.

"You are right." She nodded, the light of earnest need shining in her eyes. Stray curls caressed her cheek. He suppressed the urge to wipe them aside, to smooth the worry creasing her brow.

"I do neither one of us a service in procrastinating. Rourke, I must beg a small boon from you. It is my fervent hope that your . . . experiences over the last five years will allow you to see your way toward granting it."

His heart hammered, ready to promise her anything. His better sense, honed over the bitter years apart, kept a tight fist on his tongue's reins. "My experiences—as you put them—have taught me not to make blind promises."

Hell, hadn't he promised himself a hundred times over that he'd never allow himself to melt again into the liquid appeal in her gaze just as he was doing at this very moment? Ready to do whatever she bid?

He was a fool to have come here at all without making sure she was gone. "Tell me what you want from me and I'll consider the matter."

She sighed and glanced away, the line of her shoulders tightening. "You will allow me nothing in this, will you."

A statement, not a question. But still no answer to the dilemma facing her, the problem she wished him to solve.

"Perhaps that is for the best." Her gaze locked with his again. "I shall state my situation baldly and expect the same in return."

She paused, searching his face as if seeking his agreement to this, at least. He nodded.

"After years of refusing to return your father's bride price, my brother found another match for me a little over a month ago. I have no desire to marry his choice. Not now and not ever. Once Eoghan returns the money to your father, my alternatives will be eliminated. Time is short. Only your father's illness has delayed matters this long."

"Indeed?"

"Aye." She nodded again, though her soft skin had paled to a luminous pearl. "I need you to help me, Rourke."

I need you. He ground his teeth together.

"How?"

"I want you to help me in the only way that will stop my brother permanently. As I said, I believe your experiences . . . your new life in Dublin . . . make you the best choice for the task."

She paused for breath and Rourke could only stare at her. Did she expect him to murder her brother? To somehow discourage her new prospective groom?

"Aileen, what is it you want from me?"

She straightened her all-but-bare shoulders and lifted her chin, a clear signal of troubled waters ahead.

"I want you to ruin me, Rourke. Take my virginity. It is the only way."

The words rang in Aileen's ears in concert with the rapid thumping of her heart. Right up until the moment the proposition fell from her lips, she hadn't been sure she possessed the courage to speak her request so plainly. Yet she had done it with Rourke standing before her so tall, so remote, and so desperately out of place in the home generations of his family had occupied.

Opportunity does not often come more than once, Aileen. Let none pass you by. She had acted on his father's words. Would he?

With his elegantly tailored evening attire, polished boots, and distant demeanor it was hard to see past the man he had become and seek the boy she had once known. The kindred soul she had once loved and needed more than her next breath. Despite his outward refinements, his entire body exuded a raw power to accomplish anything he put his mind to. He could more than fulfill her request, there was no question.

But would he? Her thoughts and doubts circled like screeching gulls.

Her heartbeat drummed faster still as a flash of some emotion she couldn't name played over his features. Horror? Revulsion? Hunger? His face paled to a shade only just darker than his elaborately tied cravat. She had shocked him to his core.

Her heart sank a little, but then she had known her words would shock him. Shock she could deal with. Denial she would not accept.

"You want me to *what?*"

He bit out his question in a low, deadly-quiet voice. His lips barely moved while his entire body seemed frozen, save for the narrowing of his eyes as his outraged gaze bore into hers.

"I . . . I want you to . . . remove me as a matrimonial prize for my brother to award where he sees fit." If she were not so desperate she was quite certain she would hike up her skirts and run from the room, faced with his glowering countenance.

Rourke closed his eyes. Tension stood out along the column of his throat as he swallowed. His fists bunched and flexed as though he restrained himself from throttling her. She bit her lip and straightened her spine, along with her resolve. She could not allow his recoiling from the actions necessary for her escape plan stop her. Candlelight and shadows flickered over the harsh planes of his once-beloved face.

The peat fire hissed derision, mocking her determination.

"Impossible," Rourke ground out at last.

He opened his eyes and strode past her without another glance, pulling the door shut behind him. His booted footsteps rang against the flagstones before he crossed to the mantel and stared down into the flames. Every line of his shoulders and stiff back screamed his affront at her suggestion. His denial.

The desire to gather her skirts and flee the hall surged. She wanted nothing more than to leave him behind, along with the turmoil of emotions just the sight of him evoked.

She had anticipated his initial resistance, but she had not considered her own desperate need for his acceptance and the devastation his refusal sparked in her soul. It tore afresh the pain she'd felt when she discovered him packing to leave after Ranall's death. When she'd begged him to stay. Begged him to take her with him.

She shuddered. She would not beg. Never again. But neither could she give up without a fight. Five years of loneliness had taught her that.

She mustered her arguments and marched across the rug to join him by the fire. "Surely such an idea is not impossible for one who leads the sort of life you do in Dublin? Will you at least hear me out?"

He fired her a scornful look and reached for the decanter of whiskey on the mantel. "What do you know of my life in Dublin, Aileen? What could you possibly say to convince me that this is the only course open to you? And, most of all, why me?"

"Because you are my last hope." She watched as he poured himself a tumbler-full of his father's finest spirits before shooting his shuttered gaze back toward her.

"Too bad." The grim finality in his voice lanced her heart as he raised his glass in a mocking salute. "Care to join me?"

An occasional sherry or glass of wine was all the Claddagh king allowed his ward of eight years. But the king was dying and she would soon be at her brother's mercy if she failed to convince Rourke to help her. She nodded, willing to meet any gauntlet he tossed. He quirked a brow and poured a lesser amount in one of the cut-crystal glasses before handing it to her.

"*Slainte.*" He raised his glass and tossed back a healthy swallow.

She took a sip and struggled not to choke on the fiery liquor as it numbed her mouth and burned down her throat, bringing the sting of tears to her eyes.

She drew in a much-needed breath. She could not give up. "Why won't you even consider what I ask?"

"What made you think I would?" he retorted.

She gripped her glass tighter and forced herself to hold his gaze. "There was a time when I could have asked anything of you. When we were friends."

The glitter in his eyes made her look away. "I know that friendship died along with Ranall. I know I am to blame for how you have lived, for . . . what you have done since you left."

A snarl of amusement twisted his mouth. "How can you know what I have done? How I have lived?"

"I am not the naive girl you left behind." She took another sip of the whiskey, welcoming its peat-smoke taste and the warmth it brought to her frozen heart. Courage to continue flowed in its fiery wake.

She faced her quarry squarely.

"I know that you have lived a wastrel's life, gambling and drinking. Carousing with your new friends in dens of iniquity or visiting houses of ill repute. Your father kept an eye on you, even at this distance. I found the accounts of your activities in his desk."

Rourke's dark gaze never wavered from hers, though his lips pressed to a thin line.

"I know how much your fall into disgrace has cost him," she pressed on. "He used to be so proud of you."

He grimaced. The muscles in his jaw tightened as he took another swig from his glass. "So what makes you want to lie with a man who holds so little honor in your eyes? So little promise?"

"We were friends once," she repeated, trying to suppress the memory that they had been far more. Those feelings had not been enough to hold him then; she could not allow them to halt her plan now. "Better one night with a devil you know than a lifetime in hell with a stranger."

"Were none of the local lads willing to help you with your predicament?" Ire edged his tone.

"Jasper Farley, the man my brother would sell me to, could exact a high vengeance. Not to mention Eoghan's fury at losing not only your father's bride price, but the fat purse Farley has offered him to replace it. How could I ask one of your people to live with that?"

"Yet you ask it of me?" He rubbed a hand over his shoulder and moved a step closer.

She stood her ground. "You don't live here anymore. You've made it plain you will leave once you have paid your respects to your father. The new king will be under no obligation to honor the friendship between our fathers that brought me here in the first place, that has offered me shelter all these years."

For a moment his gaze slid from hers and his jaw worked. *Please God, let me be getting through to him.* "It is enough that I will lose my own reputation without soiling another's. You are my only choice if I am to gain my independence. Surely you, of all people, can understand that."

Again his jaw worked in silence for a moment before he answered her. "You have *honored* me with your proposal because I am a devil without honor, without a reputation to lose and no ties to the area. The lesser of two evils."

She nodded. Hardly the persuasion she had hoped to use to move him. So much for dressing seductively and gaining his acquiescence through feminine wiles.

"I may be a devil, Aileen. I may hold little that resembles honor, but that does not make me a despoiler of virgins, no matter how willing."

"I . . . I can make it worth your effort." She forced the words out as her own sense of honor shuddered inside her. "I don't expect your cooperation to come without a price."

"What?" He choked on his swallow of whiskey and thunked his glass down. The contents sloshed on the mantel. "Are you really offering to *pay* me for my services? You truly do think I have sunk into the muck."

She was lost. She knew it to her very core, but she could not stop now. "Under the Brehon Law your people still follow, I can claim my virtue price from you when Eoghan returns the bride price due to my . . . new ineligibility. In six months time I will come into my inheritance from my mother. I can pay you back, with interest, then. Surely such an arrangement will help maintain your Dublin lifestyle."

Rourke stepped closer still, looming over her. His blue eyes glittered darkly in the firelight. Without warning, he gripped her shoulders so tight her glass fell from her hand. The crystal shattered against the hearthstones. "A woman can claim her virtue price only if she is unwilling."

His gaze ravaged her lips as he pulled her roughly against him. The rough texture of his brushed wool jacket scoured her bare flesh almost as thoroughly as the scorn in his voice.

"You are not offering to pay me for my cooperation, are you, Aileen? You would have me force myself on you. Is that truly what you want, *muirneach?* Are you so desperate to escape this Farley you would sell yourself and damn us both completely with this deception?"

His fingers dug into her tender skin. Her satiny gown offered too little protection from his assault. The truth was her only defense. She tilted her head up to meet his gaze and cursed them both. "Aye."

For a breathless moment he held perfectly still, looking so intently into her eyes she swore he could see her very soul.

"Hell—"

His lips claimed hers. But this was no repeat of the spontaneous embrace they had shared on a hillside so long ago. His kiss purposefully plundered her this time. As though he meant to strip away any artifice, and render her defenseless. But despite the anger she could feel thrumming through his body, raw sensuality poured from him, tormenting her, punishing them both for the past they couldn't change and the future she had dared to propose.

His tongue pressed past her lips and thrust against her own. Fire, so blazing hot it stunned her, rushed through her veins. She melted against him, unable to do anything but accept his anger and the passion blazing to life between them.

His hand slid along her back, rough yet gentle, to cradle her neck and tilt her head up to better accommodate him. His tongue slid against her own, tasting of peat-laced whiskey. He groaned into her mouth, laving her teeth and tongue without mercy.

All the lonely days and nights of missing him roiled inside her. All the anger at his desertion, and the guilt over her role in his departure, seethed to the surface. She wanted no mercy. And she would grant him none.

She wound her arms around his waist, pulling herself further into his embrace, pulling him closer. He smelled just as she remembered, fresh and beautiful, like ocean breezes ruffling blue sage shrubs along the sandy paths in the hills behind Claddagh. The pain and the years separating them dissolved. This was Rourke, the boy who had tempted her days and tormented her dreams. Rourke, the man who had returned just as she had prayed he would for so very long.

Rourke the stranger who would break her heart again.

Tears broke loose inside her and streamed down her cheeks as his fingers arched through her hair and massaged her scalp and neck. The myriad sensations his kiss unleashed raged through her with the ferocity of a late summer storm blowing in from the open sea. Her breasts, crushed against his chest, tingled in response to the wild thundering of her heart.

Without warning, he released her mouth and stepped back, leaving her bereft and dizzy. All the wild things he had unleashed swirled on inside her at a breathless pace. She had never realized desire for a man could be so overpowering. She felt open, exposed—ready for anything he asked of her.

She swayed and clung to him to keep herself standing. His hand cupped her cheek and he brushed the pad of his thumb over her tear-damp skin. Regret and desire warred across his features. For the briefest moment, his gaze softened and she thought he meant to kiss her again.

Instead he placed his hands back on her shoulders and firmly pushed her away.

"You are a tasty enough morsel, I warrant." His words stung. "Probably well worth the price of a little scandal, with a tidy profit thrown in."

He looked her up and down with an arched brow. "Shall I rip the dress off you here and have my way with you on the hearth? Rend your virginity amid the shards of crystal? Or would you prefer me to drag you off to the comfort of your bedchamber?"

With her defenses already lowered, his barbs struck hard, but the cold gleam in his eyes stung worse. Her hands shook as she reached for the mantel and gripped it tight to keep more trembling at bay.

She drew in a deep breath and gathered strength to speak. "One night is all I ask. One night and then we can be done with one another."

He raised a brow. "Perhaps I haven't changed as much as you think, Aileen. As much as I had hoped."

He snatched up his whiskey glass and turned away. "Devil or not, a night such as you require is more than I have to give. More than even you can ask of me."

The door slammed shut behind him and he was gone. More so than if he had never arrived.

The finality of his repudiation echoed through her for a long time as she stood racked by dry sobs of despair.

Three

Rourke reached for the latch on his father's chamber door just as it sprang inward. Muire stepped back with a start, carrying a tray of barely touched gruel.

"Master Rourke. I was not expecting ye to call on yer father so early." She spoke overloud as she looked him up and down. "I trust ye passed a comfortable night?"

Comfortable did not come close to the night he had passed. Between his concern for his father and his consternation over Aileen, he'd spent most of the night pacing his chamber or looking out at the moon reflected on the harbor. Trying to shove aside the taunting appeal of a seductress in lavender satin. Of a friend he had loved and lost.

One night and then we can be done with one another.

Would that that could be so, but he knew better. Knew to his very core. The damnable scent of wisteria haunted his every attempt to push her proposal far from his thoughts, to ignore the emptiness in his arms when he'd pushed her away.

Better one night with a devil you know than a lifetime in hell with a stranger.

He'd struggled through the darkness to squash the desire that flared with the rough kiss he'd pressed on her to try and scare some sense into her. The feel of Aileen in his arms, of her breasts pressed so tightly to his chest he could feel her heart thumping wildly against his own, of her lips soft and yielding, stirred him beyond reason. Beyond sanity.

Tempted as he might be to satisfy momentary lust, he knew the solution she sought would only compound her troubles. And would torment him for a lifetime. The sins that had once enticed them could not be allowed to find new life in a lie that would haunt them both forever. He carried enough shame.

One night is all I ask. There were some wounds that should never be reopened. His was Aileen Joyce.

"Master Rourke? Did ye have an uncomfortable night?" Muire prompted, repeating herself.

Comfort had nothing to do with this entire visit. The sooner he had his interview with his father, the sooner he could put Claddagh behind him for good. At least in Dublin he had his work with Garrett and the rest of the Green Dragon's compatriots to help him expiate his past transgressions.

"Comfortable enough under the circumstances," he answered at last. He nodded toward the chamber's interior. "Is he awake then? Has he broken his fast?"

"He refuses to eat 'this pap,' as he put it." Muire shook her head, avoiding his gaze. "But he can stomach little else."

Rourke's gut churned when she looked away as though hiding the depths of her worry.

"Let me try." He took the tray from her.

Her gaze rose to his then, surprise lighting the soft blue depths. Her gentle smile took the edge off his jagged feelings for a moment. Muire Ahearne was almost as dear to him as his own mother.

"Ye always were soft-hearted. Mayhap ye have not changed as much with yer wild Dublin ways as ye think." She patted his cheek as she squeezed past him into the hall with a soft chuckle. "Seeing yer face will do himself good. Perhaps his appetite for pap will return, as well."

He stepped inside his father's room, doubting the first of her pronouncements, but hoping for the last. Muire swung the door closed behind him and plunged the room into almost total darkness. A lone lamp burned low on the washstand, casting eerie shadows into the gloom.

"Da?" he called. "It's Rourke, come to see that you eat as you should so you will get well."

He could barely make out the furniture in the chamber, the light was so dim. Thick cloth covered the windows and long curtains shrouded the massive carved bed his parents had once shared. Though not nearly as rank as he expected, the air was stifling.

His gut wrenched anew. With his wife and sons gone, had the Claddagh king given up as Aileen said? Overwhelmed by all the problems with no respite, no one to share his burdens?

Though no one save Aileen had given voice to such recriminations, these charges surely lay behind the wary glances and appraising looks he received since making landfall, the forgiveness he'd felt in Muire's touch just now. How many suspected the real reason he'd left? The reason he'd stayed away all these years?

"Da?"

He advanced a few steps. Perhaps the old man slept and he should come back later.

The image of his father stooped with age and worry, withered with illness, harrowed him. How different a picture from the robust, hearty man who had raised his sons to wrest their living from the sea and exact a fair profit for their community's catches in Galway's marketplace. A man of principles and honor. A leader born who deserved a better legacy than the son he had left—the Abel who as good as slew Cain over a woman he coveted.

The image of Aileen, leaning on the mantel as he walked away last night, rose anew. He still coveted her, still damned himself over her.

One night is all I ask.

She had no idea what she asked. Look at the price their forbidden feelings had already exacted. His brother lost at sea and his father left with only a faithless son. A son sure to disappoint him no matter the penance he paid to offset his guilt.

He turned to quit the chamber.

"Rourke?"

He barely recognized the reed-thin whisper issuing from the depths of the bed. Where once his father's voice had seemed to boom across the water and fill the very harbor, this answer rasped like dry seaweed against a salty deck. "Is that you, my son? Have you returned home at last?"

Rourke's heart thundered with the sins he'd carried through the years. With the lifestyle he openly led. Had those reports Aileen spoke of contributed to his father's decline? How could he add further to his father's afflictions by unburdening his soul of its black millstone of shame? A short visit then, a farewell if need be, and nothing more.

He set the tray on a small table and walked to the windows. "Aye, Da. Let me open the curtains so we can see one another."

He whipped the drapery back from the casement and swung the glass open. Morning sunlight and a fresh breeze carrying the cries of the gulls over the harbor streamed into the room.

"That's better, don't you think?" He spoke in a jolly voice, trying to quell rampant disquiet when he turned to see the figure huddled under a mountain of coverlets.

"The light hurts my eyes." The plaintive invalid's voice issuing from the mound could never have commanded a boat, let alone a fishing fleet the envy of all Ireland. Even in Dublin, the tales of the Claddagh's heritage in strength and honor were legendary—and their king, elected by the fleet—his Da—was the best.

Fear twisted Rourke's gut and he drew the curtains half-closed once again. As a lad scrambling over the decks and docks, he'd always thought of his da like the granite outcrop on the harbor edge—solid and immutable. Sailing in yesterday, he'd noted shifts in the rock formation, weathered changes in alignment and shape.

Time must have worn down his da, too. Time and a family lost to betrayal.

"Come closer so I may see you, my son." A hand snaked from the mound of coverlets to gesture him closer. "I have waited so long to talk to you. You were nearly too late."

Rourke scooped up the tray and approached the bed with a wary eye and a heavy heart. Between the dark velvet bed-curtains and the coverings, he still could not see much detail of his father's condition.

He reached out and took the hand that had first shown him how to steer a hooker and set a sail. It was cool for all his da's bundling, and nearly as firm as he remembered. But the profile he saw in the gloom tore at him. His father's eyes were closed. His skin, pallid in the shadows.

"I'm here, Da. I've come home."

His father nodded and gave Rourke's hand a feeble squeeze. "Every lad must unfurl his sails and drift with the currents for a bit. The lucky ones make it safely back to harbor. You're a man full-grown now, Rourke. Not near as soft as I expected from your city life."

Your father kept an eye on you even at this distance. I found the accounts of your activities in his desk. He should have known. It rankled a little that he had not. It rankled more that his father had kept an unseen tether tied to him all these years. That in his father's eye he had not been building a new life, but merely been away.

He shoved a burgeoning tide of resentment back.

He had not journeyed all this way to indulge in re-criminations against a dying man. He had come to make his peace. He proffered the tray. "You need to eat, Da. How else will you regain your strength? The fleet needs you."

His father grimaced and waved the congealing gruel away.

"Have you seen the lads then?" His voice held a heartier edge. "How was the catch? Liam will need you to negotiate a fair price. He can read the wind and the waters, but he can't grasp the subtleties of the marketplace."

"The fleet is still out in Ishmore's Killarney Bay. I believe Liam said they are due back by week's end. I doubt he'd appreciate any interference from me. You always said he was the shrewdest man you knew."

"Liam is not the only one who needs you, Rourke. Sit down. We have much to discuss." The tone of command had not entirely left the Claddagh king, no matter his condition.

Rourke put down the gruel and pulled a chair over to the side of the bed. Much to discuss indeed. Should he start with his reasons for leaving Claddagh? Should he tell his father that his wild-appearing Dublin life-style held a dual purpose? Dare he try to explain that his exploits with the Green Dragon made his public demeanor key to the actions they undertook—actions in aid of those less fortunate. Actions that made it possible for him to bear the burden that his brother had died in his place.

These same questions had echoed through him all

the way from Dublin. Now there was the question of what to do about Aileen.

One night is all I ask. While he could not do what she wanted in the way she wanted, surely there was some choice available to free her from her unwanted marriage. "Aye, Da, I have so much to say I hardly know where to begin."

"Begin with the matters nearest your heart, my son—"

The door to the chamber flung open with a crash.

"Master Rourke."

Jenna puffed into the room, clutching her apron in one hand, her cap askew and her chest heaving as she fought for breath and clung to the doorknob with her other hand. "Muire asks that ye come at once. Miss Aileen's brother is here, demanding to see yer father and promising not to leave until Miss Aileen comes with him. Even if he has to drag her out."

"Bastard." Da sucked in a sharp breath. "Can't he let a man die in peace?"

Rourke stood, wondering what he could do, but certain the situation must be nearly out of hand already if Muire had sent for him.

"See to this for me, son." His father's voice was tight. "We can talk later."

Jenna wrinkled her nose. "And he brought that fat fella that tried to kiss Miss Aileen last time they were here. The one what beat his last wife near to death, more than once."

Rourke was already striding for the door. Images of Aileen in his own arms, melting against him last night—and then struggling in the unwelcome embrace of a bounder added speed to his departure.

"Stay here," he told Jenna.

"Just remember, Rourke," his father called, "opportunity does not often come more than once. Let none pass you by."

Opportunity and Aileen. The irony scoured him.

Better one night with a devil you know than a lifetime in hell with a stranger.

In spurning Aileen, had he condemned her?

"You must cease this blustering, Eoghan." Aileen faced her half brother and her unwanted suitor, striving to keep her fright and disgust from her voice. "You know full well I can not leave here until the matter of my original betrothal contract is resolved. You were the one who signed the document that sent me here in the first place."

She remained poised by the settee, clutching its carved back for support as the brother who only remembered their familial connection when there was a profit for him paced by her in his expensively tailored suit.

Ten years her senior and given to dissipation, her father's son by his first wife looked closer to twice her twenty years. How soon before the effects of excess began to wear similarly at Rourke? And why did the thought pain her so deeply when he made it clear last night he had no lingering tenderness for her?

She shoved the pointless frustration aside for later consideration and concentrated on the problem before her. Knowing Eoghan was selling her to the highest bidder to keep such fine garments on his back, galled her.

If only another six months could have passed before she had drawn the attention of Galway's most influential and ruthless merchant. In six months she would have gained her majority and her inheritance from her mother. She could have taken the money and disappeared. She could have had a chance at avoiding this confrontation without resorting to the desperate proposition she had tried to foist on Rourke last night.

All I ask is one night. But he couldn't even spare her that. Why, after a silence of five years, had she thought he would?

"If only that old fishmonger McAfferty would get on with the business of dying and settle this matter." Eoghan glanced warily at Jasper Farley, who stood silently by the hearth, rubbing his chin and perusing her with an arched brow. His silent scrutiny made Aileen's skin crawl as if she stood before him stripped of all attire.

"Eoghan, at the very least, show some respect while you are in the man's household," she protested.

"What I meant was that with your betrothed long dead . . ." Her brother raked a hand across his thinning pate, obviously struggling to maintain some decorum in front of her prospective groom. ". . . there is no need for you to linger here. You are not family. It is time you proceeded to live your life."

"For eight years this family has been all I've known. I *owe* Niall McAfferty the consideration you seem so willing to have me throw away. Surely this matter can wait a few days longer."

"I am a forbearing man, my dear." Jasper spoke for the first time. He was a rugged man, despite his advancing years and the corpulence of his stomach—broad-shouldered with large hands. At one time, girls must have thought him handsome with his dark hair and eyes, but there was a hardness in his features and a harsh light in his eyes that had repulsed Aileen ever since his interest settled on her several months ago.

"Willing to wait for what I want," he continued, adjusting his cuffs and taking his top hat in hand. He stepped over to the settee. "But only up to a point. This matter, as you put it, has tried my patience long enough. I have promised your brother double the price McAfferty paid. But only on delivery."

He seemed to loom over her, all the more menacing because of the reasonable tone he took. Aileen struggled to stop herself from backing up. From turning and running out of the room. Weakness was something she could not afford to show this man.

"I have business that will take me to Belfast soon. We can take our time on the way home, make a fine wedding trip of the journey." The smell of rosewater and sweat nearly overpowered her as he leaned close.

Better one night with a devil you know than a lifetime in hell with a stranger. Rourke's refusal had condemned her.

Jasper brought his meaty fingers up to stroke her cheek. She couldn't help recoiling from the gesture. He chuckled, a gleam of triumph sparking in his assessing gaze. "Don't be alarmed, my dear. I enjoy a challenge and know just how to handle skittish virgins. Soon you'll be eager to please me in every way."

Dropping his hand to the edge of her chemise, just above her bodice, he rubbed the linen between his fingers. "And when you are mine, I'll dress you in the finest silks and imported lace. No more homespun wool or linen. No more cleaning or household duties beyond catering to your husband's desires."

She did step back this time, pulling herself out of Jasper's grasp and out of his reach for the moment. The smile curling his lip foretold how much he would relish the challenge once they were wed.

"There, you see?" She jumped as Eoghan spoke from just behind her. She was trapped between the two men. If they tried to carry her off at this moment she'd have no defense. She should have let Muire stay with her, but she hadn't wanted to further distress the older woman, not with all her cares for the king. Jenna was in the kitchen, too. Liam, at the docks. And Rourke, closeted with his father.

"You'll have a fine life," her half brother continued in a cajoling voice. "Why don't you just come with us now and let me sort out the legal gibberish. You don't belong here any longer."

"And just where do you think she belongs?"

They all turned as Rourke strode into the room. A wave of relief rushed through Aileen as he joined them.

He hardly looked the part of a citified wastrel. Clad in his shirtsleeves, he looked very at home, very much a prince of the bay. Broad shoulders stretched the seams of his white lawn shirt with their power. His embroidered waistcoat tapered over a flat stomach worthy of his sailing heritage, of the generations of McAffertys who pulled teeming nets from Galway's bounty.

"I had no idea you'd come back." Her brother spoke as if the idea was more distasteful than surprising, although he offered his hand.

"And I had no idea I'd find you here, Joyce." Rourke ignored Eoghan's outstretched hand, favoring him instead with a curt nod. "You never called during those first years your sister fostered here."

Eoghan's cheeks flushed an alarming red and he dropped his hand to his side. "May I present Mr. Jasper Farley, Aileen's intended."

Rourke nodded to Jasper. He looked relaxed enough, but Aileen noted the taut line of his shoulders and the set of his jaw. When he'd held that look years ago, he'd always been intent on gaining what he'd set his mind to. And she'd never seen him fail.

"You mean the man who intends to become her intended," Rourke replied affably enough. He stepped closer and managed to wedge himself right next her, extricating her from between the two other men. She breathed easier.

"You have no say in the matter. She was betrothed to your brother, not you, after all." Eoghan's color heightened further.

"Quite right," Rourke nodded agreeably enough. "But that gibberish, as you put it, still leaves her tied to Claddagh. Best wait until my father is feeling up to sorting it all out with you."

"Has he improved?" Jasper asked, frowning.

"Definitely. In fact I have come down expressly to

find Aileen." Rourke touched her shoulder and nodded to the door to the stairs. "He'd like you to continue the story you were reading to him yesterday. Said you left off at a most interesting place."

What an adroit liar he had become. He knew she had not seen his father in over a month. She'd told him so herself. Still, she was not going to pass up the escape he'd granted her. Even if it was only a temporary one. "I'll go at once. Thank you."

"Good day, Eoghan. Mr. Farley." She hastened across the room, gratitude pounding in her chest.

"Perhaps my father will be ready to discuss terms upon your return from Belfast . . ."

She knew without having to look back that Rourke was escorting her guests to the door as he spoke.

". . . I wish you a safe journey."

Harsh worry pricked her. While today's skirmish might have ended for the good, however would she avoid being shackled to Jasper Farley in the end?

Four

Rourke reached the top of the stairs, his boots heavier with each step, weighted down with the images spinning through his mind. He stopped, decanter in hand, to swirl the dusky amber liquid and shoot a gaze down the length of the darkened hall.

Was this really what he wanted to do?

The question twisted his lips with derisive humor. He'd downed enough whiskey to mistrust his motives, but he wasn't so drunk he didn't realize he was avoiding the real issue. He wanted to make love to Aileen. Had wanted to with a raw kind of hunger that ate at his soul and his honor for far too long to doubt something so basic. But was he ready to live with tonight's actions for the rest of his life?

Opportunity does not often come more than once, his father had said. *Let none pass you by.*

Opportunity—this idea, born while on the docks with Liam, helping the fleetmaster and Sean O'Toole make repairs to Sean's boat so he could rejoin the fleet, had burgeoned as the day wore on. Working in the waning sun, with the gulls overhead and the sparkling water lapping at the dock, had fostered the ghosts haunting him and created a touchstone to the life he'd left behind.

He refused all attempts to socialize further and ate his evening meal alone in the hall that echoed with old memories—Ranall laughing and daring him into races across the rigging; Mama and Da walking the path to St. Brendan's, arms laced together; Aileen arriving, alone and scared, abandoned by the only family she had left; Aileen on a windswept hillside, laughter and berries, and a kiss that had changed everything; Aileen dressed to seduce last night; and finally, Aileen as he had seen her this morning, strained and harassed.

Could he love her and then walk away forever as she proposed?

Denial arced through him. He could no more make love to her and leave her now than he could have five years ago. Then the pain had been too fresh and the guilt too raw for there to be anything else. Now, just by making her proposition, by expecting his compliance, she brought one burning truth home to him. Despite the desire he had tasted on her sweet lips, any regard she might have once held for him, any respect, had been shattered by Ranall's death.

In truth he could not blame her for the way she felt. But no matter what lay between them, he was obligated to help with her current situation.

If not for his transgression so long ago, she would be married to his brother by now. Married and safe from her brother's schemes, safe from the likes of Jasper Farley or any other dissipated swine her brother came across. Rourke had met more than his share of men like Farley. Men who haunted the taverns and brothels that had made up the hunting grounds of the Green Dragon. Garret and the others frequented many places, places that would have set Aileen a-shudder, for the express purpose of identifying men such as Farley, men who exacted unfair rents and perpetrated crimes against their tenants with impunity. Men whom the law did not bother to police.

His forays with the Green Dragon had saved many from Farley's ilk and repaired a portion of the damage they ravaged on this beleaguered land. Rourke's shoulder yet bore the mark of their latest encounter with iniquity, saving a tenant lass taken in lieu of rent and sold to a vile brothel owner. Would such exploits raise him in Aileen's estimation?

I can make it worth your effort. Aileen's words echoed back to him.

The small bag of coins he gripped chinked against the decanter in tuneless harmony with his thoughts. Her offer had stung far more than she could know. The depths she thought he wallowed in burned across his heart. He had loved her. He ground his teeth together as fresh pain loomed. Damnation, if he was honest with himself he'd have to admit that he still cared too much. Enough to risk both their souls in an effort to give her anything she wished. But not the way she proposed it. Never that way.

Enough dawdling. It mattered little what she thought of him or what his intentions might have been if events had played differently.

He forced himself to put his plan in motion, his footsteps silent across the thick Persian rugs in the hall. Aileen would have to settle for a loan to aid her escape from her predatory would-be husband. A loan and the promise of help in attaining control of her inheritance when she reached her majority. Independence for a spinster was rare, but if anyone could convince a judge that her brother was incompetent, Garrett's friend, Daniel O'Connell, could.

He blew out a quick breath. This scenario alone would salve his conscience, help save his sanity, and make him feel that coming here was not entirely wasted. He may have had no further interviews with his father, but at least he would save Aileen from either wasting herself or condemning herself to a future she would abhor.

A small wash of light edged the bottom of her door. Good. At least his nocturnal visit would not startle her from sleep. He grasped the knob and turned it before doubts could still his intent. If he was going to convince her there was another way to prevent her marriage, this was the best time. Who knew what tomorrow would bring?

He opened the door without knocking. "Aileen—"

The sight of her stilled his tongue. Dressed in a sheer white night rail, she stood by the fire, packing a small valise, her ripe womanly shape outlined by the glowing flames. Her golden hair rippled loose over her shoulders and down her slender back.

Rourke swallowed, his mouth dry and his thoughts a muddy quagmire of mingled lust, honorable intentions, and the certainty that he would not leave here unscathed.

She took a startled step back and swivelled to look at him.

"Rourke." She sucked in a breath and clutched the brown skirt she was folding. "I . . . I . . . wasn't expecting to see you."

"Indeed." The word nearly shook out of him. With an inward grimace, he forced a nonchalance he was far from feeling. He leaned against the door jamb and tried to still the hot blood rushing through his veins.

"I brought you a nightcap." He waved the decanter to encompass her attire and the invitingly turned down coverlets atop her bed. "It would seem you are more than ready for any man who might stop by. And in all-too-appropriate virginal white at that. Or have I arrived too late for you to retain that claim?"

Red stained her fair cheeks and caressed her rounded breasts before disappearing beneath the low edge of her gown. She shook her head. "I await no man."

"Indeed." She was far too alluring in the white gown. His body reacted to every inch of her. The whiskey he'd downed burned away in the heat of the desire pounding through him. His mouth grew dry, his muscles tensed.

As her surprise at his intrusion died away, her eyes took on a different glitter. The light of anger blazed in her depths and her chin raised. "It's late, Rourke. I don't care for a drink. You should go."

Images of her in his arms taunted him. Her lips locked with his, her arms entwining him. Not in the lavender confection of last night, not even in the diaphanous white she wore at the moment. The thought of her stripped of all coverings suffused him. Wisteria-scented skin pliant beneath his every caress. Her heated breath washing across his chest as he put an end to the torment of too many years and buried himself within her.

He should go. Somehow he had to stop himself from accomplishing the very deed she had asked of him only last night. But if he left now she would go on with her packing. Go on with what appeared to be her present decision to run away before he could offer his assistance.

"I didn't invite you here, Rourke." Her voice rose a notch, in volume and firmness. "You should leave."

He raised a brow, unable to resist tormenting her with the very proposal she had thrust at him the night before. The proposal that had haunted him unmercifully. "Your . . . *invitation* last night did not seem to hold an expiration. Did you rescind it somewhere along the way? Or perhaps you have changed your mind and you're packing to join your swain, Farley."

Anger and fear snapped in her eyes. She shuddered and balled the skirt into a tight wad, her full breasts swaying beneath her nightgown with her movements. His groin tightened in response.

"You know I have no wish to wed Jasper. I have no wish to marry any man." She threw the rumpled garment into the valise on the stool beside her. "I would never have come to you as I did last night if I wished to follow my brother's dictates. I thought you of all people would know me well enough to understand that. It would seem I was mistaken."

Her words lashed him raw in an instant. He was far too vulnerable to everything about her. Her words, her needs, and the corresponding spark they fanned within him. Anger followed hard on the heels of desire. He pushed away from the door frame and kicked the door shut with one booted foot. It slammed closed with enough force to rattle the hinges.

Aileen jumped at the sound and her eyes widened as he came closer. Rourke spared a quick thanks that Aileen's room was far enough away from his father's so as not to disturb him. Then he could spare thoughts for nothing but her and the wild emotions she wrought inside him. Desire, guilt, compassion, and anger rocketed through him whenever he so much as looked at her.

"Rourke—"

"What, Aileen?" He closed the distance between them still further, ignoring the alarm bells ringing in his head. "What else do you want to say to me? What more can there be beyond your low opinion of me and your determination to do just as you wish?"

She did not retreat from him, holding her ground despite the slight trembling of her chin. She straightened her shoulders, an unfortunate motion that thrust her breasts even more boldly against the sheer fabric of her gown. He ground his teeth together and tried to ignore the tempting sight of her rosy nipples and how desperately he wanted to taste them. To taste her and all the passion he suspected her capable of.

"So you have come to torment me with my own words? To reopen old wounds and tear my heart to shreds one last time?" Angry tears shimmered in her eyes. "If those are the true reasons for your visit, you may consider your mission completed, Rourke McAfferty. I am defeated. I will not marry Jasper Farley. I can no longer hide behind your father and the good people of Claddagh. However I escape this, I must do it on my own."

Firelight glinted in her golden hair and glistened in the tears at the edges of her eyes. He could have groaned with the longing that suffused him to gather her close and kiss those tears away. But he knew it would not stop there. He searched for his anger of only a moment ago.

"Your help was the only aid I sought. The only choice I thought I could make, short of fleeing altogether or giving in." She nearly spit her condemnation at him. "I do not have it in me to become a whore, not even within the sanctity of the marriage Jasper proposes."

"Yet you offered yourself to me." He stepped closer still and thumped down the decanter and the bag of coins, enjoying the discordant clink of metal against crystal, a perfect complement to the pain and lust roiling inside him, swirling in the air around them.

"Nay."

"Aye, you did, only last night." He deliberately let his gaze wander from her facedown over her high, rounded breasts. To torment her. Yet all he succeeded in doing was tormenting himself. Her breath quickened beneath his perusal.

"You displayed your wares as skillfully as any harlot in the street and begged me to take you."

"Nay, I did not beg." She shook her head and exposed the soft curve of her neck, the tender pulse point at her collar.

"Aye." He cut off her denial. "And you do it even

now. How could any man deny what is so freely offered?"

Boldly he cupped one full, soft breast. She tensed at his touch, but her chin lifted further and she refused to retreat from him.

He fondled her, a leisurely caress that fanned the flames already plaguing him higher still. Her nipple tightened against his palm. Hot blood thundered through him, engorging his flesh to painful limits. He locked his gaze with hers and brushed her nipple with his thumb.

A sound, part gasp, part moan, escaped her. He brushed the sensitive tip again and she shuddered and closed her eyes. One tear traced a slow path over her cheek as she fixed her sparkling gaze on his once again.

"I did not beg last night, Rourke." She reminded him in a husky tone that tore at the slender thread he still held on his control. The final strand of sanity he possessed. "Your decision must be freely made. I will never beg you for anything again."

"Never again." She did not pull away from him as he expected. She stepped closer instead. Soft, pliant, wisteria-scented skin beckoned. She was the girl of his dreams and the woman of his nightmares. Stolen kisses that belonged to no other.

Pain thrummed again inside him. He could remember all too clearly the last time she had begged anything of him—a dark night, a windswept dock, the sweet boon of love she offered him. He had refused her and lived to suffer all the lonely days and nights that followed.

Could he face that again?

"Never again." He repeated, unsure whom he answered. He slid one arm around her and drew her soft body against his own hard length. The scent of rain-washed wisteria and Aileen filled him. She was heaven and hell in his arms. More than a man could ask for. He wanted her, nay, needed her, more than his next breath. How could he deny what she asked of him when it was the very thing he wanted? Had wanted for more than five long years?

"I didn't come here for this," he told her as he drew her closer still. Hunger clamored hot in his veins. Pain and longing far sharper than anything he'd ever felt all but choked him. "I cannot give you what you want, Aileen."

"Give me what you can," she whispered, her gaze clear and strong. "Take from me what I offer."

Raw desire bit into his soul with sharp teeth, shredding his good intentions.

"Hell."

He caught her soft lips beneath his own. Words were useless between them, useless when all he wanted to do was love her until there was no strength left in his body. Tomorrow would sort out the rest of the world. For tonight nothing mattered but the feel of her against him and the fiery need she stirred inside him. Tonight he would have her and damn the morrow.

Tears pricked Aileen's eyelids as Rourke's mouth plundered her own. Her heart hammered. She had succeeded all too well. He would indeed take her virginity. She knew that down to the soles of her feet. To the depths of her soul.

His warm lips demanded her all and she drank her full measure from his, tasting his whiskey-laden breath against her tongue. Last night she had been ready for this, armored to get through her outrageous proposal without allowing her wayward feelings to interfere or snag her regret. Tonight her defenses lay scattered to the four provinces.

His hands caressed her back, kneading her flesh through the thin linen of her gown and sending whirls of heat through her. He was wearing only the laborer's shirt he had worn while working at the docks with Liam all day. The muscles of his chest were hard and demanding against her breasts. Her heart beat wildly.

She could not reconstruct the barricades demolished by his timely rescue of her from her brother and her suitor. Especially not with his tongue laving hers, or his lips suckling a hot trail down her neck and back up to recapture her lips and pull her closer and closer.

There was naught she could do to protect herself from his passion or from the desire leaping to life inside her. She could not quell the old love and hope singing through her veins. She was his. His so thoroughly it would be useless to deny it. He nibbled her ear, his hot breath fanning through her.

Tomorrow would bring such pain, but for tonight all things were possible and she would grasp with both hands the opportunity to taste his love, if only for this one night. This was Rourke. Her Rourke. And despite the circumstances she could deny him nothing. He claimed her lips and rimmed them with his tongue over and over until he plunged boldly into the gasp of pleasure he drew from her.

Tonight, she was his and he was hers. She threaded her fingers through his hair and pressed closer to him still. Cupping her body to his. Cradling the hot evidence of his desire for her against her belly. She teased his lips with her tongue, enjoying their smoothness in contrast to the texture of his stubbled chin.

He groaned and released her mouth. "Dear God, Aileen." He shuddered against her, his breath hot against her ear.

"Aye." She more than understood. The fire between them was far more than she had ever expected. "Make love to me, Rourke. If only for tonight."

"Hell." He closed his eyes on that soft curse, spoken under his breath. She could almost read his thoughts. He wanted to deny her. To deny them both, but the need raging between them had a life of its own.

The blaze in his blue-eyed gaze raked her, stripping her of everything but her raw need for him. Here and now. No past. No tomorrow.

"So be it." Anger tightened his jaw. He would deny them if he could, despite the rigid evidence of his desire strained against her belly. He set her from him, grasped the front of his shirt and tore free of the buttons, shrugging the fabric to the floor.

Firelight flicked his torso with glowing tongues. His chest was broad and strong. No longer a boy's. A man. His arms were sculpted muscle laced with dark, silky hair she longed to stroke. A jagged scar puckered one shoulder. A trophy from a duel, perhaps? A prize from his life outside this room. Tonight the stuff of his life, of hers, did not matter. She would ask him later.

Her gazed skimmed further down his chest. He tapered at the waist as another sprinkling of dark hair scattered over his belly and disappeared beneath the edges of his trousers.

Heat swelled inside her, along with a quiver of fear.

His gaze scoured her features. "And now, Aileen, is this still what you want?"

"Aye." She managed the word despite the breath locked in her chest.

With slower movements, his gaze never leaving her face, he reached for the fastenings to his trousers. One button, two—Aileen's heartbeat drummed in her ears—three, and then the fabric lowered, slipping down his hips. She caught her breath as they inched lower still until his turgid flesh sprang free and proud. His trousers slid to the floor and he kicked his feet out of both them and his boots in short order.

Her gaze was caught in fascination on the hard thrust of flesh sprouting from his body. Dark hair thatched the base, akin to the curls between her own thighs. He was thick and hard and long.

A spiral of heat shot through her belly. Her tongue edged her lips. The tip of him was rounded and thicker still, glistening with a tiny drop of moisture.

Arousal. The word thrummed in her mind.

She licked her lips again. He groaned and further moisture glistened against his bulbous apex. The urge to touch him overwhelmed her, to slide her fingers over his glistening flesh and test the feel of him.

"Rourke." She could do naught but breathe his name.

"Aye." Desire sparkled hot in the depths of his eyes. He took a step toward her and she almost retreated.

He was so strong, so overwhelmingly male. She held her ground with an effort.

"And now you, lovely Aileen."

As his gaze held hers, his hands traced her fingers and then up over her arms in a slow caress. She shivered as he reached her shoulders and his gaze told her everything she needed to know. He tugged at the soft linen and lace.

Five

Aileen's nightgown drooped over her shoulders and hung low against the tips of her breasts.

"So very lovely." Rourke pulled her against him and kissed her lips soft, warm, and slow as he moved them both toward the bed.

Lazy heat spiraled down her spine, rising again to tingle and swell in her breasts. The scent of blue sage and Rourke nearly overpowered her. Then his mouth touched her neck, pressing hot, moist kisses that shivered through her. He moved to tantalize the hollow of her shoulder with his tongue. She was pliant in his arms, absorbing all that he poured into her with his touch, with his lips.

He tugged at her gown again, baring her breasts. "Beautiful," he whispered, his breath teasing her taut nipples.

He seated himself at the edge of the bed and settled her between his thighs. Her arms were tangled in the night rail he held bunched behind her.

"So very lovely," he repeated. She basked in the warmth of his husky compliments.

Her breath locked as he dipped his head to her

breasts. And then his mouth was on her nipple. Heat pooled low in her belly and swirled through her heart as he suckled her.

"Oh, Rourke." Mindless pleasure spiraled outward from the touch of his lips against her flesh. He nipped her, grazing her with his teeth, and she shuddered, completely his to command. He released the first nipple only to repeat his delicious treatment on the second. Her knees grew weak.

He released the gown from his grasp and it sighed to the floor to puddle around her feet. She grasped his shoulders, grateful to have something to cling to.

His hands swept her back, buttocks, and thighs, stroking her, testing her as he continued to lave and suckle her nipples. She shuddered beneath his touch as he squeezed her buttocks and then stroked a soft pathway around to the front of her thighs. His fingers brushed lightly between her thighs and she couldn't restrain the sound that welled from deep within her.

Part gasp, part groan, she did not recognize the sound. But she ached to have him touch her there again, despite the heat searing her cheeks.

He did not disappoint her, his fingers flicking over the very center of the pleasure radiating through her.

"Open for me," he commanded, his breath hot against her wet nipple.

She spread her thighs, unable to deny him. His fingers returned, probing more boldly against her flesh. She shivered with each touch.

He cupped the back of her neck and drew her down toward him. His gaze glittered at her. She wanted to sink into it. To sink into him.

"You are mine, Aileen." His words rasped over her as his fingers continued their exploration of her slick flesh. "Mine."

And then he offered her a kiss that seared her soul as his fingers pressed up inside her. Wildfire raced along her nerve endings at the sensation of having the tips of his fingers enter her body. Her breasts brushed his chest as his lips plundered her. She shuddered and he sucked her tongue deep into his mouth, his fingers pressing further, higher, and then, higher still.

A quick thrill of pain lanced the sensual haze he wove around her and through her. She gasped, breaking the kiss.

The harsh sound of their mingled breathing echoed as a log crashed in upon itself in the hearth.

"I . . . I . . ." Words escaped her.

"You are no longer a virgin, Aileen." Rourke's gaze glittered darkly up at her, his fingers encased deep inside her, brushing her womb. "I have taken your maidenhead. You are free."

Pain clogged her throat at his words. She would never be free of the things he made her feel. The things she still longed to feel. She had bargained for this one night. And it was all hers.

"Make love to me," she repeated even as his thumb brushed her damp curls and pleasure spiraled through her once more. "Make love to me all night, Rourke."

"Aye—"

She cut off his reply as she bent and covered his mouth with her own, boldly thrusting her tongue into his mouth. She would have everything she could from this night, for it was all she would ever have.

His thumb brushed again and then again, and then harder, more insistent, spiraling wild heat and dark-honeyed pleasure through her. And then his fingers moved inside her again, turning the echo of pain into a slow, sweet friction. His tongue and hers matched the rhythm of his sensual invasion.

Pressure built inside her, higher and higher, in perfect tempo with his fingers and his thumb, until she thought she could bear no more, and then it went higher still. She arched her hips toward him, needing and yet unable to name her need. And then sudden uncontrollable shudders wracked her. Pleasure broke over her, rippling out from her very center in wave after feverish wave. Rourke caught her as she collapsed against him.

"Oh, Rourke." She panted against his neck, grateful to have his strong arms about her. "That was . . ."

"Aye, beloved." He kissed her brow and cradled her against him as a soft chuckle rumbled through his chest. The hot evidence of his own desire probed her hip. "And that was only the beginning."

"There is more?"

"Indeed."

Aileen sounded so stunned Rourke couldn't hold back his smile. She was indeed every bit as passionate as he had always known she might be. His beautiful Aileen. She had made weak, flimsy things out of the barriers he had erected around his heart.

"There is much more," he promised, and she smiled.

He kissed her, softly at first, letting her float through the hazy pleasure she had just experienced and draw back toward the desire that still flamed hot inside him.

Gradually he deepened the kiss, sliding his tongue against hers, tasting the pleasure on her lips. And when she returned his pressure and looped her hands behind his head to draw him closer he knew she was ready.

He leaned back on the bed, drawing her with him. Her body slid against his, extracting a groan from him at the sweet torment of her wisteria-scented skin moving against his. Hot and pliant, just as he'd dreamed over a thousand nights.

Her breasts pressed against his chest and her belly cradled his aching manhood. God, he had never wanted a woman so much. She returned each stroke of his tongue with her own, threading her fingers through his hair.

He slid his hands over her velvety flesh, cupping her breasts, stroking her belly, fondling the plump roundness of her buttocks. He nudged her legs down his hips, arching her wet heat against him. Twin groans echoed as his flesh thrust intimately against her. She was so wet, and so ready for him.

"I need you, Aileen," he ground out. "I need you now."

"Then have me," came her quick acquiescence. "Have all of me, Rourke. For tonight I am yours and you are mine."

"Aye." He more than agreed. The tip of him slid against her folds and he shuddered. "Oh, aye."

He grasped her hips and guided her in slow torture over his hard length. She took him, inch by maddening inch, until he was deep inside her.

"Mine." He managed the one word as he claimed her lips for a lingering kiss and then he could hold himself still no longer. He moved deep within her and her body gripped him tight.

Heaven.

Hell.

Both.

Tangled in a world that he could no longer define.

She gasped atop him and arched her neck back. Her golden hair brushed his thighs. Fire and moonlight danced over her skin. She was more than beautiful. She was woman personified with a power and majesty all her own.

"Aileen . . ." Words failed him. He could not describe how she made him feel. Not if he had a thousand nights before him. He slid his hands over her—her thighs, her breasts, her slender waist.

"Aye, Rourke, it is the same for me." Husky-voiced, she lowered her sparkling gaze to his.

Thunder rumbled in the distance. Far out beyond the bay. Out in the open sea. Thunder and lightning roiled within him, a storm of passion and emotion revolving around this woman.

His throat tightened and the need to mate himself to her blazed fully through him.

"Aye, indeed." He gripped her hips and lifted her slightly, watching her face as the movement slid him partially out of her. Anticipation pounded through him.

Pleasure tightened her features and widened her violet-gray eyes as he slid her back down his length again. He repeated the movement, watching her. Pride, power, and incredible tenderness warred in his chest.

"This was meant to be." He slid into her again. She was so tight. So hot. So slick.

"Aye." Her agreement came husky and breathless.

He wound his fingers into her hair and tugged her down for a hungry kiss, tasting the truth of his words on her lips and the power of the connection between them. Cradling her in his arms, he rolled her beneath him and thrust deeper still into the sultry confines of her body.

There could be no other woman for him. He moved within her, capturing a primal rhythm that was more than mere lovemaking, more than a man and a woman finding pleasure for a night. Seeking solace from old wounds or a haven from the future. He was pledging his life and his soul to her. There would be no turning back, no leaving her behind this time.

She shuddered beneath him with each thrust, her tongue tangling over and over with his. Her legs twined high about his waist, accepting all of him as a rhythm older than time and stronger than thought took over.

He needed her. Needed each deep thrust. And then to thrust deeper still, as she caught his rhythm and echoed it back to him. He needed the tight sheathing of her body, the warm, wet caress as he moved within her.

Harder.

Faster.

Driving himself into her over and over again, while she clung to him. Her sleek sheath gripped him tight and then tighter still as broken cries fell from her lips to echo against the solid stone walls. His name, over and over again. And then he could hold out no longer as he followed her with his own pleasure, shuddering deep inside her.

Complete.

Silence held in the room, broken only by the hissing fire in the hearth and the sound of their mingled breathing.

"Rourke?"

"Aye?"

"Thank you for—"

"Hush now." He didn't want her gratitude. He had not fulfilled the bargain she had proposed. That was not what he had done. He didn't have the strength to explain it now. Now, he could barely move.

"But, Rourke—"

"Hush." He caught her lips with his and kissed her very softly, enjoying the lingering sensuality.

She sighed and looped her arms around his neck, kissing him back measure for slow, delectable measure. Her tongue teased his lips. Wisteria and woman filled his senses.

Pleasure began a distant burn inside him and he smiled against her lips.

"What are you smiling about?"

He moved ever so slightly inside her, allowing her to feel his flesh burgeoning to insistent life once more.

Her eyes widened and she sucked in a breath. "Oh, my."

"Indeed."

"We can . . . do it . . . again?" The wonder in her tone forced a chuckle from him. She arched her neck up and kissed the hollow by his throat. Waves of desire shot through him to pulse in his groin.

"Aye, beloved. I've a feeling I will never get enough of you."

She kissed a soft trail of burning kisses along his

collarbone in answer. Until she reached his scarred shoulder and pulled back.

"Rourke, I need—"

"I have much to tell you. We have much to share. But for now all that matters is this." He kissed her soft lips. "There is no one in my heart save you."

He captured her lips for another kiss. He throbbed inside her and she wiggled delectably in response. "Our questions can wait."

"Aye." She arched her neck and met his lips again.

Aileen snuggled into a warm hollow in the pillows as Rourke kissed her temple and pulled the quilt over her shoulders. She was tired, deliciously tired, as she drifted near sleep, listening to him dress and ease out of her chamber in the gray, rainy dawn.

She took a deep breath—blue sage and ocean breeze lingered on her coverings. She ached in places she hadn't realized could ache, but the pangs were welcome—they signaled her freedom not only from Eoghan and Farley's plans for her, but from years of questions and doubt, years of loneliness and longing.

For the first time she dared to hope. To look into the future and see more than gloom and desolate dreams.

Even if all she ever shared with Rourke was one night of passion, the sweet heat of his kisses and the memory of him deep inside her would echo beyond the physical coupling.

He had saved her. Despite himself. And in doing so he had shown her that what had once been severed, what they had once felt for one another, could live again. Richer, fuller, more complete.

She stretched, her body still thrumming from the waves of passion he had wrought from her. She conjured the sight of Rourke naked beside her and savored the memory of his hard flesh against hers, within her. Each kiss and caress burned on inside her heart as though branded against her soul.

Heat crept over her cheeks at the bold direction of her thoughts. How would she face him this morning? Their intimacy was so fresh and new. And what of Muire and Jenna? Would anyone notice her change from desperate girl to woman?

She wanted—needed—to hug that knowledge to herself, and keep it hidden a while longer. She was Rourke's. He had claimed her with his actions and his words. What she had intended to be an end felt far more like a beginning.

But what of Rourke? Had he fulfilled her request only to turn away or did he feel the rebirth of the connection between them? Would he stay in Claddagh or return to Dublin? The raw wound in his shoulder, barely healed, must have shown him how dangerous the ways of a wastrel could be. Could she convince him to give that life up? To start a new life with her?

But what if the wound had come from a duel over a woman? Unreasoned jealousy flared. She knew there had been others, there had to have been. *There is no one in my heart save you,* he'd whispered in the night. She hugged his words to her.

Somehow, surrounded by the scent of their lovemaking—her body still branded by his caresses—somehow, she could not despair for their future. They had come too far.

The bell from St. Brendan's tolled twice, signaling the end of early Mass. She shoved the covers aside, along with the hovering doubts and uncertainty. The Claddagh women would be gathering to make food baskets for Galway's poor in a few minutes. She'd have to hurry if she was going to take bread to Mrs. Gilkelly beforehand.

As she dressed, she spied the ring on the mantel where she'd placed it last night, determined not to take the reminder of her broken betrothal, her shattered future, with her. She had worn the special ring on a chain for eight years, first because it was too big, and later as a reminder. It had once been Rourke's mother's ring. The emerald heart had always fascinated her with its green fire. She slipped it in her pocket to take down with her and leave in the king's desk for safekeeping.

Later she would seek Rourke out and try to determine what the future might hold for the two of them.

Together.

Six

Rourke entered his father's sickroom and stumbled to a halt. The window draperies were already open, as were the windows themselves. Despite the clouds outside, light played on the polished oak furnishings and highlighted the lush colors of the Persian rugs and wall hangings, decorating the chamber's floors and walls.

He had forgotten how warm and welcoming this room had always felt, especially when his mother was alive. When he and Ranall had spent wintery evenings playing chess by the fire with Da or listening to Mama's stories about the Fian of old.

The soft sound of rain pelting the thick walls beyond the casement filled the chamber along with the scent of rain-washed granite. Much better than his last visit, only yesterday? But then the whole world seemed a different place this morning.

He'd left Aileen's bed as dawn lightened the gray skies over the harbor. A soft kiss to her temple as she snuggled into the pillows, a final whiff of her enticing wisteria scent from the golden hair splayed behind her, then he tucked the coverlet over her creamy white shoulder. Donning his scattered clothes, he'd returned to his own room before anyone was the wiser regarding the monumental shift their one night of lovemaking had made in the universe.

He hadn't planned on making love to her when he'd gone to her. But what had begun so innocently years ago had decreed that end, no matter their denials or better intentions. He could not deny that it had felt more right than anything he had done in his life.

Regret no longer had a place in what they shared.

Muire had interrupted the rut he had been pacing steadily into the floor of his own chamber and summoned him to see his father, effectively ending his debate over whether to remain where he was or return to Aileen and hold her in his arms once again.

Now he would have to find a way to overcome the obstacles placed in their path five years ago. To make his Da understand that he was taking his advice and seizing the opportunity that he'd been graced to find a second time. *Let none pass you by,* the old man had said.

There was no way he could leave Aileen behind again. He would take her to Dublin and marry her there, if she would have him. She must. It was the only solution he could conceive. Her brother, the memory of his, her bridal price and contracts be damned. Aileen was his as surely as he breathed.

"Da?"

He strode over toward the carved four-poster, determined to tell his father everything, to seek his understanding if not his blessing. For too long they had suffered from guilt and recriminations, denied themselves their fragile hope of happiness. No more.

The bed was empty. The mass of coverlets, heaped there only yesterday, lay smooth and flat.

"Da?" He called louder this time, concern pricking him.

"I am here, son." His father's voice beckoned from behind him—quiet, confident, and very unlike the invalid's reedy whisper of only one day ago.

Rourke swivelled in surprise. Sure enough, there sat his father in the far corner of the room by the hearth. More weathered than the last time he'd seen the old man in the light of day, Niall McAfferty still bore the regal air of a man used to command. Gray might streak more of his black hair and his tan was paler than usual, but he bore little resemblance to the fragile invalid Rourke had seen in the shadows just yesterday. Confusion snared him.

"You . . . you appear to be feeling somewhat better today, sir." Suspicion tinged his voice despite his efforts to keep it out. "Or is it that you have not been quite so ill as you let on?"

Fully dressed in boots, trousers, and a simple shirt, his father quirked one eyebrow and nodded. "I feel better than I have in quite some time. Will you join me? We have much to say to one another, I believe."

The Claddagh king gestured to the leather-padded chair separated from his by a low table set with a tall teapot, some mugs, and several steaming dishes.

Dumbfounded at the seeming miracle unfolded before him, Rourke settled into the chair and leaned forward, intent on getting to the bottom of whatever artifice his father was foisting on him. Either the old man was masterfully putting on the front of a well man, or he had perpetrated a cunning fraud by faking his illness to lure his remaining son home.

Niall McAfferty returned Rourke's scrutiny without further comment until Rourke could no longer stand the silence. "Which is it, Da, are you dying or no?"

His father shrugged and offered a slight smile. "The priests at St. Brendan's will tell you that all men are born in preparation for death. Who am I to argue?"

Relief, leavened by days of regret and miles of fearful worry, coursed through Rourke. He pushed from the chair and paced over to the hearth. His father was not dying. Not yet. The hanging over the mantel depicted a single-masted boat yawing in a fierce storm only a few feet from the safety of shore, exactly how he felt.

Should he be grateful or angry? Both or neither?

He picked up the black king from the chessboard still set by the fire and twirled it against his palm. The wily king, protected by all the other pieces, no matter the cost. He turned and glared at his father. "Who else knows? Is the whole village a party to this deception?"

Was Aileen?

"Liam and Muire are my only confidants. And before you can accuse her, Aileen is innocent. I could not tell her my plan, nor could I deceive her for long. That is why I have kept her away from me for all this time."

Chattel for her brother, duped by his father. No wonder she had been desperate enough to make her outrageous proposal his first night home. What could his father have been thinking to serve her thus?

"How could you play such a trick when she needed

you most? She has been alone and heartsick over you—and her brother's vile plan to wed her for a fat purse." He slammed the chess piece down, rattling the board on its small table. "While you hid in your room. I can not imagine how—"

"Enough, Rourke." His father cut off his protest and shook his head. "I did what had to be done. I could not resolve this dispute with Eoghan Joyce by myself. I needed you."

Rourke snorted. His father had never needed anyone.

"Drop anchor, Rourke." Da gestured to the chair again. "And furl your sails for a moment."

Rourke held his place for a few heartbeats more, but his father had never been willing to settle halfway when he bore the wind in his sails. Rourke returned to his seat.

The king nodded. "Had I merely sent for you, you would have wasted precious time wrestling with unnecessary regrets and misspent blame. I waited five long years for you to come to your senses, for you to come home. My pride prevented me from sending for you long ago. Aileen could not afford to let yours delay your return."

Rourke managed to keep from squirming in his chair. He had begun the journey home on more than one occasion, only to find some reason at the last moment to delay the trip. Da's ruse had been a desperate act for certain, but an effective one.

And if it had been to benefit Aileen he could at least listen to the rest. Echoes of her soft, passionate cries and the memory of her in his arms affirmed his resolve to at least hear his father out.

Da poured tea into the mugs on the side table and helped himself to a scone from a small basket.

"Have one," he said. "Muire put currants in them, the way you like. As I said, we have much to discuss. I'd like to begin with the day you left here so abruptly. And how you have spent the last years in Dublin. I have spent many sleepless nights wishing I could go back and change things."

Rourke shook his head, refusing the biscuit his father proffered, his mouth dry as bleached whale bones on the shore.

The time had come—the righteous indignation and blame he'd avoided like a coward all these years, recriminations for the life he had given every appearance of living ever since. He would face his father's condemnation at last, knowing that there was no blame in Aileen's heart.

What was done was done; it was time to stow his regrets and get on with the business of ensuring their future. He could not change the past. But he could do something about what was to come.

"I owe you an apology, Rourke." His father leaned forward and fixed his gaze with Rourke's. "I was too paralyzed by the loss of your brother following so hard in the wake of your mother's death to think about you, to realize how you must have felt. To realize you blamed yourself for Ranall's ship capsizing."

"It was my fault. All mine." Rourke swallowed against the tightening in his throat. Aileen's golden curls blowing in the wind and a forbidden kiss that tasted of sweet berries and sweeter love. No matter the yearnings of his heart, he had trespassed where in honor he did not belong. There had been a sound on the rocks behind them and he'd turned in time to see Ranall hastening away.

"You can not take responsibility for the wind and the waves. The storm blew in too quickly. Ranall was an excellent sailor. If anyone could have ridden the storm out it would have been him." Da leaned closer and grasped Rourke's forearm.

"But it was my turn to scout the currents." He'd started to scramble after Ranall, to explain, but Aileen turned her ankle on a stone. By the time they'd hobbled back home, Ranall was sailing away from the docks. Too late for explanations. Too late.

Self-loathing tore at him.

"Ranall knew how you felt about Aileen." Da's grip tightened as he practically forced Rourke to look into the blazing honesty of his blue gaze. "How she felt about you. We all did. He did not begrudge either of you. There was a girl on Inishmore who had caught his eye. Just that day he had asked to be let out of the betrothal. He went in search of you to tell you, but when he couldn't find you he went out. It was as simple as that."

Ranall knew how you felt. We all did. There was a girl on Inishmore . . . The truth in his father's words pounded through Rourke.

He did not begrudge either of you. "Why didn't he say anything? Why didn't you? Especially after . . . ?"

Da pressed his lips into a thin line; regret deepened the lines at the corners of his mouth and his eyes. "At first we were busy with the search. The day we found his boat is the day you left. I lost you both. I thought you would come home, given time. Come to your senses."

"I did." Garrett had saved him, pulled him from the gutter quite literally and showed him how to put what was left of his life to some use.

"Does Aileen know Ranall's intentions? Did she?"

Da shook his head. "She was devastated. You were gone. Ranall dead. How could I tell her that neither of you had wanted her? Do you know she takes flowers to his marker every week when she takes them to your mother's grave? All she will say is that she owes him."

The truth sluiced through Rourke, washing through the darkness shrouding his soul. "He saw us that day. Saw us together in the hills. He must have left to give us privacy. And then she hurt her ankle."

Da nodded. "And so you were late and Ranall went out. Surely you have paid enough, done enough atonement risking Dublin's hangman's noose to come home now. To claim your heritage and the woman you loved. The Green Dragon's work will go on without you. There are plenty of rights to be wronged on this side of the island as well."

So Da knew about his exploits with the Green Dragon, with Garrett, the friend who had saved him from himself. Somehow, after everything else, he was not surprised. "Those are almost his exact words to me when I told him I was coming here."

The bells of St. Brendan's tolled for the second time this morning. Extra services for some forgotten saint? Gooseflesh prickled Rourke's neck. He knew that was not the reason even before he saw his father tense and turn to the windows.

"The bell rang for service hours ago," Da said, rising from his chair. Rourke was already striding to the window. "Every week the Claddagh women gather there to make baskets for Galway's poor. Galway townfolk may look down on us, but the hungry are glad for the sharing of our bounty."

Rourke could just make out the church spire over the cottages. The bell continued to peal a definite alarm.

"No sign of smoke." Da joined him and they both strained to see what lay behind the warning.

A small figure in flapping black puffed down the path from the village toward them at a awkward gait. The prickling of Rourke's flesh turned to cold sweat as the woman made her way far too slowly.

"We'd best go down."

His father clapped his shoulder. He winced, but nodded. *Aileen.* Fear pounded through him.

They opened the massive front doors and met the stooped figure of an old woman just as she collapsed against the stone arch entrance, clutching her rain-sodden shawl around her shoulders.

"Mrs. Gilkelly, what is it?" His father put his arm around the wizened figure and eased her onto a small bench.

"Ye must . . . come . . . at once . . . sir," she wheezed and struggled for her breath. "They've taken her."

"Come where, taken who?" Dread poured through Rourke carrying the certainty that he already knew the answer to the last one. He'd known as soon as the bell tolled.

"Fetch the widow a drink, Rourke."

Everything in him screamed. There was no time for niceties. But there was no time to argue, either. He turned.

"Wait," Mrs. Gilkelly protested. "It's Miss Aileen."

His gut froze. He turned back. "What of Aileen?"

"She brought me some of Muire Ahearne's scones like she always does every week." Mrs. Gilkelly nodded. The breeze blew scraggly wisps of her white hair into her face and she swiped them away. "She takes the napkins I launder up fer the baskets and on the way she puts flowers on my Donal's grave along with yer dear mother's and yer brother's."

Rourke could have shaken the woman to have her get to the point. His father still kept a bracing arm around her and shot him a quelling look.

"What happened, Mrs. Gilkelly?" he asked with far more patience than Rourke would ever muster.

To hell with waiting for her answer. Telling him the bell tolling had to do with Aileen was enough for him. He started forward toward the village.

His father shot his hand out and stopped him. "Best know what kind of seas we face before we set our sails."

Mrs. Gilkelly frowned. "Two men and that sly-lookin' brother of hers was waiting. They snatched her right up. Clamped a hand over her mouth and picked her right up."

Eoghan Joyce. He'd throttle the man when he found

him, Aileen's brother or not. Especially if she'd been hurt. Jasper Farley must be behind this.

Mrs. Gilkelly shook the rain droplets from her head in sorrow. "Miss Aileen gave 'em a good fight, but they put her in that carriage anyway and took off faster than a gull skimming the waves fer scraps. I came off my stoop and headed here as fast as I could, meeting little Jenna and Muire. Jenna's to the docks to fetch Master Ahearne. Muire's sounding the alarm."

Da's gaze locked with Rourke's. Grim determination shone in their depths. "My pistols are in my desk, Rourke. I'll fetch them and meet you at the stables."

Grateful to be in motion at last, Rourke nodded and turned away.

"Thank you, Mrs. Gilkelly. Come inside and rest—there's water and some spirits in the study as well," he heard his father say as he rounded the corner.

Seven

Aileen's head pounded; waves of yellow pulsing through black spiraled in tight circles through her. Her mouth was dry and her arms felt as if they were weighted down with a basket of wet laundry. She struggled to open one eye and thought better of the action as light pierced her and set off a fresh wave of nausea.

"Good, you are beginning to rouse." Jasper Farley's voice boomed through her. "I was afraid that fool of a brother of yours had given you too great a dose of laudanum in his haste to deliver you to me." Jasper offered a sniff of disapproval as her head spun. "I would never have used that on you."

Eoghan.

The vile potion he'd forced her to drink. Confusion and fear nearly pulled her back into the comforting blackness. She fought to keep a hold on her senses, to pull herself out of the drug-induced haze and lethargy weighing her down.

"Where . . . where. . . ." Her voice came thready and weak. She hated the feeble sound, and hated having to ask. The cushions beneath her shook, not just from Jasper's loud tones. They were moving. She did not recline on a settee, but a coach-seat directly opposite him. She struggled to sit up, to open her eyes. To swallow back the bile swirling up from her stomach.

What had Eoghan done? Dread flooded her as she remembered her abduction. Her struggles had done little beyond angering Eoghan and his men. After the laudanum she remembered nothing more until waking here. Wherever here was.

"Let me help you, my dear." Jasper leaned forward and grasped her arm just below her elbow, and tugged her upright. She swayed against the coach's jouncing rhythm. Jasper's grip at least kept her from falling flat on her face until she regained her balance.

He smiled at her as she struggled to meet his gaze. "We are on the Belfast road. On our way to our wedding. I told you I had business there."

The Belfast road. She blinked and shielded her eyes from the light. Despite curtains, the coach's interior still seemed too bright. They were miles from Claddagh. Miles from anyone who could help her. From Rourke. Would he have realized she was gone by now? Would he come after her? Certainty brought a single ray of warmth to her heart and stilled some of her rising anxieties. Aye, he would, she was certain of it. But when? And how?

Jasper released his grip; his hand trailed along her sleeve, almost brushing the side of her breast. Aileen nearly choked on her inner scream of protest. She took a deep breath and tried to clear the thick wad of netting from her mind.

"Wed . . . wedding?" she stammered out stupidly and blinked at him on the opposite side of the coach.

His smile deepened with satisfaction, creasing his broad face. "We discussed this, my dear. Just yesterday. But then you have had an exciting time of it, haven't you?"

He patted her knee. She jerked away, her stomach continuing its slow roil as the darkness beckoned once again.

Jasper clucked his tongue at her and settled back against the seat cushions. "Your maidenly sensibilities please me. You are indeed a suitable candidate to grace my table. And my bed."

He chuckled, pleased with himself. His broad face held the satisfied look of Claddagh's dock cats when tossed a fat fish. "But, you have nothing to fear from me. This prenuptial trip may seem a bit unconventional, but I will not tamper with your delicate sensibilities until you are my wife in the eyes of God and man. You truly have nothing to fear from me, my dear. I intend to honor you above all things."

His dark gaze gleamed as he perused her person quite thoroughly. Even in the shadowed interior of the carriage as it lurched along the road, she could feel his gaze weighing every inch of her before him as though he inspected new merchandise.

She could only imagine what his idea of honor was. A man who would stoop to thievery in order to get what he wanted held no honor, but then she doubted he would even understand such a concept.

Eoghan had as good as sold her to this man. A man who would view her as his property, as his to do with as he pleased, for his pleasure in any way he saw fit. The buttons of Jasper's jacket strained to contain his girth. And now he sought to marry her. She could not stave off the image of him, naked and sweating on top of her, inside her.

No, gut-deep denial surged. She belonged with Rourke. She shuddered and hugged her arms around herself. Somehow she must find a way to escape. Perhaps they were not too far outside the city yet and she could scream for aid from a passerby.

"I . . . I . . . need some air. The laudanum," she choked out and reached for the curtain.

His hand clamped on her wrist, tightening for just an instant with a warning of pain against her tender flesh. Her gaze flashed back to his and she read his determination and a flash of something deadly in his soul. "I prefer we maintain our privacy for the time being. We will be stopping to change horses in an hour or so."

She shuddered again and tried to pull herself free. He held on and leaned forward. The sickly-sweet smell of his rosewater cologne filled her with dread.

Help me, Rourke.

"If you are cold, you will find a new pelisse and bonnet on the seat beside you." Jasper brought her hand to his puffy lips and pressed a wet kiss to her palm, his mouth open against her skin. She could have sworn she felt the tip of his tongue flick her.

She jerked her hand away.

"Very sweet," he said and quirked a brow at her. "You may thank me for them properly later, after you have modeled the other garments I provided for you."

He released her again. She rubbed her wrist and eyed him as he settled himself back against his plush seat. For an instant the temptation to reveal that she was no longer the virginal bride he was expecting flared. But despite his efforts to present a civilized countenance there was something very uncivilized lurking deep within Jasper Farley's eyes. Telling him his prize had been given to another man would not sit well with him. And at the moment it was the only thing about her that he seemed to value.

She flirted with the idea of flinging herself from the moving coach, then abandoned it. Even if she managed to open the door, the injuries she might suffer would hamper her efforts to get away.

Lulling him into thinking he had her well and truly trapped, that her reluctance sprang from innocence, seemed the safest ploy for now. Until she could get away.

"You . . . you . . . said you . . . that we . . . would not . . ." She grimaced inwardly at the weak sound of her purposely naive stammer.

Jasper chuckled again, the sound mirthless and hollow. A harbinger of his plans. "There are many pleasures a man and woman can share without actual consummation. Many games that do not involve premature breaching of a maidenhead. We will have several nights together for me to initiate you slowly into the pleasures of the marriage bed."

He leaned forward and licked his lip. "I have no reason to rush you or to force you too soon. I have had a great deal of time to plan this, Aileen. You will not suffer a lack of passion at my hands, I assure you. You needn't fret, I will be a very attentive lover. You will learn to meet my expectations."

She was horrified.

"Why have you chosen me?"

She could not help asking, although she wasn't sure she really wanted to know. Just having this intimate conversation with Jasper made her feel as if a trap were closing mercilessly around her. Breathing his air choked her with hopelessness.

"I noticed you in the marketplace one day." A faraway look edged Jasper's eyes, softening their hard glint. His gaze drifted to a point just beyond her shoulder as he rubbed his chin. "Taking baskets from a wagon and handing them to the beggars."

"You stood out in the crowd like a beacon. So gentle, so beautiful and regal. When I investigated and learned of your circumstances, I knew I had to rescue you. I couldn't allow you to stay where you were less than you should be. You didn't belong there in that dirty place with those fishermen." He spat the last word as though he could think of nothing worse.

"Rescue me?" She forced herself to breath evenly, to remain calm in the face of this incredible assertion. He certainly believed his motive; she could not afford to anger him while they were still alone and she barely had strength to sit, let alone run. *He* was the one she needed rescuing from. What could he possibly mean?

"Your brother was a fool to waste a gem like you on those lowlife people. They are little better than Gypsies . . ."

Outrage boiled. For the McAffertys, the Ahearnes, Mrs. Gilkelly, and all the other people of Claddagh who had welcomed her into their homes and their lives.

". . . Thank goodness you were not forced to actually go through with the alliance. But I have taken you away from all that and now your life will be as it should be. You are too beautiful and too fine to waste on anything less than perfection." He stretched his back, making his paunch thrust forward to strain his buttons further, obviously quite comfortable spouting his prejudice.

Perfection. She swallowed back the need to defend all of the Claddagh from Jasper's opinion. What a warped sense of himself and of her he carried. He didn't know her at all and really didn't care, despite his protestations to the contrary. The most perfect place she could imagine for herself was with Rourke at her side and all of Claddagh to care for.

Jasper ignored her silence, still caught up in his memories. "Luring your brother into deeper and deeper play and then buying up all his vowels was definitely a masterstroke. Once I had him in my debt, it was easy to dangle more coins and persuade him to fetch you back from McAfferty."

Ice shivered through her at his words. That he would so blatantly reveal such a thing with no thought to how she might react chilled her blood. She bit her lip to keep from railing at him. Eoghan had not willingly traded on her future a second time. But the knowledge brought cold comfort.

Silence held for a moment as Jasper's gaze perused her features.

"You do not agree with my assessments. No matter." He waved a pudgy hand. "I expected that your ideals may have been muddied by spending so much time with those fishmongers. I am ready to deal with that as well. Have no fear, Aileen. In time you will come to appreciate all I have done for you. One day you will realize just how much you owe me."

And what price did he expect her to pay for that gratitude? She shivered just trying to imagine the cost.

After digging for a moment, Jasper pulled a snowy white square of linen from his trouser pocket and mopped his face. "You look flushed, my dear. Perhaps you would like to loosen your bodice?"

Not on a hot day in the devil's realm. Aileen shook her head as he proffered the cloth to her.

"Suit yourself." He shrugged and swiped his brow again, subsiding into silence.

She closed her eyes, hoping to gain a respite before their carriage stopped. Images from the night flowed through her. Rourke in the doorway. Rourke claiming her for an angry kiss and then for sensual ones that turned her bones to supple wax. Rourke, naked and proud as the firelight played on his muscles. Rourke beneath her, above her, making them one.

She'd never consent to the attentions Jasper Farley thought to foist on her. Never. Married or no. There had to be a way for her to get back to Claddagh, to Rourke. A way to delay this journey until he could find her.

There is only you in my heart, Rourke had said.

Hurry, Rourke, hurry. Half plea, half prayer, the words thrummed through her over and over as the wheels churned down the road carrying her further and further away from him.

When a gunshot split the air outside, causing the horses to scream and the carriage to lurch and slow, she caught her breath. Hope thundered through her despite the tiny voice that warned it might not be the rescue she'd been praying for.

"What is the meaning of this outrage?" Jasper thumped on the roof with a silver-headed walking stick. "Why are you stopping, driver? Move along, man. What are you waiting for?"

"Rourke," Aileen breathed.

Jasper shot her a narrowed gaze. "You'd best pray it's not." With a speed his bulk belied, Jasper snatched her by the shoulders and huddled her against his side. "He has no claim here. You are mine. And you will remain so. He can not have you."

His fetid breath fanned her cheeks. His eyes glittered as they narrowed to scrutinize her. She very much feared he intended to brand her with a kiss. She would gag for sure if that occurred. Suppose this was not Rourke, but a highwayman!

The carriage continued, slowing to a stop. Would a highwayman be willing to rescue her for a price to be paid on her return to her rightful place? She tensed, willing to try any avenue of escape.

This had to be Rourke. Oh, please let it be Rourke. She forced herself to meet Jasper's gaze squarely without quailing in his grasp. His fingers tightened painfully against her arms.

The carriage door wrenched open. Strong sunlight streamed into the interior of the compartment, washing away the gloom. A powerful figure stood bathed in the light. There was no mistaking that strong silhouette or the pleasure that coursed through her at the sight of him.

Rourke. Elation soared in Aileen.

"Allow Miss Joyce to step outside." Polite words, but Rourke offered them with a deliberate edge.

Aileen appeared unharmed, at least, although he had to hold himself back from climbing in and wresting her from the bear-grasp Farley was foisting on her.

"Release her, Farley," he growled again. "I won't repeat myself."

Gratitude played on the expression she turned to him—gratitude and overwhelming joy. Stray wisps of blond hair escaped the simple knot she'd gathered her hair into. She looked weary, but unharmed. A portion of the worry he had carried for too many hours and too many miles eased.

"Let's discuss this as reasonable men, McAfferty. Miss Joyce and I will be wed by week's end." Farley let her go anyway and smoothed his hands on his trousers. "Her brother has given us his blessing. You have no right."

Aileen scrambled for the door, straight into his arms. He pulled her to him and breathed a deep breath of wisteria and relief. She flung her arms around his neck and clung to him as he spun her away from the carriage.

"Is that so?" Da proclaimed his skepticism to Farley, and anyone else listening, in his most regal tones. "I believe he has had a change of heart. Shall we ask him?"

Aileen's mouth dropped and she turned to look at him. "You are out of bed? You are well?"

"I'm sorry for the worry I cost you, lass. It was necessary."

Still held firmly in Rourke's embrace, Aileen nodded. A look of sheer happiness and relief suffused her soft features as she smiled up at his father.

"Did he harm you in any way?" the king asked.

"I'm fine, now," she assured them both. She looked long into Rourke's eyes, the gray-violet of her gaze shimmering with honesty. "Truly."

She was so warm and vibrant, he was certain he would never be willing to let her out of his arms, let alone his sight.

Never again.

Farley hefted himself from the carriage, his top hat askew, his face an alarming red from thwarted perfidy. He clutched a long walking stick and stared at Aileen pressed close to Rourke's side. His mouth opened and shut several times in rapid succession, looking for all the world like a giant puffer fish gasping on a deck.

Rourke could have laughed from the sight and from the relief. Aileen was safe. Aileen was right where she belonged.

"Unhand my wife-to-be, you jackanapes! Get your fishy hands off of her or I'll charge you with kidnaping," Farley blustered.

"Forget it," Rourke growled.

"She will never be your wife, Farley. Give it up," his father added.

"Ahhh, the father's ridden to the rescue, too. Amazing recovery, *your majesty,*" Farley jeered and sketched a mock bow.

Da bowed his head. "Recountings of my impending demise were premature, it would seem."

"But even such as you are subject to the laws of the land. My agreement with her brother can not be gainsaid. I paid a hefty price for the gel. Instruct your son to do what is no more than right and unhand her at once."

"My son has not needed my instruction to do what is right for years."

"Aileen will never be yours, no matter what price you paid. In fact, I believe her brother will say as much himself," Rourke added, pleased with his father's words despite the present conditions. Aileen's grip tightened on his collar.

"Eoghan," Rourke called, using his sternest voice.

They'd tracked him down in Galway and forced him first to tell them the whole story of how he'd come to hand his sister over to Farley. And then they made him ride with them after the couple so there could be no question he was rescinding his consent.

Eoghan came around the side of the carriage and dismounted. He looked a little the worse for wear. "It's true, Jasper. The original betrothal agreement stands. You cannot have her for your wife. Not without a long fight and her cooperation."

"Never." Aileen sucked in a deep breath.

"What nonsense," Farley bellowed. "I settled your debts and gave you a tidy profit. She is mine, bought and delivered."

"My agreement supercedes yours, Farley. Take this . . ." Da tossed a bag of coins to Farley. It thumped and chinked on the ground by his feet, ". . . to settle any expenses and be glad Eoghan has decided against pressing charges for the scurrilous debt you forced him into."

"Joyce!" Ever the businessman, Farley paused in his tirade to scoop the bag up. He took a step toward Aileen.

Rourke moved between them and her erstwhile suitor thought better of the action, weighing the bag in his hand instead. His gaze swept from one to the other of his opponents as his jaw worked and he, no doubt, calculated the contents.

"Your eldest son is dead—how can the agreement still be in force?" he asked at last.

"Because she is mine." Rourke tightened his hold on Aileen's shoulder as he claimed her. He looked down at her. "If she will have me."

The light sparkling in her eyes and the smile she favored him with, a smile that warmed his soul, told him yes even before the word came out of her sweet lips.

"Aye."

He pulled her to him for a blazing kiss to seal the bargain. She was his. The only woman who would ever claim his heart.

"I love you," he whispered into her hair, refusing to be hurried in this, even with Farley's glowering disapproval boring into his back.

"And I you," she answered. "But how—"

"The agreement that brought you to our household only states that you are to wed my son," Da spoke up. "While we intended that to be Ranall, the wording allows Rourke to fulfill the contract. Can you forgive me for not clarifying this years ago?"

Aileen nodded and reached a hand out to the king.

Farley snorted in disgust. The creak of carriage springs showed he'd given up at last. A moment later his driver pulled off with a clatter of hoofbeats and a ᵘd of dust.

"Let's talk this through at home," Rourke said. "We have years of catching up to do. Stories to tell."

He boosted her onto the mount that had carried Eoghan out of the city.

"What of me?" her brother protested. "Am I to walk? You took whatever the moneylender left me to add to the purse you just sent off with Jasper."

"Eoghan . . ." Aileen warned.

"Here." Da reached into his pocket and pulled out a smaller purse. He tossed it to Eoghan. "I hear America is a good place for a man to seek his fortune. I wish you a happy journey and I advise you to begin before Farley returns from his trip to Belfast."

"But—"

"Never argue with the Claddagh king, Eoghan. You will not win." Aileen smiled at him. "Good luck. Let us know how you make out."

With that they wheeled away, setting the horses to a fair clip. Aileen tossed one final glance over her shoulder at her brother before they rounded a curve in the road to see the half-salute he waved as he turned in the opposite direction. And then he was lost from sight.

When they slowed, they had a chance to talk a little.

"Stories?" Aileen asked.

Rourke nodded.

"Like how you hurt your shoulder?"

"You've hurt your shoulder?" Da frowned at him for a moment and then raised a brow. "The Green Dragon?"

Aileen shook her head with a puzzled frown furrowing her brow. "This had better be good."

Aileen finished brushing her hair and turned to look at her husband waiting for her in bed. Things were so good between them, she had to keep reminding herself that they were real. That she was not dreaming.

Her body still sang with the echoes of their lovemaking earlier. The heights of passion and the depth of his love astounded her. The emerald ring on her finger twinkled in the soft candlelight bathing the chamber. Two hands for friendship, an emerald heart for love, and a crown for loyalty. The Claddagh ring.

Not so very long ago she had not believed she deserved to wear this ring. Only a few weeks before she had not believed it possible to find forgiveness enough to make her worthy.

Rourke had shown her—together they had discovered—that this ring bound them to the past—to his mother and his father's love, and to their memories of his brother.

And from the moment Rourke slid it on her finger, this ring represented the freedom of their future.

He held out his hand from the bed. "Come here, wife. It is far too lonely without you for sleep."

One lazy grin and a quirked brow and the passion he always raised in her flowered anew. "I believe sleep is not your true concern at the moment."

Laughter mingled with their kisses as she joined him once more and as lazy heat spiraled through her with his every touch she knew they had found their way together at last.

About the Author

Elizabeth Keys is the pseudonym for Mary Lou Frank and Susan C. Stevenson, who live in southern New Jersey. Finalists in Romance Writers of America's RITA 2001 Awards, these lifelong friends deliver tales of achieving your heart's desire through love's special magic.

To find out what other books have been published by Kensington visit their Web site at: www.elizabethkeys.com